I've travelled the world twice over,
Met the famous: saints and sinners,
Poets and artists, kings and queens,
Old stars and hopeful beginners,
I've been where no-one's been before,
Learned secrets from writers and cooks
All with one library ticket
To the wonderful world of books.

WALK IN THE
PARADISE GARDEN

Justine Charles comes to Chrysolaki, a Greek island where dark and ancient superstitions lie just below the sun-drenched surface, with her fiancé Louis d'Arrancourt, in order to get to know him better and to meet his older sister. However, once on the island Justine becomes engrossed in the life of Elaine, a strange young girl, a mute of angelic beauty, and is then drawn into conflict with the villagers, into great physical danger, and into passions for which she is not prepared.

Books by Anne Maybury in the
Ulverscroft Large Print Series:

THE JEWELLED DAUGHTER
RADIANCE
JESSAMY COURT
I AM GABRIELLA!
WALK IN THE PARADISE GARDEN

ANNE MAYBURY

WALK IN THE PARADISE GARDEN

Complete and Unabridged

ULVERSCROFT
Leicester

First published in Great Britain 1973 by
William Collins Sons & Co. Ltd.,
London

First Large Print Edition
published August 1983

British Library CIP Data

Maybury, Anne
Walk in the Paradise Garden.—
Large print ed.
(Ulverscroft large print series: romance)
I. Title
823'.914[F]   PR6063.A885

ISBN 0-7089-1004-1

Published by
F. A. Thorpe (Publishing) Ltd.,
Anstey, Leicestershire
Printed and Bound in Great Britain by
T. J. Press (Padstow) Ltd., Padstow, Cornwall

FOR IONE

Love is
a time of enchantment:
in it all days are fair and all fields
green. Youth is blest by it,
old age made benign: the eyes of love see
roses blooming in December,
and sunshine through rain. Verily
is the time of true-love
a time of enchantment—and
Oh! how eager is woman
to be bewitched!

1

THERE are things that at the moment of happening are infinitesimal in themselves—a shadow, a voice, a waft of scent—and yet which, in retrospect, are seen as pointers that change the whole of life.

For me it was the moment when, in Constitution Square in Athens, Louis and I sat drinking coffee and killing time before catching the ferry to Hydra and from there to the small island of Chrysolaki. I had been glorying in the sun and watching the people and the traffic, as heedless and busy as in any capital city in the world. Then, turning to see who sat at the other tables, I caught sight of the paperback novel lying discarded on a chair just behind me. I picked it up and riffled through it.

Odd sentences, odd words meant nothing until I came to two lines which sprang at me from one of the pages.

The most important thing in the lives of all of us is to be aware, not of the past nor of the

1

future, but of the everlasting present.

I read the words twice and then, keeping the place with one finger, I looked on the cover for the book's title and the author's name. *Not Without Honour*, by Matthew Braddon. Although I hadn't read any of his books, I recognized the name as that of one of Britain's best-selling novelists.

"Read that," I said, and passed the book to Louis, pointing to the lines.

There was a little coffee left in my cup. Louis had asked the waiter for *Sketo*, explaining to me, "That's one Greek word for you. It means 'without sugar.'" It was wonderfully refreshing, very hot and strong and fragrant, and I drank it, watching Louis as he read the words in the paperback.

I had known him for such a short time, yet his marvelous looks still excited me. His dark-gold hair sprang back from a broad, not too high forehead, his profile was very straight and clear-cut and his eyes already had the tiny creases that were the beginnings of laughter lines. I was busy assessing his mouth—lips deeply molded, sensuous—and trying to think of some more apt adjective when he looked up, sunlight dancing in his eyes.

2

"Approval?"

"Of course."

"Well, then." He closed the book and slid it across the table to me. "Let's decide to agree with Matthew Braddon—Matt to me, since I know him. The everlasting present. That's now." He leaned sideways and kissed me. "And I'm content with it."

I laid my hand on his and closed my eyes and felt that to passers-by I must look rather like a cat satiated with the warm indolent perfection of life. For three incredible weeks before we arrived in Athens I had ridden the crest of dizzy happiness that a small traitorous asp of common sense told me could not last. I had denied the faint warning as the natural disbelief that life could be that wonderful. I still denied it. *I am happy now. Let it be!* I laughed aloud.

By my side, Louis said, "This is one of those times when I could kick myself for having packed my camera. I'd like to have a permanent picture of you as you are at this moment—"

"In a sidewalk café, squinting into the sun?"

"Just like that. You look marvelous. Why didn't the Greeks ever have a goddess of joy?

3

Never mind, when we get to Chrysolaki I'll take a hundred photographs of you and then I'll have a one-man show in London and you'll make my fortune." A waiter passed our table. Louis spoke to him in easy Greek and paid for our coffees. "Come on." He swept the paperback novel from the table onto my lap. "We've got two long boat journeys ahead of us and I know by experience that I shall get bored with looking out at islands I've seen dozens of times, and probably fall asleep. You may not. Matt's book seems to have been well read and discarded, so you may as well take it and at least skim through it, because you'll be meeting him. He lives on Chrysolaki."

We raced to the taxi rank in the Square, fell into the first cab in the line and drove to Piraeus. The ferry would take us to Hydra, where we would have to spend the night and, in the morning, catch another boat east to Chrysolaki.

Wise to the mad scramble for seats on the island ferries, Louis strode in front of me, his bright head towering above the rest of the travelers, and found us two corner places on the upper deck. "You only have cabins if you travel at night," he had said.

We sailed at two o'clock—for some reason

or other, half an hour late—and immediately the little ship's nose turned into the choppy, hyacinth-tinted water.

Louis demanded food. We had bought luncheon boxes in Athens and, comfortable in our so-called reclining seats, we unwrapped fresh bread and cheese, a bunch of grapes glowing with the smooth patina of alabaster and cartons of yoghurt mixed with honey which we dipped into with little plastic spoons.

Islands came and went in the golden haze, many of them covered only with scrub and looking like camels' humps. Neither the ceaseless, incomprehensible chatter around us, the strong, silky onslaught of the wind, nor the pulsating of the ship's engine broke the peace which lay like a gilded wing over the Aegean. For four hours we slid through seas ruffled by the strong *meltemi*, the wind which blows almost every summer day from the northeast and cools the blazing islands.

At first, like Louis, I watched the broken coastline and half drowsed in my chair. Then, satiated with the loneliness of the pale-jade and ochre islands, I took out a small pad from my purse and the pencil Louis had given me. It had belonged to his grandmother and had come from Kashmir. Rubies and turquoise were inset in the beautifully chased gold.

"What are you doing?"

"Making a list of the people I have to send postcards to."

"Then you'd better remember to buy them in Hydra. You won't find any in Chrysolaki."

I finished my list, put pen and pad away and picked up Matthew Braddon's book and began to read.

The very first paragraph had an impact that made me want to read on.

There was no escape. Johnson had built his own way of life, bloody and anguished, and he found that there was neither man nor woman who would walk it with him. He travelled alone which, for a man with stern dreams, was the only way he could go.

I read through a brief résumé of the man, Johnson's background and became so engrossed that I jumped like a startled cat when Louis spoke to me.

"You're going to meet Matt Braddon, so you'd better shut that book and listen to a bit of his history. If you don't, you may drop a fine clangor, and you wouldn't want that, would you?"

I closed the book, put on my sunglasses and lay back, looking ahead of me at the islands on the skyline. "Tell me and then I'll be able to see how much of him he has put in his book."

"The most important thing for you to know is something that was mentioned so briefly in the English newspapers that you probably won't remember—and anyway, people's memories, where they aren't personally involved, are very short." He leaned forward, pointing out two dolphins rolling with friendly curiosity alongside the boat. When at last they dived and disappeared, I curled my legs up under me, and in that not very comfortable position, asked, "What wouldn't I remember?"

"A startling news item about Matt which appeared a year ago in the London papers."

Made indolent by the rocking of the boat and the heat, I asked flippantly, "What did he do to warrant that publicity? Swim the Aegean or murder his mistress?" It wasn't funny, it wasn't clever, and I didn't blame Louis for not laughing.

"Matt had a sister, who used to come and

stay for weeks at a time at Chrysolaki, Helen Braddon. Last summer, the morning after her arrival at Marathon (that's the name of Matt's house), she was found dead at the foot of a huge rock that juts out into the sea near his home."

There was the sound of string music from somewhere behind us: swift, exciting, very loud—like an invitation to wild dancing. I listened to it and watched a caïque with tawny sails pass us.

"There was an inquest," Louis said, "and the verdict was, in our vernacular, 'Accidental death.' "

"She fell . . . ?"

Louis's silence was too long; it denied my comment.

"Well, go on. If she didn't fall, then . . . ?"

"Nobody knows. The facts were simply that she was found on the boulders at the foot of the cliff with her neck broken. The islanders call the cliff the Dark Sister—not a particularly romantic name—but the relationship is in a way applicable because there are two of them; the other, the Green Sister, is only a few kilometers away."

I asked again, "The verdict was that she

8

fell, but you don't believe it. Is that what you're saying?"

"I can't imagine a woman like Helen Braddon climbing a cliff, interesting only to sea birds, late at night."

"Perhaps she was athletic."

"Not she!"

"Then she went there to meet someone."

"There are plenty of places on the island for lovers without climbing a goat track to keep a rendezvous. I'll be showing you some."

I slid round the inference, and kept the interest on Helen Braddon. "Did you know her?"

"Yes, but I wasn't here when the so-called accident happened. Kate told me when I arrived a few days later. She said there were whispers and rumors galore. One, that Matt and his sister had been heard to quarrel that night, but none of the villagers would give evidence against Matt, they just shrugged their shoulders and looked blankly at the police whenever they came to question. They've always liked Matt and they didn't like Helen and I don't blame them. She never bothered to make herself agreeable to the islanders. She just came as a sophisticated

9

Londoner, patronized them, used their island to tan her gorgeous body and then returned to England without so much as a backward smile. She lived entirely for herself and, dear heaven, according to the stories that circulated, she was wild!"

I took a fig from a small basket and ate it.

"She was twenty-six when she died, five years younger than Matt."

"They were close—as brother and sister?"

"I doubt if they had a thing in common and I never understood why she came to Chrysolaki—the Bahamas or the Costa Esmeralda were more her kind of places. When she did come, there were always quarrels—they both had fiendish tempers. Then, after a few bricks had been thrown between them, back she'd go to London, all raven-haired beauty and blazing anger and lovely clothes."

"She was rich?"

He laughed. "Her lovers were—she saw to that."

We wiped fig juice from our fingers and tossed the tissues overboard.

"Ludmilla hated Helen."

"Who's she?"

"The Caucasian woman who housekeeps for Matt—he happens to be a bachelor—and

10

she used to say, 'She bad. She bring hell.' You'll meet Ludmilla, I suppose. She looks like a rag bag, but don't be fooled by that. She's a marvelous servant, a fine cook and keeps a spotless house. You'll find she talks without using verbs, but that doesn't stop her speaking her mind to Matt and anyone else who crosses her. She's a good judge of character, too—at least, she was right about Helen, and it was she who found her lying on the rocks of the Dark Sister."

I said incredulously, "You're inferring that a man of Matthew Braddon's fame killed his own sister? Oh, really, Louis!"

"One of those facts that can be stranger than fiction, my darling," Louis said. "Dictators can kill; doctors commit murder. So why not a writer? They aren't sacrosanct, you know. Anyway, the villagers all believe it. According to them, Matt tipped his sister off the cliff. And since she was a bitch, by all accounts, it was justice. So they ganged up against the law and nothing was proven against one of the great best-seller writers of the day."

"Did you like Helen?"

"She wasn't my type." He reached out and twisted a strand of my hair round his finger

11

like a rope. "Why are we wasting time talking of someone no one will ever see again? *We* are the important people to us. Justine . . . Justine—who chose that name for you?"

"My mother."

As if I hadn't spoken, he said in a low, tranced voice. "Justine . . . I want you completely and absolutely. But you know that, don't you?"

He drew me into an uncomfortable hug. The bouquet of the wine we had drunk with our lunch hung around our lips as we kissed.

The sun sank lower and became wreathed in vermilion haze, and the man playing the guitar moved away towards the stern of the boat, so that his music was faint and thin, as pagan as the islands couched in the purple sea.

I lay back, gazing out at nothing in particular, feeling only the stirrings of excitement that I would soon be on the soil where the old gods had reigned so magnificently.

"And then," Louis said after a long silence, "There is Elaine."

"Who is she?"

"Helen's daughter. Matt has made her his responsibility. She's only fourteen, pretty if you like pale-gold girls, and she lives permanently at Marathon."

"And goes to the island school?"

"Education on Chrysolaki?" He laughed. "Oh, the islanders submit to the minimum, but they fight it with every bit of Greek rebel instinct. They live off the sea and the land, and if their children have bigger ambitions they must leave the island. Religion mixed with superstition rules here."

"Then Matt is her teacher?"

"She is unteachable—what they call retarded. For some reason or other, her brain ceased to develop after the age of five. Until a year ago, she was looked after by Helen's mother, but she died. Matt went over for the funeral and when he came back to the island, he brought Helen and her child with him. That was the afternoon of the night she died. The rumor is, according to my sister Kate, who knows every scrap of village gossip, that Helen wanted Matt to take Elaine, arguing that he could employ a companion to look after her, and that the alternative would be that she would be put into a home for retarded children. They say that this was what they quarreled about on the evening of their arrival."

13

"But surely Helen's husband had a say in what was happening to Elaine?"

"She wasn't married."

"Oh, and the lover—?"

"First find him among the legion."

"But for a man to have to look after a maladjusted child—" I began and looked incredulously at Louis.

"She's not exactly that." He yawned, and stretched with the complete unselfconsciousness of a lion.

"Then what *is* she?"

"In Kate's words, she's sweet and vacant and easy to deal with. Kate adores her—but then she doesn't have to live with her."

"And nobody can do anything for this child?"

"No. After Helen's death Matt took her to experts in the States and in Europe, but they all told him that she would never mature."

Never grow up . . . never grow old . . .

The wind was dying down and it sang in the rigging of the ship like the beating of swans in flight.

I said, "It'll be interesting meeting Matthew Braddon."

"But not too interesting!" he said.

I was so enveloped in my own gilded happi-

14

ness that I scarcely heard him; I certainly knew that there was no need to reply. But as I lay, my eyes heavy with drowsy contentment, my mind too lulled with sea and air to be really alert, I felt a vague sympathy for the unknown Elaine . . . Elaine Braddon for want of her father's name. And so, still thinking of her, I must have slept, for it was a quarter of an hour later when I looked at my watch and heard Louis call.

"Come and have your first glimpse of Hydra."

I got up and joined him at the rail, our hands linked as we leaned over watching the little boat edge her way into the smooth waters of the harbor, and in the dying daylight I saw the campanile ahead of us and the white walls of the gabled houses stained pink by the low sun.

There was no ferry to Chrysolaki until the following afternoon and so we spent the night at a hotel near the harbor.

The strings of lights hung like diadems across the curve of the bay, the voluble Greek voices, the strange hint of the east in the smells, which were a mixture of Turkish tobacco, burning charcoal and spices, acted on me like an enchanter's wand. I could, that

15

night, have let Louis share my bed. That he did not was due to my insistence that we knew that our physical need for one another was not in question. To me, the important thing was to be able to prove that ours was not a brief, emotional fantasy with no more substance than fool's gold. It was useless to say: *We know we are attracted physically to one another, therefore everything else will be right, too . . .*

Life wasn't so simple; there had to be something left when passion died, and although Louis began by laughing at my arguments, he had said finally, "If that's the only way I can get you to Chrysolaki, then virtuously is the way we'll go. But at least we're engaged."

I didn't even want that and I said so. "We'll go as friends."

"You're asking a very great deal if you imagine I won't make love to you."

"Let time take care of it all."

"That sounds pretentious."

"I'm sorry, darling, I didn't mean it like that. What I mean is, let what we now feel develop into what we believe it can."

"And you think we can stay like that?"

16

"I'm sure of it," I said and was not sure at all.

So, determined to keep the bargain we had made, I lay alone in the huge bed in the hotel at Hydra. And I fell asleep on the magical thought that the winds of the Aegean were set fair for us.

I had met Louis at a time when my life had seemed to have dropped into a pit of emptiness. My mother had died some years earlier, when I was sixteen, and I hadn't realized until then how completely my father had relied on her. A very aged aunt had said at the time, "It's such a pity you haven't brothers and sisters because you'll have to be man as well as woman in the house. For your father will just sit back looking helpless and handsome and let you cope. And you will, dear, you will!"

It had been just as she had said. My father was a dreamer, a man of great plans that never came to anything, of imaginings that belonged to a masculine cloudland, and his life had been spent in an inferior administrative job in a London office. His one hobby was sailing, and when he had been left a little money by an aunt, he bought three things—a beaver coat for my mother, a diamond brooch

17

shaped like a rose for me, and a small cabin cruiser for himself. The boat, kept at Chichester, was his great joy and at the Yacht Club he was an enormous success as an amusing raconteur. But no one offered him the marvelous job he dreamed of.

He was gay and sociable but completely unable to cope with the hard facts of living. I had to carry him over every obstacle concerning our small house, to cope with our financial affairs and ease every complication that left him waiting, charming and inefficient, for me to settle.

We spent most summer weekends on the little boat in the small horseshoe bay, and that was the only place where my father enjoyed taking control. I became a willing and, since I loved the sea, competent "crew."

Suddenly, without any pre-warning, my father died. By that time I had been so conditioned to taking responsibility that I was lost without my role as prop. I found myself in a sudden limbo, working mechanically—and no longer with interest—at the temporary job I had taken at the Tate Gallery and at weekends going to Chichester to show prospective buyers over the beloved boat I could not afford to keep and had advertised for sale.

A week after my father had died, Louis joined the Yacht Club, bringing his shining new cabin cruiser, his charm, and a gaiety which delighted the women who haunted the little harbor. Someone called him the Butterfly Blond, but that was unfair, for he was all male and quickly proved himself a fine sailor.

I was somewhere on the perimeter of the women who clustered around him until, looking over their heads in the bar one night, he saw me, put down his glass and walked straight through them to where I sat depressed and annoyed because I had lost in a deal over the sale of the boat. I knew its worth but the man who had made me an offer had taken advantage of the fact that I was negotiating alone and was quite certain he could beat me, a mere girl, down in price. He couldn't, and I sat drinking a Pimms No. 1, slumped in an emotional void from which I couldn't escape by myself. My father had demanded so much of me that, on my own, I was nothing.

And then, there before me was Louis d'Arrancourt smiling, saying he'd seen me on the last few weekends at the Yacht Club and wasn't it time we met?

I knew already that he was a photographer

by profession, and I quickly realized when he took me to dinner that night that he was also a perfectionist. He had worked for some years as assistant to a distinguished commercial photographer, had placed third and then second in two international photographic competitions, and on the strength of them, had opened his own studio in Knightsbridge. He was acknowledged as versatile, for while the experts praised him for the clarity and directness of his studies, he could also produce work of poetic romanticism. He had spent his first years collecting cameras of all kinds, experimenting, testing, searching for what he really wanted until, when I went to his studio, I found that he had narrowed the field to two cameras. His work excited me: I knew by instinct that he was good; that one day he would be ranked highly. In the meantime he suffered from my father's weakness, an inability to cope with responsibility other than that he took so gladly with his camera. His business affairs were in such a muddled state that he ran the risk of bankruptcy.

He had told me quite frankly, over our first dinner together, of the crisis in his affairs. "Even selling my boat won't really help. And besides, why should I?"

My father would have said exactly the same and then passed the practical headache over to me. I recognized their similarity, but it didn't prejudice me against Louis. In fact, it was as if this man had walked right into the void my father had left—everything fitting: charm and looks and irresponsibility.

I discovered early what a fine photographer Louis was. He took a great many studies of me, but his first efforts in his studio were a failure. After many attempts, he had given up, saying with laughing exasperation, "What's the use of trying to get a formal portrait of you when your face changes its expression every moment? Come on, we'll get the car and go out somewhere and I'll take you in informal moments—we'll find some woods or even a place on the Thames Embankment." The photographs that he eventually took of me were vivid with the suggestion of vitality, of movement, of laughter.

During the first week we knew each other, Louis had his stroke of luck. A friend from his college days, Bill Guest, who admired Louis's work, heard of the muddle he was in with his creditors and his tax. Bill possessed a shrewd business brain, and to him the unraveling of a financial tangle was a challenge. Over a drink in a Chelsea bar he issued his ultimatum.

"If you'll get off my back, go right away from London and stay away, I'll sort out this bloody mess. But keep out of my sight for a couple of months, and if you can earn some money while you're away, then for God's sake do so."

I was not quite clear afterwards exactly what had been said between Louis and me, but I found that I had agreed to go with him to stay with his sister on Chrysolaki for seven weeks. My temporary work at the Tate Gallery was over, and I was in love and eager for a holiday. It was as if Louis had dropped a piece of perfection right into my lap.

"Yes," I said. "Oh yes, I'd love to go with you."

The travel arrangements took a couple of weeks, and during that time, moment by moment, my feeling for Louis intensified like sunlight warming up a frozen land.

2

MY first glimpse of Chrysolaki was of a thin blue line of coast rising out of the darkening sea.

As the little ferry drew nearer I saw the caïques on their way to the fishing grounds and then the tawny tricorne sails of windmills on the waterfront.

Small whitewashed houses dotted the bay, and a pile of what looked, from the distance, like brown and gray sacks were huddled near the quayside. The sacks moved, lifted heads, flicked tails. They were donkeys waiting passively for any load the travelers might choose to heap upon them.

The ferry had scarcely tied up when the crowd on it surged forward.

"Luggage," Louis cried and turned to look for ours.

I picked up our overnight bags and waited while he dived through the pack of people rushing to get off the ferry as if it were in the last stages of sinking. Voices rose, calling to a scattered few waiting on the quayside. I watched black-haired women, laden with produce from the Hydra markets, stick out their brown elbows and fight their way down the gangway. I drew a long breath and the scent of spices was even stronger in the air, mixed with the haborside smell of wet rope.

On the quay I noticed that the only means of transport, apart from the donkeys, were a few bicycles and a small dark car.

"Why in the name of all that's crazy does someone go and move our suitcases to the stern of the boat?" Louis exploded, colliding with a woman carrying a basket in which lay a pathetic dead duck, snowy feathers soft and white, ruffled as if still living and fighting the last of the day's wind.

Louis apologized charmingly in Greek to the woman and disappeared, returning a few moments later loaded with our suitcases and some camera equipment.

"Come on," he hurried me. "Kate will be waiting." We were halfway down the gang-plank when he stopped dead and gave a mighty shout of dismay. "Oh, *no!*"

"What's the matter?"

"There." With no hand free, he jerked his chin towards the quay. "No Kate. But Matt Braddon. That does it!"

"Does what? . . . Does *what?*" I repeated, pushing him forward as I was being pushed by the crowd.

"I'm superstitious. And I have a 'thing' about the first person I meet at the end of a journey. I feel it sets the seal on a visit."

"Then shut your eyes," I said casually, "and when you open them again, look somewhere else. Your sister is probably over to the left by the windmills or to the right near the donkeys."

"She's not. That car is Matt's and, believe it or not, he has brought Elaine along."

I had time, during our slow approach down the gang-plank, to study the man and the girl who stood with him. First, all I could see of the man was that he was dark and of ordinary height. Then, as we drew nearer, I saw his face in greater detail. He was a very still man with a broad forehead and a strong chin. As we came face to face, the color of his eyes puzzled me—they were like clear water, and although friendly with greeting, I had a feeling that he was perhaps a solitary. Or was it just that, because of his fame, he was so much a personality that he could not help but stand alone? It was obvious that he hadn't Louis's free, friendly way nor his gift of easy

25

laughter, but I could not "type" him; he was neither the strong dark man of the clichés, nor the gentle dreamer.

The girl by his side was holding on to his arm with square, sun-tanned hands. Her hair was cut very short and curled like feathers over her head. Her features were small and charmingly blunt, and had it not been for the empty expression in her violet eyes she would have been beautiful.

A young man in blue denims seized our luggage and carried it to the dark-green car. From somewhere behind me I heard thin piping music, and drawing in breaths of scented air, I felt Louis's arm round my shoulders.

A little girl with bare feet and wearing a red dress too long for her ran laughing past me. Turning to look at her, I nearly fell over a fishing net laid out slap in the path of the arriving passengers. Louis steadied me. "On Chrysolaki, darling, you're incidental. The fishes come first."

"Then why don't they throw out their nets and catch them instead of catching me?" I extricated the toe of one shoe, got caught up again by my other shoe, said "Damn!" and looked up into the face of Matthew Braddon. Simultaneously we laughed.

26

"Kate asked me to meet you," he said to Louis. "Her car has broken down and won't be ready till tomorrow."

"It always does break down at crucial moments. Nice of you to bother. Justine, this is Matthew Braddon, whose novel you're hugging in that garish bag of yours. Matt, this is Justine Charles. I'm going to marry her."

It wasn't the moment to argue the point that I was not even engaged and I let the comment go.

Matthew was saying, "I hope you'll like our island."

"I'm sure I will." I looked around me at the small town of Hagharos lying under the tangerine sunlight which stained the white walls of the houses.

Matt was introducing Elaine. "My niece . . ."

I held out my free hand to her and smiled. But her arm remained at her side and I realized that she didn't understand about greetings. I said "Hullo, Elaine," and touched her fingers. They were cool and limp and her expression was gentle, but the emptiness remained in her eyes as if I were nothing more than a remote moving image across her vision. She was nearly as tall as I, her legs long and slim, her pale-green dress clinging lightly to her immature body.

"It's only a short drive to our village," Matt said and opened the car doors.

I sat in the back with Louis and listened to the flow of conversation. Names which meant nothing to me yet were tossed across from the back to the front of the car. Jock Anderson . . . Niko . . . Kouvakis . . . Stephanides . . . I gathered that Anderson was a retired doctor living on the island, and in between voluntary visits to people who had minor injuries, sat in the *tavernas* drinking *ouzo*.

Matt said, "I'm still agitating for some sort of clinic here. It's crazy to have to send for an air ambulance if someone is taken really ill, but at least I've managed to get the authorities in Athens to lengthen that suicidal airstrip at Hagharos."

"I doubt if it's used much," Louis said. "Chrysolakians never seem to die and there's always Kate to run around with her first-aid box doing her good deeds."

The little car jerked and dipped and swayed. Matt glanced in the rear mirror at me and said, "Our roads are horrible. I'm sorry. You know there's a saying that the Greeks never bother to build a road when there's water to take on the job of moving people from place to place."

"Or mules, or donkeys," Louis said. "I suppose no one has yet thought of opening the island up to tourists?"

"No, God be thanked by we who are isolationists. We haven't the oracle of Delphi nor the lions of Delos. We have nothing that attracts—"

Louis said, "You wait until someone starts to dig."

"If the archaeologists had thought there was anything here, they'd have brought their spades and pails by now."

I leaned forward and touched Elaine on the shoulder. "You must love living here."

She half turned at my touch.

Matt said quickly, "Don't you know? She can't speak."

A small shock quivered through me. I sat back in my corner of the car with a sense that, in all innocence, I had been guilty of a major error in tact.

As if he knew how I felt, Matt said, "It's all right, Justine. Elaine understands very little of what is being said; there's a block between herself and the rest of the world. What she understands is mostly by instinct."

29

To say "I'm sorry" would be banal; to ask questions would be impertinent at this early stage of our meeting, so I stayed silent, very aware of the small, pretty head in the seat in front of me, aureoled in corn-colored hair. Dumb as well as retarded, that gentle child . . .

Yet to see her next to Matthew Braddon, no one would dream of her poignant limitations; she sat so quietly, so obviously relaxed, so undemanding.

The country on either side of the rough road was splashed like a painter's palette with the dark green of palms and fig trees, and plantations of oleanders and bougainvillaea spilling over walls. The sunset emerged from a cloud like dragon's fire.

A woman with a stick like a shepherd's crook urged forward a group of reluctant geese, and between groups of trees, we caught an occasional glimpse of the sea, swiftly darkening.

Louis and Matthew Braddon interrupted their conversation to point things out to me.

"That's a mastic grove—they use the resin to flavor *ouzo*, which," Louis added, "you'll only enjoy if you like aniseed." Soon after that we passed a broken arch and Matthew said, "On that pediment you can still just see

30

the same words that were carved at Delphi—and, by the way, you should try to visit it while you're here—it's the loveliest spot in all Greece."

"What are the words?" I asked.

" 'Know Thyself.' "

"Who does?" Louis said lightly. "And, come to that, who wants to?"

No one answered him.

We came to a village of scattered houses and a small arid square framed in pepper trees.

"Kentulakis," Matt said, "our nearest village."

I looked at the low-built houses, carefully whitewashed or ochre-colored. Geraniums flowed over balconies; women stopped and watched us. They were tall and strong, clad funereally in black, and walked with the natural peasant grace of an ancient people. Scantily dressed children played in the dust, also pausing, when they saw the car, to watch gravely. Matt waved to them; they lifted their hands in their own small salutes.

After Kentulakis, the land on either side grew more wild and lonely. Tangles of tall grass encroached on the road, so that in places we drove along little more than a track.

31

There was a sprinkling of olive orchards and distant vineyards on the few hills.

The two men talked and I wondered about Matthew Braddon. Writers and artists made colonies on islands in warm seas, but according to Louis, Chrysolaki was so remote that not even tourists visited it. Yet the man at the wheel looked essentially civilized.

What had taught him the value of the moment? Perhaps the great philosophers of the past? But did one ever learn to live from the experience of others? Then something in his own life? Helen's death, or the poignancy of the eternally silent girl by his side. It must surely have been some experience of personal tragedy that had brought him to his own philosophy for happiness and his chosen isolation.

Louis touched my arm. "Look to your left."

I saw a gaunt hill rising sharply out of the flat land. "They call it the Green Sister."

"She's bald on top," I said.

Elaine turned and looked at Matt, hearing his laughter. Even in profile I saw that although she was aware of us and of our conversation and our laughter, she had no contact with it.

"That bald patch, as you call it," Matt said, "is a geological freak. There are only two other known places in the world where it exists, one in the North of England and one in China."

"I've seen plenty of bare rocks."

"Ah, but not ones that, when struck, sound as if bells are ringing. Most of the Green Sister is scrub, but if you could get closer you would see that the rocks at the top are great porous boulders. I don't advise you ever to go and see for yourself, though."

"I'll take your advice; I'm no mountain goat."

"Oh the climb isn't as steep as it looks. But the local people are very superstitious about it. If they heard the stones toll—and to them, they toll—they would take it that the gods are warning of evil in their midst, and heaven knows what chaos you'd start up on the island."

Our track had wound outwards towards the sea and there was now a ruby patina over the water. Groups of pines, lighter than those I knew in England, broke up the shore and a flock of birds flew over a huge cliff that was as unexpected on that flat shore as the Green Sister had been beyond the olive orchards.

"Storks," Louis said. "Flying over the Dark Sister."

"Another one? The island seems to like relationships."

"Oh, our corner of Chrysolaki is in a kind of pincer-grip between the two Sisters," Louis said. "Kate once told me that she sometimes has nightmares that one day the hills will come together like nutcrackers and Argus, Kate's house, will be annihilated."

I ducked so that I could see the Dark Sister more easily out of the car window. "It looks even less friendly than the other. And the sea here is very wild, isn't it?"

No one answered me. The silence was full of a sudden tension. As soon as I sensed it I remembered what Louis had told me. At the foot of that cliff they had found Matthew Braddon's sister, Helen, lying dead.

I changed the subject quickly, saying over-brightly, "There's a house through those trees."

"Argus," Matt and Louis said together.

34

3

THE tall gates were open and I saw the avenue, so dark that it seemed that night had already fallen under the cypresses leading to the house where Kate d'Arrancourt lived.

It stood square and gray and solid, with a flat roof and tall windows. As we drew closer I saw that the gray stone façade of the house was pitted with criss-cross lines, as if a fine net had fallen between us, so that we represented reality, and the house the setting for some dream sequence in a ballet.

But it was real; the windows were lit up and someone moved across a room; then the hall was flooded with light.

As we got out of the car, the headlamps streamed onto yellow cactus flowers on a low wall, and roses, full-blown and hot with sun. At the sight of them the house lost some of its eeriness.

Louis took my hand and we walked towards the woman who had opened the door and stood at the top of three steps waiting for us.

We looked at one another, politely, expectantly—strangers who wanted to like and be liked. The woman was perhaps thirty-five, but I was always so bad at guessing ages that she could have been much younger, with a face that had been roughened and aged by continual exposure to merciless sun. She was, as I had expected from the photograph Louis had shown me in England, short and square, with brown hair that sprang strongly back from her narrow forehead.

Her tanned hands were held out to me. "Justine." She leaned forward as I reached the top step and kissed me. "I'm Kate. It's lovely to have you here."

It seemed so unfair, I thought, that this woman should possess such homely plainness and her brother, the male, such beauty. Not that Kate seemed to suffer any inhibitions. She flung her arms round Louis, giving him two noisy, delighted kisses.

"Come along in, you must be tired." She led us through a cool hall. "It's a hellish journey from London. Oh, Matt, don't go! You must have a drink first. And Elaine." She put out a hand and took the girl's; the excitement that had given speed to her voice quietened and she spoke very slowly. "Dear,

36

you shall have one of my special orange drinks that I made with fruit I picked straight off the tree. You know, don't you, that this lady is Justine and that Louis is going to marry her?"

"Don't bewilder her with words," Matt said quietly.

Kate turned to him. "Oh, but I think she is gradually getting to understand more than you realize."

It was the faintest brush of wills—scarcely more than the stroke of a feather. The little moment came and went, and we entered a large room with oriental rugs on a mosaic floor and furniture that was ornate and heavy and out of place in a room that cried out for lightness and grace.

Kate bustled about, collecting bottles and glasses for the iced drinks which, she said, was always Louis's priority when he came to visit her.

She explained with excited laughter, "He says that before anything else, he has to wash away the dust of our terrible roads with a drink."

Elaine sat quietly in the chair in which Kate had seated her, and as I watched her I realized how ignorant I was about retarded children. I had not known that some could be so quiet and gentle and appear so superficially normal. In the car it had seemed that she scarcely moved, but in Kate's living room, as she sat opposite me, I saw that Elaine's square, tanned hands were moving slightly all the time, twisting and weaving in her lap as if she were making drawings with her fingers on the skirt of her smooth green dress.

Then Kate laughed at something Louis said and which I had not heard. Startled, I looked from Elaine to Matthew Braddon, and although he had not been glancing directly my way, I knew he was aware of me. It made me so nervous that I said the first thing that came into my head. "Have you been on the island long?"

"Eight years. I'm almost accepted as a native."

"And you don't intend to return to England?"

"You should know the answer to that, Miss Charles."

Matt's chair was near mine, and under cover of the small bits of news Kate was giving Louis, I said with an answering impatience, annoyed that this stranger could embarrass me, "I can't read your mind any more than you can read mine, so there's my question, Mr. Braddon. Are you planning to return to England one day?"

His laugh was so unexpected and spontaneous that it made him seem suddenly very much younger. "You misunderstood me. What I meant was that you must know perfectly well nobody can be so certain of the future that they can say definitely, 'I shall do this' or 'I shall do that.' "

"Oh, but we can—"

"We can what?" Louis came quickly into the conversation.

I told him and he said, "Of course there are things we know are going to happen. For one, that Justine and I are going to be married."

"I'm so happy about it!" Kate looked over her shoulder, holding up a crystal jug. "I hope you like Negronis because I make them rather well, don't I, Louis?"

I said I had never tasted one but that I'd enjoy trying, and as I spoke I made an involuntary movement towards a long, ornate wall mirror. Kate saw and immediately set down the jug.

"Oh, but how thoughtless of me! Just because Louis expects a drink the minute he arrives is no reason why you shouldn't see your room and freshen up. Dear, I'm so sorry. You see? That's what comes of living this isolated life, one tends to follow the usual pattern—in my case, Louis's demands. I'll take you upstairs. Louis can pour out the drinks."

Matt rose. "I'll say goodbye, Miss Charles."

"Oh no"—Kate turned to him quickly—"you must stay for a while and talk to Louis; it's so long since you've seen each other."

"You can also," Louis said, "stop calling her 'Miss Charles.' She's Justine." He held up the drink he had poured out and the light glowed on the rose-colored liquid as if it were a jewel caught in crystal. "Odd, I haven't tasted a Negroni since I was last here."

In the hall Kate paused, a hand on my arm. "That green baize door leads to the kitchen quarters and over here"—she crossed to a door opposite and threw it open—"is where we dump all the things we can't be bothered to take upstairs. You can hang your swimsuit here, or anything you like. You see?" She pointed and laughed. "There's my awful old sun hat and my golfing umbrella. I can't think why I brought it out here with me except perhaps to remind me of the lovely lush grass of England." There was a touch of wistfulness in her voice.

The green-and-yellow umbrella was propped in a corner next to an ebony stick with a serpent's head for a handle; the sun hat had a bright red ribbon round it and there was a pair of shabby overshoes, which I doubted she ever wore on this island of little rain and no snow.

"Now come up and see your room," Kate said.

The staircase was narrow at the base and wide at the top like an outspread fan, and the room we entered, on the left of the wide corridor, had two tall windows. Kate crossed to them and pushed open the shutters.

"Now you can see it better." But the swift flame of the sunset sky had died and Kate corrected herself: "Or no, you can't, can you?" and went back to the door and flicked the light switch.

My first glance fell on two large oil paintings.

"Great-great-grandparents," she said. "You see how fair the woman is? She was Swedish and that is where Louis gets his golden look from." She spoke with pride.

The furniture in the room was an extraordinary conglomeration of period pieces. Over a huge Empire bed was flung a silk coverlet magnificently embroidered with a peacock motif in worn and faded blue and green and gold. A gilt ormolu desk stood cornerwise and served as a dressing table, the mirror crowned by two rather shabby cupids. There were two chairs, one enormous and covered in yellow brocade, and on the bedside table was a two-handled vase, obviously Athenian, which had been converted into a lamp. There were also some books and a biscuit tin.

"I hope," Kate said, anxiously watching me, "that you'll find you have everything you want. But if I've forgotten something you have only to ask Ruth or me. Ruth, by the way, runs the house. She has been in our family ever since I can remember and is devoted to us. Thank heaven she has taken to life out here, even to the extent of learning enough of the language to be able to go shopping."

"This is an interesting room."

"Oh, the house is filled with the last relics of our grandeur." She spoke with mockery.

42

"And how grand the d'Arrancourts were at one time! But that was long before I was born. I had to sell our house in London about ten years ago, and with that money and the proceeds from what remained in the way of furniture and porcelain, I could have lived extremely comfortably, but I speculated and lost most of it. I'm now existing on what is left." She shrugged her thick shoulders. "Well, it's something to be able to live on such a beautiful island, I suppose."

I wandered to one of the windows and Kate moved up behind me. The sea was just visible in the darkening sky and immediately below us was the garden.

"You can't see it at night, but over there, straight ahead of us"—Kate pointed—"is another island. Palacanthus. It is owned by Costos Machelevos, a Greek millionaire and a bachelor, and some way to the left is the Dark Sister."

"Louis pointed it out as we drove here. It's an odd name to give a cliff."

"The origin of it is lost in time." She turned away and went to the second window. "From here, in daylight, you can see its twin, the Green Sister."

I shaded my eyes against the lights of the

room and could just make out the pyramid shape against the heavily starred sky.

"The Aegean is full of legends and Chrysolaki has its own," Kate said. "But I suppose Louis told you."

I laughed. "He doesn't go in much for storytelling, but Matt said that the rocks of the Green Sister make sounds like bells tolling when they're struck."

"No one who is alive now has ever heard them, but everyone on the island believes the story that if the tolling of the rocks is heard it means impending disaster. There was an earthquake here hundreds of years ago and the stones rang and warned the people in time. Then a century ago they rang again. The women fled, taking their children. But the men laughed at their superstition and remained. The next night a tidal wave struck the island and most of the male population on the west coast was wiped out. Of course, I don't believe the story. At the same time, when you live among people steeped in ancient lore, something rubs off on you. If I heard the stones, I really believe, against my own sane reasoning, that I'd wonder what evil was afoot on the island. But that's foolish of me. The stones are a natural formation and the old gods are dead—or rather, they never existed." She made an odd little gesture, crossing her fingers as if asking forgiveness of those gods whose reality she had denied.

She had moved near enough for me to notice how unusual her eyes were—pupil and iris of the same color, giving her an odd, slightly wistful monkey look.

Her fingers touched my arm. "How happy I am for you both. If you could be married from here—"

I said as gently as I could, "We haven't even agreed to an engagement yet. We thought we needed time to know one another better."

She shook her head, smiling. "Oh, but now I've met you I have no doubts about the future. You and Louis will be so splendid together. I couldn't have wished him to have loved anyone better."

The lights chose that moment to dip, shudder and steady again.

Kate laughed. "You mustn't be alarmed if you suddenly find yourself in the dark. Our electricity supply is very capricious. It has cost us—Matt and our doctor friend Jock Anderson and I—a great deal of money to have it brought to our houses from Hagharos, bypassing Kentulakis. The rest of the island lives by oil lamps. You see how primitive we are."

Her last words were drowned by a sudden cacophony of sound. I leapt round, staring at the wall.

"Oh dear, you are being swiftly introduced to all the hazards of the house, aren't you? Those are my clocks—or rather, Louis's and mine, since they are family heirlooms. They span many centuries and, poor though I suppose I am, I can never sell them."

She spoke through the orgy of chiming, of notes vying with one another, light and sonorous, tinkling and growling like violins merging with cellos, drums with flutes— many striking simultaneously, but a few trailing behind and one, raucous and throaty, bringing up the rear.

"I do hope you'll get used to them. But then, I'm sure you will, as I have done. I never even hear them."

I said politely, "I have an apartment on a busy main street, I'm used to traffic noises."

"I'm so glad because, you see, there isn't another room to offer you. The house isn't as large as it looks from the outside, and apart from Ruth's room and the one Louis has always had and which is full of his photographic paraphernalia, we only have a little box room which I keep for Elaine. There are times when Matt has to go away, and Ludmilla, his housekeeper, sleeps rather heavily and if Elaine becomes restless in the night, as she sometimes does, Ludmilla would never wake. So, I have her here. Of course, when Matt is home, she is perfectly safe at Marathon. He sleeps, as he puts it, like a spy on the run." She laughed.

The last of the clocks in the adjoining room made a poor, pathetic little *peep* of sound, striking eight.

When Kate left me, her quick footsteps running down the fan-shaped staircase, I wandered to the east window, opened it and stepped out onto a small balcony curved like a pulpit in a church.

It was quiet except for the hiss and lap of the sea somewhere behind the house and the murmur of conversation from the room below me. In the far distance, to the left, I could see the quiver of lights which I guessed was Hagharos, and directly in front of me the Green Sister loomed against a sky frozen blue-white by a full-risen moon.

As I turned away I saw Louis's photograph

47

in a carved wooden frame on the dressing table. I picked it up and turned it towards the mirror. To see anything reflected—an object or a reproduction of a person—was to see differently, perhaps more truly.

Looking at Louis's photograph, I wondered if I knew the man whom I had so suddenly loved, and if he held my photograph up to a mirror, would I seem different to him? I laid the heavy frame back on the dressing table, tipped out my overnight bag, washed and chose a fresh dress from my suitcase, then made up my face.

From somewhere below me came the soft tinkling of a bell. Every sound and sight in this hot, ancient world filled me with curiosity and I went out onto the balcony again. A goat, milk-white in the silver night, was tethered just beyond the garden. The full moonlight struck it as it shook its head, so that the bell below its bearded chin danced. I caught a glimpse of a horn—just one, as if it were no goat I saw, but an animal from the world of legend, a unicorn. Whether or not it had another horn perhaps hidden by the shadow of the trees I didn't know, for someone moving in the garden below made me lean over and look below.

A woman stood quite still, and I wondered how long she had been there. It was obvious that she knew I had seen her, but she didn't speak and it was I who broke the silence.

"I'm sorry. I can't say 'Good evening' in Greek, but perhaps you understand English."

"I am Ruth." She spoke slowly and very clearly, without raising her voice.

"Oh, of course. Louis has told me about you."

She moved towards the side of the house, saying as she went, "If there is anything you want, please let me know, Miss Charles." She had vanished before she had even finished her sentence, so that my name came from out of the emptiness of the garden.

4

LAMPS glowed in the sitting room and small white moths were already starting their compulsive dances of death against the closed screen doors that led to the terrace.

The people in the room were very still. Kate sat on the faded yellow settee with Elaine at her side, two hands clasping a mug.

Louis moved from the window towards me and his hand touched my cheek. "You look like something that has just come out of its cellophane wrapping."

"From the grocer's."

"No, darling, from the florist's. And you smell good, too."

It was a brief, laughing, personal exchange, and as I sat down, Matt moved away from the fireplace, his hand brushing the tall green fern fronds in the bronze urn that stood where a fire would probably burn in winter.

"Elaine and I must go." He took the mug from her and pulled her lightly to her feet. Then, holding her hand, he turned to me. "We'll meet," he said.

I touched Elaine's hand. "We'll meet too."

I had no idea whether her smile was one of understanding or just a pretty formation of her long, up-curled mouth, and a moment of wonder crossed my mind as to what hereditary forces had made her what she was.

Louis went with them out to the car, and Kate pushed open a screen door and walked onto the terrace. "The air is so scented tonight," she said and gestured to me to join her.

We could just see, to our left where the light streamed from the open front door, the three people walking to Matt's car.

"How lovely Elaine is!" I said.

"Louis has told you, of course."

"But it's so hard to believe—that is, until you look at her eyes."

"It's also hard for even us, who know her well, to be quite certain how much she understands of what is said to her. Before her mother's dreadful death she could speak—oh, childishly, enunciating words with difficulty; but at least we could understand. Now . . . now, we don't even know if she has forgotten the words she knew before that tragedy."

"Yet she sat so quietly while we talked, watching us as if she found it all interesting."

51

"Oh, she watches; but Matt is certain that she understands very little. She can do simple things like dressing herself, with a great deal of help from Ludmilla. And if her food is cut up for her she will eat it. She loves food, especially peaches." Kate's face softened. "To see Elaine eating a peach is to watch, for a few minutes, a perfectly normal child."

The car doors closed and Matt's car purred to life.

I said, "If Elaine was born subnormal how is it she was so upset by her mother's death? How was it she understood?"

"Even animals know fear. And Helen's death coincided with one of Elaine's restless moods. At those times she doesn't sleep and has to be watched carefully; otherwise she gets up out of bed and wanders out of the house. She has been found in the olive orchard, on the road and even down by the beach, which is most frightening of all for us because she doesn't know fear and might walk into the water. On the night her mother was killed, Elaine was found on the beach crouched at the foot of our great rock. Tears were running down her face and she was trembling, but no sound came. It was terrible. We are certain she must have seen her mother fall but couldn't tell us."

"You think she saw who it was with her mother?"

Kate shook her head. "We don't know. But if she did, she seems to have forgotten who it was. There is nobody here whom she fears."

We stared into the distance and there was nothing I could say that would not sound banal.

Kate broke our silence. "I have sometimes tried to bring Elaine back—oh, gently of course, to that night just to see if by recalling it, the shock could be broken and we might get a lead to the facts of Helen's death. But it's no use. I think—subconsciously since Elaine knows no logic—she has chosen to blank that terrible experience out of her mind."

"Could Helen have committed suicide?"

Kate's eyes opened wide. "She loved life too much to destroy herself, and in spite of all her wildness she never drank too much. So those weren't the causes of her . . . accident!" The hesitation before the last word was deliberate. "So the question is, Who was the man?"

"Or woman?"

"I doubt if Helen Braddon would take a

moonlit walk with someone of her own sex. No, I think she climbed that goat track on the Dark Sister with a man and they had an argument and fought—Helen was not averse to fighting with fists if she had to."

"And Elaine saw?"

"We shall never know what she saw."

"But she looks so happy."

"Why not? She is loved and cherished by everyone here, and as she has no memory, the incident—whatever it was—is forgotten."

"I've always thought retarded children were troubled and frustrated."

"The doctors say that there is no consistent pattern of behavior."

"And Matt took over the responsibility. How strange for a man . . ."

Kate turned and gave me an odd look. "Oh, but you see—" And then she broke off as if checking an impulse and, instead, she said matter-of-factly, "Experts told Matt that as it would be impossible to improve her condition, she would be happier living with a family; that since she is not troubled and confused herself, to exist in a home with children who were might cause her distress. You'll see, Justine. She is the most contented human being you could meet; she asks

54

nothing more than what she has, she lives for every sunny moment. And I think that is the greatest happiness." Kate turned back into the room as she spoke, and I followed.

I heard Louis return from seeing Matt off. He was whistling a tune I didn't know.

"A Greek folk song," Kate explained. "Louis has taught himself quite a lot over the years that he's been coming here for his holidays."

On a narrow table against the far wall were three tall, half-burned candles. Kate saw my glance towards them. "Those are for Elaine— sometimes I bring her here for an hour or so before she goes to bed, just to give her a change of scene or if Matt is going out, and we use those candles for her shadow pictures. She has an extraordinary gift, you know. Some people in England who work with retarded children discovered it. She sits between a light and a white wall and copies the drawings of animals and birds from books. It's a curious gift and one which nobody can explain—I feel that she is observing with her hands what normal people observe with their eyes."

"And the people around—the children of Chrysolaki? Does she play with them?"

"Matt won't allow her to. But they adore her from a distance."

"Why does he isolate her?"

"She's not isolated. There's Matt himself and Ludmilla, his housekeeper, who is wonderful with her, and then I help look after her, too. You see, I act as part-time secretary for Matt. It keeps me occupied and earns me money."

I must have been frowning, for as Louis entered the room, he said to me, "What are you looking angry about?"

"I frown when I think," I said lightly.

Kate said, "Let's go and eat. I'm sure Justine must be starving."

During the meal, she ran from kitchen to dining room with watermelon, small fresh lobsters and, finally, very sweet cakes which Kate told me were called *karidópita* and were made with walnuts and honey.

When Ruth brought coffee into the living room, Kate said, "You haven't really met, have you? This is Miss Charles."

"Oh yes." Ruth half turned and looked at me. "We met before dinner when I was in the garden. Miss Charles was on her balcony." Her voice, as earlier that evening, was polite, formal and completely flat.

A sound beat like far-off drums and I recognized it as the pulsating of a boat's engine.

Louis leapt to his feet. "It's coming here, to our landing stage! Listen . . ." His face was vivid with excitement.

"But who on earth would call on us by boat?" Kate asked. "We know no one from the other islands. I can't think—"

"Oh, *I* can!" He was out of the room in such a rush of movement that the air stirred like a cool breeze around us. We could hear his footsteps on the stone flags that led to the back of the house.

Kate turned to me. "Do you know what this is about?"

"No."

She handed me a coffee cup. "Well, we'll just have to wait. It could possibly be a boat from Hagharos bringing some photographic supplies Louis wrote and asked for. He could never exist for seven weeks without his camera and every possible piece of equipment." She stood absently pleating the corner of an English newspaper that was probably many days old, and her head was tilted, listening.

Upstairs the clocks must be pounding the

minutes away; but the room in which we waited for Louis was oppressive. There was a kind of poignancy about Kate d'Arrancourt—a woman in her late thirties living out her life in this too-large and not very beautiful house on an isolated island, with the clocks and Matthew Braddon's typewriter over at Marathon all ticking her life away.

I was drinking the last of my coffee when Louis returned. No one could inject more gaiety into a place than Louis when he chose. He came by way of the terrace, flinging open the screen doors and bounding into the room waving a piece of crested paper.

"I've got news—from Palacanthus." He swept round us, arms outstretched, saying to me, "And that, my darling, is Costos Machelevos's island."

"What news?"

"I'm going to see him tomorrow. This is an invitation."

Kate said in dismay, "Oh, Louis dear, don't get any grand ideas. You couldn't possibly afford to keep up with his magnificence."

"This is a piece of professional business." He began walking up and down the room. "I didn't tell you," he said, stopping again in front of me, "in case it fell through and Machelevos didn't even bother to answer my letter, but I decided to try and earn some money while I was over here. I told you that Bill's parting words to me before I left the studio were, 'If you can find some work to do while you're over there, for God's sake take it.' He also said, 'Talent's no bloody good unless it's applied to something that brings in the cash.' So I had a flash of inspiration. I wrote to Costos Machelevos—told him when I was coming to Chrysolaki and suggested that he might like to discuss with me an idea I had."

"What idea?"

"That I go over and photograph his island, take hundreds of pictures of his house, the treasures in it, his grounds, his guests. And out of them he might like to select enough to make a splendid book of color photographs of life on Palacanthus. The book could be published privately and copies given to his friends as Christmas presents. I even went into details: a large book, bound perhaps in dark-red morocco with gilt lettering. No expense spared."

"And the launch we heard was from the island?" Kate asked.

He nodded, unfolding the letter again. "He wants me to take over some of my work for him to see—I brought quite a variety, just in case—fashion stuff, girls' faces, glamour, even some travel advertisements—" He paused and some of the light went out of his face. "But what am I getting so damned excited about? Good photographers aren't that rare these days. It could be that Machelevos will take my idea and give it to some Greek professional."

Kate said briskly, "Nonsense! Stop being beaten before you start. All you have to do is show him the samples of work you've brought over and remember that he is a man who likes self-confidence in others."

"But, hell, I came over here to be with Justine. I must have been crazy to suggest this job."

"But you did and it'll probably be the turning point in your life. How long will it take?"

"The letter says that if we agree on fundamentals, it will only be for about four weeks because he goes to America at the end of the month."

"Then that's fine," she said, smiling. "You and Justine will have a nice time together when it is finished, and this man Bill—I hope he's honest!—will be delighted that you've been working. I'm sure Justine will understand." She smiled at me.

"Of course."

"Well, then, it's working out perfectly. Justine will always be here when you get back." She looked happy and complacent. "Machelevos is highly influential. If you please him, you'll please half Europe and your fortune will be made. You must remember you've now got Justine to think of, too."

I would like to have said, "Oh, Kate, for the time, leave me out of Louis's plans." But I couldn't; her bright, hopeful face silenced me.

After an hour of talking, Kate urged us to go for a walk. "It's a lovely night, so don't stay indoors." She interpreted my swift glance at Louis correctly. "You mustn't mind leaving me alone. I have Ruth if I want to talk to someone and there's the radio and a pile of new books—I order batches of them and then never somehow seem to finish one. I don't know why. I think I prefer magazines—those lovely glossy ones I used to see in England. I'm not particularly intelligent, you know."

She smiled as I protested "Oh, no!" and made a mental note to send her a gift of a subscription to a glossy when I returned to London.

Louis reached for my hand. "Come and I'll show you Chrysolaki by moonlight."

Each stone step from the terrace down to the garden was clearly outlined in pearly light. I looked back as we walked down a path between the tidy flower beds, and saw Kate twisting the knobs of the radio on a carved chest. I wondered if she was so used to her quiet, confined life on the remote island that she felt a relief at not having to entertain me. Perhaps she was no longer conditioned to put herself out for strangers, although I was certain that she had meant it when she said she would do everything she could to make my stay enjoyable and I was equally certain that her first impressions of me were favorable.

If Louis was successful in the Palacanthus proposition and would need to be away a great deal, I was determined not to hang around the house waiting to be entertained. Louis had not told me that this might be a partial working holiday, but I didn't mind—I had an island to explore, the sun and the sea to enjoy. Time was going to be nothing.

We walked through a little gate into an olive grove. The moon silvered the leaves of the crooked trees and as we went in silence, I had the strange sensation of having drifted to Chrysolaki without any effort on my part—the air journey, the wait in Athens, the night's stay in Hydra, and the crowded ferries had melted into unreality. At some moment in London, while I slept, an enchanter had touched me and transported me to this place where strange scents and sights and sounds brought such a sense of timelessness that I could have been wandering in an Olympic legend.

Together Louis and I came out of the grove and crossed a patch of wild grass to a place where worn stone steps led down to a piece of hollow ground lined with cypresses and scented firs. My arm brushed a flurry of cup-shaped blossoms and Louis laughed, pulling branches aside for me to pass. "Arbutus," he said. "Like everything else in this place, it grows and multiplies. Careful—" And just in time he pulled me up sharply and I did a short leap over a fallen stone.

I bent down and touched it. It was smooth

63

as silk, clearly veined in the moonlight, cool as only marble can be.

"It's a piece of an old column," I said. "Louis, what is this place?"

"Nobody here can remember when it wasn't called the Paradise Garden. Archaeologists abandoned it years ago when they decided that they hadn't come upon the remains of a temple, but just some rich ancient Greek's house, which had perhaps been destroyed in the earthquake centuries ago. The place is just a wilderness of flowers and moss and broken bits of marble. The islanders don't bother with it—there's nothing here that can help them make a living. So it's ours." He folded me in his arms.

I remembered how I had stood on the balcony of my room at Argus and breathed in the scents of the island. This seemed to be the place where they were concentrated, dispersed perhaps by some mysterious alchemy in the moon's light, since there was no wind to blow them east or west.

Patches of oleander and hibiscus flowers defied the incandescent light and burned crimson against their dark leaves. Some lines, learned in childhood and forgotten for so long, came back on the rolls of memory.

> Fruit of the Hesperides
> Burnish take on Eden-trees
> The Muses sacred grove be wet
> With the red dew of Olivet . . .

And on this spot had some Dionysian revelries once taken place? I stood still and, fantasy becoming fact, thought I could hear the thin reed music of pipes that had played long ago, in the age of fable, while naked youths had danced.

Enchanted by the garden, bewitched by the scents, I turned impulsively to Louis and laid my face against him. "Darling."

He had an athlete's agility. In what seemed a single movement I was lying on the mossy ground and he was beside me, resting on his hands, looking down at me. The moon was behind him, so that his face was in shadow, mine was exposed to the full white glare above the trees. My heart was pounding; I felt the pillow-softness of moss behind my head.

Louis took my face in his hands. "Let me look at you. The moon turns you milk-white like a ghost, and when you speak gently your voice is so light that if there was a wind, it would blow it away." I felt his fingers on my closed lids. "You have lovely, tufty eyelashes, short but thick . . ." He brushed his lips across my throat so lightly that it might have been thistledown blown on me. "That's just the apéritif," he said and moved so that his whole weight was on me.

I put my arm across my eyes, hiding from his laughing, passionate face, cutting him off from contact with my mouth. He slid to my side. "All right, darling, maddening girl, we'll move more slowly."

His body no longer blocked the silver garden, and I rested back against a moss-encircled tree, looking into the lovely hollow of the Garden where broken pieces of marble lay like patches of snow among the wild lilies and the rosemary.

Something moved in the distance. Leaves in the wind? But there was no wind. I shut my eyes and opened them again. The distant movement continued softly, smoothly towards us.

"There's someone there," I said.

"Rabbits and hares." He spoke with his lips against my throat. "Or gnats ready to bite—"

"Elaine."

Louis's arm slackened and he looked over his shoulder. "Oh, damn it to hell!"

She had stopped walking and was standing half in and half out of the shadows. She wore a long flowing dress of some material so soft that it molded her figure in the seductive way of a Greek statue; her hair was aureoled in light.

I wondered how long she had been watching us and how much she understood of what she had seen. A man and a woman lying together: whispers, bodies close. But no more.

I scrambled to my feet and as I went towards her I realized that she was wearing a nylon nightdress that reached her bare feet.

Louis said impatiently, "So she's on this game again, wandering about the countryside when she's supposed to be in bed and asleep. If they can't look after her properly, then they should send her back to England and put her in a place where she'll be locked in."

I could understand his irritation; in a way, I felt it, too. In such a place of bewitchment, all my reasonable resolutions, all my fine arguments would have been dissolved and we would have made love.

As it was, we went towards Elaine and I said her name gently, uncertain as to whether she remembered that we had met or whether we were strangers to her. I was careful not to let my voice alarm her. "It's Louis and Justine. You came down to the boat to meet us, didn't you?"

Louis's voice cut sharply across mine. "Go home, Elaine."

She didn't move.

"*Go—home—*"

She was so still that she could have been a statue: a Galatea into which life had not yet been breathed. I reached out and took her hand, and as she didn't draw away I knew she was not afraid of me.

"Do you like going for walks in the moonlight?"

"You've been told that it's useless to ask her questions. She can't answer you; she doesn't even understand what you're saying. We'll have to take her home." He peered at her. "She isn't sleepwalking, is she?"

"No. Her eyes follow us. She's wide awake." I led her towards the four broken marble steps that were the way out of the Garden. She came, walking sure-footedly, and Louis went first along a path that ran to the left of the one we had taken from Argus. In the distance the sea was as still as glass.

Louis said, "I'll make a bet that she was actually looking for you. You're someone new and you talked to her. People don't, you know—except Kate and Matt and Ludmilla. The rest leave her alone."

"Kate said the village people loved her."

"I don't know about that. But she's pretty and strange and they're odd here—shut away from the enlightened islands. Simple people often attach some sort of superstitious devotion to things they don't understand—at least, that's how Kate puts it. She says that children do it, and even the mothers on this island are little more than that. Oh, they work hard and have large families, but they're riddled with magic notions. Anything that is out of their normal rut they treat as miraculous—or evil."

We had been discussing Elaine as if she weren't there, and glancing at her I realized that she was quite unaffected by it. Her world was inside herself, shut away, exclusive and God knew how empty . . .

We had rounded a bend in the path and I heard symphony music and saw the lights of a house.

"Marathon," Louis said. "Elaine—hurry; you're home." He pushed open a tall wrought-iron gate and we went down an avenue of flowering bushes. I was afraid that Elaine would be cold and I wished I had a coat with me to put round her shoulders. But when I touched her hand I found that in spite of the thin nightdress, her fingers were warm.

The house at the end of the drive was white and two-storied. Huge rounded windows curved out of sight and I realized that from the far side of them, there must be, as at Argus, a view of the sea. Lamps shone from an upstairs curtained window, lighting the delicate tracery of the wrought-iron balcony, so that its sea-horse motif was clear-cut, the little animals prancing one after the other the length of the house.

The leaves of the trees rustled in a wind so light that I couldn't feel it. It was a strange sensation—as if something living but invisible hovered above us, playing among the cypresses.

Another light shone in a downstairs room and a man sat in a huge armchair with his back to us. I recognized Matt by the strong, dark swirls of his hair.

Elaine's hand was limp and warm and

trusting in mine, and when I glanced at her I saw that the little half-smile was still on her face, as if she had achieved what she had left her bed to do.

It was quite impossible that Louis was right and she had come to find me, not really knowing where to look but following the sound of voices. Inquisitive as a lonely pony in a field, she could have walked through the night to look for someone who she knew in her vague mind was closer to her own age than those who ordinarily surrounded her.

5

WE crossed the garden to the last lovely movement of Haydn's Clock Symphony. Simultaneous with our footsteps on the paved patio, there was a movement from the chair, and Matt sprang to his feet and turned to the windows. He could not have heard our approach through the sound of the music, yet, alert as a cat, he had sensed an alien presence. For a moment his stance had the fierceness of some violent defense, then he relaxed visibly and came towards us.

A white moth flew across my face, and Elaine put up her hand to touch it. As it escaped her, Matt stepped out to meet us.

"Your niece!" Louis said with a wave of his hand that was a mockery of polite formality.

"Come in."

As if on cue, the gramophone switched itself off with a click; we entered the big room, and Matt pulled forward a chair. "Where did you find Elaine?"

"Watching us," Louis said, "in the Paradise Garden."

Elaine sat on the floor near a sleeping cat, sleek and gray, with pointed ears that twitched as I bent to stroke it. It roused itself sufficiently to yawn at me, the muscles of its back rippling at my foot, then settled again, curling its head near Elaine's foot.

Matt left abruptly and I looked about me at the large room whose dominant feature was the splendid picture window that looked out across a patio to the spangled sea.

Matt returned and I watched him move, so sparingly, every gesture controlled. "I've just been to check the back door. It was unlocked. I'm sorry about this, but please stay and have a drink."

I said I wanted nothing and Louis asked with alacrity for a whiskey.

While he poured out two drinks into finely engraved tumblers, Matt said, "Elaine has bouts of night-wandering and so we try to keep the outside doors locked. She doesn't understand how to twist keys, and the only doors that are left open are the French ones in this room when I'm home. I'm afraid Ludmilla forgot to lock the back door tonight and Elaine wandered out."

"She wasn't even wearing slippers," I said.

"Oh, she's used to that. The soles of her feet are very tough and physically she's extremely healthy." He glanced at her as she sat curled up beside the cat. "She can stay here for a few minutes and then I'll take her upstairs and get her to bed after"—he added ruefully—"washing her feet."

Elaine saw him glance at them and pushed one forward, examining it. It was a perfectly shaped little foot with scraps of dry earth clinging to her toes.

"The trouble is"—Matt sipped his drink—"that Ludmilla sleeps like the dead and because she works so hard during the day, I haven't the heart to disturb her now. But sometimes she's absent-minded—that door should have been checked."

Louis was completely uninterested in Elaine. He changed the subject firmly. "Now that I'm here, I want to ask you something. You know Costos Machelevos, don't you?"

"We meet sometimes on his island and talk, but I never go to his many enormous parties. I detest such gatherings, where only inanities are exchanged. But Costos as a man, I like. Why do you ask?"

While Louis told him, I watched Matt,

74

wondering again why such an obviously sophisticated man was living on an isolated island where there was not even a colony of English-speaking people to join for amusement and diversion. Why had he not chosen Rhodes or Crete where there would have been companionship for him?

Chrysolaki was probably very beautiful and the weather perfect, but a man like Matthew Braddon surely needed the exchange of good conversation with intelligent minds and, from what I had already heard from Louis of the island's lack of a "foreign intellectual set," I doubted he would find it here.

Suddenly Elaine moved. She rose from the floor with a smooth grace and ran to the far end of the room, standing between a lamp and the wall. Looking down at the large illustrated book lying open on a table, she lifted her hands, twisting them in slow, careful movements. The lights in the room were soft but, even so, the shadows Elaine implanted on the white wall were clear. The slender gray line of a stalking tiger slowly came to life as if I were watching its sun shadow on a wild African plain. The likeness remained for only a moment or two and then Elaine looked down at the book again, resting her hands only momentarily in her lap before lifting them once more, weaving and arranging her fingers into the unmistakable shadow of a camel.

Matt said, "She can copy from a book but she can't copy any moving thing. We've tried her and we have always failed. An object has to be inanimate for her to be able to make its likeness."

Yet movement was the essence of Elaine's animals. The square fingers with their small, spatulate nails had the lovely fluid lines of a shadow ballet. It was as if her brain existed in her broad, sun-tanned hands.

"That's enough for now, Elaine." Matt's voice was firm and quiet. "You must go to bed."

She looked at him half over her shoulder, lifted her hands again and, this time without looking at the book on the table before her, twisted her fingers into a strange humped shape. A tortoise? A toad! Something she had seen in a field? One finger shot out and then back again like a long tongue. Perhaps somewhere on the island she had seen a snake and watched its tongue flash out. Were there snakes on Chrysolaki? Of all the animals and birds she had produced during the five or six minutes she had been silently performing, the last was the only unrecognizable one.

"That's the one shadow she doesn't copy from the book. No one understands it," Matt said.

Elaine looked at me as she held her hands' pose, as if to demand if I could understand. But I couldn't. In a way I had a strange feeling that she was trying to bring me into her silent world. But what was it that last hand-shadow was trying to convey?

"Elaine . . ."

She dropped her hands at Matt's voice and rose like an obedient child. He said to me, "You must excuse me for a few minutes while I tuck her into bed. Don't go, please."

"If you'd let me take Elaine up to her bed, you and Louis could talk," I said. "You must have a lot to say to one another."

"I couldn't let you."

"Why not? I wouldn't suggest it if I didn't want to."

The offer was an impulse, I had no idea why I wanted to tuck Elaine in her bed. It could just be an unconscious maternal instinct or the fascination of a beautiful subnormal child who could only convey what she enjoyed doing through her fingers.

I heard Louis laugh. "Do you know, Matt, I only met Justine two and a half weeks ago, but I've already learned that she takes to responsibility like a duck to water."

"So," I said, crossing to Elaine, "I win?" I looked at Matt and then held out my hand. "Will you show me your bedroom, Elaine?"

"She doesn't understand," Matt said. "Her room is the second on the left—that is, if you really—"

"I really do."

Unlike the stairs at Argus, these were carpeted in a cool green, although the side treads were of stone. A gallery ran round three sides of the upper floor, and a long passage led off it. I hesitated, wondering whether Matt had meant me to find the second door along the gallery or the passage. I turned to Elaine and she went ahead of me, pausing at a door.

"Is this your room?"

She waited, watching me with her incredible rich violet-blue eyes. I turned the handle and pushed open the door, feeling for the light switch.

A thin glow from a single bulb lit up the room. It was completely empty except for one large painting on the wall facing the door.

For a moment I stood mesmerized by the strange living quality of the face looking down at me. If the painting honestly resembled the sitter, then she must be among the world's most beautiful women. Dark-auburn hair brushed back from a vivid, laughing face; eyes blue and very slightly slanting, mouth large, not too red, perfectly formed and a little cruel.

A glamorized likeness, perhaps. But who was she and why did her superb portrait hang in an empty room?

I turned to Elaine, who was leaning against the wall outside, her hands working, pleating and fretting at her dress. Quietly I switched off the light, closed the door and said, "I made a mistake, darling. Now, which is your room?"

I stood, holding her hand, looking along the passage. And suddenly I realized that Matt must have meant the second door on the left along the gallery.

I was right. When I opened that door, it was a small, pretty bedroom decorated in green and white—a young girl's room—*with four bars across the window.*

But of course, they had to protect her. Since, Kate had told me, Elaine had no fear, she could decide to jump from the window for the sheer fun of it. Yet those bars haunted me as I sat her down near the washbasin and cleaned the island dust off her feet.

"Now, bed," I said.

She turned and suddenly ducked her head and laid it for a moment against my shoulder. It was a small, charming little gesture and I kissed her cheek. She turned, as if satisfied, and climbed into bed and lay smiling up at me. I was wondering if I should sit with her until she went off to sleep when Matt's voice called me.

"Come down, Justine. Turn off the light. She'll sleep now. But leave the door open."

Her eyes were already closed and her hair curled over the pale-pink pillow. For one moment an overwhelming pity for that beautiful child swept over me. Then I remembered what Kate said: "She is always happy." And I wondered if that were not, after all, the most precious gift of the gods.

When I entered the living room Matt was at the far end, standing by the window.

"She's in bed," I said, "and I think she's asleep."

"It was kind of you, but I can't risk this night walking again. I shall have to change the rooms round so that Ludmilla sleeps in the one Elaine now has and she sleeps in the inner communicating room. I thought of doing that last time she had a period of wandering. If Ludmilla keeps her door locked, Elaine won't be able to get out."

"Has she always wandered?"

"Ever since she came to the island she has had bouts of it."

Since the night Helen died . . .

Louis gave me an almost imperceptible shake of his head and I changed the subject.

"If Elaine can make those lovely shadow pictures, she must be able to draw."

Matt shook his head. "A pen or a pencil means nothing to her."

"Does she understand what she's doing?"

"What is understanding? A thing of reasoning, which Elaine doesn't possess? Or is it an instinct, like a blackbird beating on the earth with its feet in order to lure the worms into thinking there's rain? I don't know. But since her development is permanently arrested, I don't think it matters much as long as the atmosphere around her is a happy one."

"I'd like to take her out sometimes if I may."

When Matt smiled his face changed, grew

81

less remote, less like that of a cold observer. "That's kind. But you won't find her companionable."

"Because she can't speak? But companionship doesn't need words."

"No, but it does need an awareness of the other person."

"I think she has that, and while Louis is over at Palacanthus working, perhaps I can establish some sort of relationship with Elaine. That would be wonderful."

"I'm afraid you won't be able to."

"And you'd rather I didn't try?"

Matt must have misread the tone of my voice or an unfortunate choice of words, for a shadow of anger crossed his face. He got up quickly from his chair and walked the length of the long room. The sea lay gleaming beyond the great window. "You think I enjoy the everlasting watchfulness that has to be kept? You imagine that I am, perhaps, a prison guard *manqué?*" His back was to us but his voice was filled with a quiet anger.

"I'm sorry. I didn't mean to sound critical. I suppose I just—didn't understand."

He turned and faced me and again his smile softened his face. "Don't mind me. I'm touchy on the subject of my guardianship of

Elaine. Experience has made me so. Twice I've engaged people from England who I thought were young enough to find some rapport with her, but it didn't work either time. *They* were the ones who became bored and frustrated; Elaine was quite untroubled, but they found they couldn't stand her silence. Now there is just Ludmilla and I—oh, and, of course, Kate. I don't know what I'd do without her."

"But the children in the villages here—"

"If she joined them it's more than likely she would be distressed, because she couldn't understand what they were trying to communicate to her and then they would grow bored with her *because* they couldn't communicate. And children can be so cruel. We who live with her don't try to make her understand, so in that way we don't bewilder her. I can't expect you to understand. Only someone trained in the treatment of retarded children could do that. You see, Justine, it isn't a simple case of one type of retarded growth—there is a very broad range of disabilities for these children. So—" He broke off, and I sensed by his gesture of impatience that explanations did not come easily to him.

"All right, you've warned me, but I would still like to take her out."

Louis leaned over and touched my knee, saying lightly, "Justine is very feminine, but she has a streak of persistence that would shake most men. I like it. I think I'm going to enjoy being bullied by her when we're married." He drained his drink. "Come, darling, home."

I rose and Matt did not try to stop us from leaving. On a carved table in the hall I saw a brightly colored rubber ball and a little pile of silver bells tied together with scarlet ribbon.

"Elaine's toys," Matt explained. "But she prefers to be with animals, with my gardener Niko's goat and his donkey and our cat. She has an affinity with animals."

He opened the door as he spoke and we stepped out into the semi-darkness. The moon was somewhere behind the tall pines, and the stars were remote. The only light that lit us as we made our way down the drive between the hibiscus bushes was the stream of yellow that came through the open door of the house. I didn't look back, but I knew that Matt was standing on the threshold, watching us.

Louis laughed as we turned onto the track

that led home. "You nearly got yourself an enemy, my darling."

"Why?"

"Questioning Matt's wisdom concerning Elaine."

"But I didn't, I only said—"

"That you doubted that she was being allowed to live the kind of life best for her. You mentioned the idea of her mixing with the village children."

"It was a harmless comment. I'm no expert but I'm interested and—oh, Louis, I'm so sorry for her."

"Then you'd better show it in a less questioning way. Matt allows no interference and he has a temper that matched his sister's."

"By the way, had she dark-auburn hair and very blue eyes?"

"She had. Why?"

"There's an empty room at Marathon. I didn't quite understand where Elaine slept and opened the wrong door. There was nothing in that room except a portrait on the wall, and if the woman was anything like the artist's conception, then she really was glorious."

"That's Matt's sister," Louis said. "I

remember Kate telling me that when Helen died, only one of her possessions was sent out to him—that portrait. I suppose he asked for it, or else she willed it to him."

"But why shut it away? It's so lovely."

"My guess is that he doesn't want to be haunted by her every time he enters his house."

"Then why not sell it?"

"It's by Rushton and worth a lot of money. If it came on the market it would be in all the papers and there'd be talk and conjecture. Matt would hate that. His sister died in strange circumstances and he sells her portrait for a small fortune. Can you imagine what the gossips would say about that? Matt has a reputation and it mustn't include involvement with his sister's death. So he hangs it in an unused room. It's a big house and I doubt if that door has ever been opened since the picture was hung there—except by you, my darling, who, like Pandora, lifted the lid, as it were, on Matt's secret horror."

"You're being melodramatic."

"That's life. Haven't you noticed?"

"But, Louis, you can't think that—"

He stopped on the dark path under the olives and held his arms wide to me. "At this moment I'm not in the least interested in Matthew Braddon's life, only in ours. Come here, woman."

I went to him, and leaning against a tree, he pulled me to him and held me tightly, saying with his mouth against mine, "I love you, and I can't and won't live without you." He drew his head back in order to see my face in the moonlight. "Well, darling, don't you have an answer?"

"Of course. I love you."

"For always."

"I . . . I hope so."

His fingers reached up and tugged none too gently at my hair. "You use cautious words for a certainty, Justine. You don't *hope* so, you *know* so."

"We're here to find that out, and it's wonderful to love and be loved, but that's my hair, not a wig you're pulling, and it hurts."

He pulled more tightly. "Just a reminder that I'll hurt even harder if you dare to try and escape."

"At the end of seven weeks you may want me to!"

His hands stroked my throat, ran down my body lightly. "You're soft in all the right places. And stop talking nonsense."

As in the Paradise Garden, all of me wanted him, but on the road out of Matt's drive there were no mossy banks. I laid my cheek against his and closed my eyes. At the same moment the light that had streamed along the flowered drive of Marathon went out. Matt had closed the door, and we were in darkness. He could not have seen that we had paused round a bend in the road to come together with our deep physical urgency, but strangely, the extinguishing of that distant light was as intrusive as Elaine in the Paradise Garden.

I drew out of Louis's arms. "It's been a long day. Let's go home."

To my surprise, almost as if the switching off of the far light had been an intrusion for him too, Louis didn't argue. "All right, just for tonight. But, Justine—oh, darling, you're my great and terrible need."

We clung to one another and then, too tired for anything but old clichés, I said, "Tomorrow is another day," and took his hand and we walked back to Argus.

Kate was listening to the radio when we entered the living room, but she reached across, switched it off and smiled at us.

"Have you enjoyed your walk? Where did you go?"

"To the Paradise Garden." Louis threw himself into a chair. "And Elaine came too."

Alarm leapt into Kate's eyes. "You found her there—wandering again?"

"In nothing but her nightdress. If she gets picked up one night by some youth from the village who decides he likes her pretty body, Matt will only have himself to blame."

"Louis dear, don't talk like that!"

His eyes danced and he leaned back in his chair watching her. "Do you know how I'd solve the dilemma of having a subnormal child foisted on me?"

"No, and I'd rather—"

"I'd hope for some sort of crisis, so that I'd be forced to place her in a home for her kind in England. I'd see that it would not be in any way that would cause fingers to be pointed at me and people say, 'He doesn't want bad publicity and so no one must accuse him of sending her away because he couldn't be bothered with her any longer.' I'd plan it very carefully—perhaps leave a door open so that Elaine would wander out. Only I'd be cleverer than Matt—I'd see that a couple of benighted strangers didn't come along and upset the whole plan. Had Elaine not been missed until morning—"

"*Louis!*" Kate had shot up out of her chair, standing over him like some angry brown bird protecting her fledglings. "If I didn't know you so well, I'd think that you enjoy being what I can only kindly call mischievous, I'd warn you to guard your tongue while you're on the island. *You* should know that! As it is, I'm sure you'd never hint at such things outside this house. God help you, if you do!"

There was a long pause like that in a battle while the two sides considered their positions. I sat quietly, feeling awkward and uneasy. From upstairs the clocks broke the silence, groaning and chiming and rolling off the hours—eleven of them. Through the discord which neither of the combatants seemed to notice, Louis got up and put an arm round his sister and kissed her.

"Dear Kate"—his voice fought for a hearing amid the symphony of striking clocks—"take no notice. Since when have you listened to my idiocy? Well, don't start now and stop being cross." He glanced at me. "Justine thinks you mean it."

"You don't understand," Kate said

shakenly. "You haven't been here, but there's been so much awful whispering and conjecturing since Helen died that I suppose I'm sensitive to it all—for Matt's sake. I know him and I know it's not easy for him to have Elaine at Marathon, but he'd never, never send her away. That I'm certain of."

I wanted to break in and say goodnight and leave them. I got up as Louis said softly, "Why don't you start to live your own life, Kate?"

"I do. Oh, I do!"

"Running to Marathon every five minutes . . ."

"You seem to forget," she said bitterly, "that our grandparents tossed away fortunes—and I lost what was left. I have got to live—why else do you think I spend my mornings at Marathon typing for Matt? Why else do you think I live here, shut away from the cities which I love?" She broke off, and her voice changed, losing its bitterness in a small, quick laugh. "I always indulge in a moan to Louis when he comes over, but after it, I feel better."

She seemed to have forgotten Louis's strange lead-up that began her moan.

With one arm still round Kate, Louis

91

reached out. "Come here, my 'other woman,' and say goodnight nicely."

But later, as I closed the door of my room and was alone, I knew that something had been left out: some words unsaid in front of me; some explanation left unfinished. Whose? I didn't know; but I was suddenly aware that I was among people I knew little about. I lay in the wide bed with the carved headpiece and faced the fact that after our wild leap into love, there was a great deal that Louis and I had to learn about one another.

The windows behind the drawn curtains were open, but only the soft crash of the waves upon the rocks at the foot of the Dark Sister disturbed the sleep of summer on Chrysolaki.

6

ALTHOUGH the day had been long and tiring and I was normally a good sleeper, my first night at Argus was punctuated by vague awakenings when, in my swinging half-conscious state, I heard the caroling and the croaking of the clocks from the rich collection on the other side of the wall. Each time I heard them I turned over and managed to go to sleep again, telling myself that I would get as used to them as I had to the traffic which rumbled past my apartment near Chelsea Embankment.

When daylight came, however, and I was in that final light stage of sleep before complete awakening, the sound of the clocks became exaggerated, beating like a hundred drums hitting against my ears, forcing me to open my eyes a few minutes before I would have done had the room been quiet.

The knock on my door came in the relieving quiet after the clamor from the next room. Ruth entered carrying a laden tray. "Miss Kate said she thought you'd like

93

breakfast in bed this morning, but you could have it sitting at the window."

"Thank you, I'd love that." I reached for my robe and tied the sash as she set the tray down on a small table. "I was listening to the clocks," I said. "There must be dozens of them."

Her face did not relax its blank severity. "There is a fortune in that room and yet—" She stopped, pressed her lips together and turned abruptly to the door.

And yet a woman lived here who longed for city life, who typed to help keep herself . . . Perhaps it would make more sense when I knew Kate better.

I picked up the pink rose that lay on the tray. "How lovely!"

"Mr. Louis sent you that. He has already left for Palacanthus. The boat came early for him and Miss Kate wouldn't let him disturb you. He hopes to be back before lunch." She paused at the door. "You have everything?"

I said "Thank you" again and pushed open the double doors of the little balcony.

"I saw a goat out there last night. It had a single horn."

"That's Niko's animal. His name is Siphi."

94

"He was like something out of a Greek legend."

"There are a lot of things like that in this place," Ruth said and left me, closing the door quietly.

Kate came in as I was finishing my second cup of coffee and asked how I had slept.

"I never have to count sheep," I said noncommittally, wondering if she would ask if the clocks disturbed me. But she just smiled and nodded and then laid a small writing pad on the dressing table. "I'm due at Marathon in ten minutes. I would have asked Matt to let me off for a couple of days so that I could show you round, but his book has to be completed by the end of next month."

"Thank you, Kate, but you don't have to bother in the least about me. I'm rather good about being on my own."

She pointed to the pad. "I've written down a few necessary words for you that will help if you get lost. They speak an island dialect here, but it's better for you to know Athenian Greek—the people understand it. Actually, you've only got to say 'Argus' and anyone will show you the way—I'm well known here. Who else but the odd English would choose

95

to isolate themselves on an island that has no considerable foreign community?"

I already knew that laugh of hers, dry and unamused. "If you ever feel like having lunch out," she went on, "just remember that you will never go wrong if you order *souvlakia*—it's a kebab grilled on a skewer. But come home today, won't you, because Louis will be back." She bent forward and kissed me on the cheek. "I have to leave now for Marathon. We start work early so that we can relax during the heat of the day. Enjoy yourself, dear." She hustled out of the room and I heard her talking to Ruth in the passage.

When I was dressed, I made my bed and took my tray downstairs. Ruth allowed me no further than the kitchen door, took the tray from me and said, "You'll find it very pleasant on the beach, Miss Charles."

I had a feeling that she was afraid I would hang around the garden, perhaps expecting midmorning coffee, or would try to talk to her or in some way disturb her ordered life.

I gave her quick reassurance. "I think I'll explore the village we passed through last evening."

"Kentulakis? Dry, dusty," she said shortly.

"The Lord forgot rivers when he made the Greek islands." She clattered plates and I knew she wanted me to go.

On the way out I picked up a peach from a blue bowl and walked down the garden path eating it.

The sun was already hot as I went past a tamarisk-enclosed herb garden and then a very small cottage with faded blue shutters. To my left, the one-horned goat shook its head and the bell at its throat jingled.

When I reached the beach, I took off my sandals and walked barefoot across the silky-soft sand to the water's edge, tossed the peach stone into the waves and rinsed my hands in a rock pool.

At my side, the Dark Sister rose, huge and jagged and inviting only to those with cloven hooves. The blue waves slid over the rocks at its base and a pencil-thin line twisted between sharp, upthrust teeth of rocks almost to the top of the great cliff. It was up that path that Helen Braddon had probably walked on the night she died.

But that was old history, and my only reaction was a vague feeling of regret that someone as beautiful as the portrait in the empty room at Marathon should have died so young.

I turned away and tried to find a way round the Dark Sister to the other side, where there could be another and perhaps less over-shadowed bay. But the sea, washing over the boulders, was too threatening for me to risk an adventure through the angry foam, so for a while I amused myself stepping among the safer rocks on the beach, looking into little pools alive with small crabs and starfish, opalescent under the sunlit water.

I didn't stay long on the beach. Instead, I turned inland and came to the path and followed it. I found myself on a track which looked like the one Louis and I had taken the night before. Although I could see no one, I heard women's voices singing while they worked in a field, and I began recognizing other small landmarks that I had noticed in the moonlight on our walk from Matt's house—a wooden stake on which someone had tied a handful of now dead hibiscus blooms; a broken stone wall that enclosed nothing; and trees, a few pines; butterflies dancing among the scattered wild flowers and the drowsy humming of insects.

Then, as the track curved, I saw Marathon.

The tall gates were closed, but I pushed one open and walked through. Immediately I was struck by the contrast between the two villas—Argus, the dark house set in its hot, bright garden; and Marathon, no larger than Kate's house, but with whiter walls and a garden that was like a cool green oasis in the vivid morning.

The shutters at the windows were a pale jade-green, and the wrought-iron sea horses—posed in dancing attitudes across the balcony—gleamed like shining jet in the morning sun. Under the glossy leaves of an orange tree was a long rattan chair with yellow cotton cushions. I could hear the sound of a typewriter being pounded as I walked round the house.

Matt Braddon was standing outside a vine-covered patio, and I paused, uncertain, after the ease with which I had found my way to his house, of the rightness of what I was doing. Standing fully and squarely in Matt's vision, I realized that I should have telephoned or—since I had no idea yet whether Argus possessed such a thing—have sent a request by Kate asking if I could take Elaine with me while I explored whatever there was in the immediate surroundings of the village of Kentulakis.

Although Matt seemed to be looking directly at me, he did not speak. I took a few embarrassed steps forward and the fantailed pigeons strutting between us wheeled up, encircling the garden, and found sanctuary in the poplars.

"I'm sorry, Matt, if I've disturbed you. But I came to ask if I might take Elaine out."

"Oh, Justine . . ." He had obviously been oblivious to me and I had jolted him into the present.

"If I could take Elaine—"

"Of course. Of course."

"I promise to look after her."

"I'm sure you will." He looked round vaguely. "I don't know where she is. Perhaps Kate knows, or Ludmilla. If not, then Niko has been asked to keep an eye on her. You probably passed his cottage on the way here and you'll see his goat in the field over there—" He nodded in the direction of the way I had come.

"With its one horn like a unicorn," I said, laughing.

"If you want to be fanciful, yes." The thought obviously amused him. "Realists

100

would just call it a freak. But it's a devil goat; let free, it eats the heads off all the flowers it can find. I believe only Elaine really loves it." He bent and picked a green sprig from a plant and crushed it. "Rosemary," he said, and picked another piece and held it out to me. "We have quite a lot of herbs here—that bronze plant is fennel; the blue-leaved one next to it is rue, and there's marjoram and tarragon."

I rubbed the rosemary between my fingertips and looked at the herb beds. "How closely they grow together."

"Of course, it's intentional. It prevents the intrusion of weeds."

"I learn something every day," I murmured, and wondered whether the change of subject was as irrelevant as it seemed, or whether by keeping me talking he was giving himself an opportunity of studying me and approving of me as a companion for his mentally retarded niece.

Then as he turned away from me, I said, "I'll go and find Elaine, and I'm sorry—"

"What for?"

"I feel I interrupted your thoughts."

"Yes, you did."

"I should have gone to the front door and

rung the bell—only I thought if I walked round the house I might see someone I could ask and that . . . well, that might disturb you less than ringing bells."

"Anything—sound or sight—disturbs me when I'm trying to think."

"I *am* sorry—"

"All right. All right." His abruptness left him and he laughed and looked up at the sky. "It's a lovely day, so enjoy it and stop apologizing. Writers are hell to live with and it's appropriate that I chose a villa named after a battle. Now, run along and see what you think of our island."

I walked away without another word, circled the house and saw no one. Then, in the field where Siphi was tethered, I saw Elaine. She was at the end furthest from the goat and from Niko's cottage, and she was kneeling in the long grass, her yellow dress splayed round her, with a donkey standing foursquare in front of her. I watched for a moment or two. She seemed to be looking the donkey straight in the eye as if they were having an intense silent conversation.

The second time I called her she turned her head and saw me. Two pairs of eyes, hers deep-violet, the donkey's slanting and darkly sad, watched me as if I were an intruder.

"I'm going for a walk," I said slowly. "Will you come with me and show me your island?"

She looked at me with a vague, sweet puzzlement, but when I held out my hand, she understood the gesture and reached out to me, her fingers curling round my palm. We left the donkey to its contemplation under the solitary tree that gave it shade, and walked out of the field.

It was a strange sensation to have a companion who could neither understand what was said nor even try to speak for herself. I had offered to take her with me on an impulse the previous night and had kept my word, but I wondered, as we followed the road that led to the village, how I was going to manage without any point of mental contact.

I was glad to see that they took trouble with her appearance. Her dress was simply cut and had a little gilt star brooch sewn to the collar, probably so that she wouldn't try to take it off and scratch herself.

My doubts about how I would cope with her did not last long. Her hand, every time I let go, sought mine and communicated a serenity. It was as if, cut off from emotions as we knew them, nothing darkened her world and she possessed that implicit trust that made contact a joy.

My sense of direction was never particularly good, and twice we found ourselves following the wrong track until, remembering my drive from Hagharos with Louis the previous evening, I used the Green Sister as a guide to Kentulakis.

There was a thin pine forest at the foot of the great pyramid of scrub and stone, and as we passed it and saw in the distance the outskirts of the village, I heard the sound of a pipe. A young shepherd, probably, but to me it was as if Pan still haunted the glades of Chrysolaki, lying somnolent in their dappled sunlight.

Occasionally Elaine stopped and pulled up a handful of grass and brushed it across her chin with a little movement of sensuous joy. Once, she stood still and watched a great bird hover above us, then, entranced, she lifted her hands and spread her fingers, looking round her, obviously searching for the shadow. When she could not see it in the noontime sun, her fingers lost their way and wove haphazardly, making nothing but restless, searching movements.

"I think it must have been a hawk," I said. "When you get home we will see if we can find one in a book for you to copy." I talked to her as I would have done to a child who could understand, and the fact that she could hear me without comprehension did not seem to worry her at all.

A crimson butterfly caught her attention and she ran after it and lost it.

Matt, of course, had been right. She did not really understand movement, but it fascinated her—flowers dipping as a bee entered them, flying insects, even the long grasses waving in the *meltemi*, that wild, dry northeast wind of the Greek islands I had first felt on the boat from Piraeus.

I wondered if Elaine's senses quickened at a scent, if color meant anything to her. Still wondering, I brushed against a honeysuckle bush growing in a shady place near a derelict cottage. I picked a creamy bloom and drew on the little capsule of sweetness; Elaine watched me and I picked another flower and gave it to her. She stood with it in her hand and I took it from her and put it to her mouth. The enchanting flavor must have reached her lips, for she smiled and tried to take the flower from me, opening her mouth like an eager fledgling.

"No. You don't eat it." I picked two more blooms and held one while she sucked the sweetness, her eyes momentarily losing their violet blankness in pleasure. If I let go she would have eaten the flowers, and we had a short and, to her, bewildering tug of war until the tiny flowers disintegrated in our rough fingers. It flashed through my mind that this might be the kind of frustration that would begin a tantrum and I steeled myself to deal with it. I was quite wrong. The moment the flowers, bruised and torn, dropped onto the path, Elaine forgot them.

Clusters of eucalyuptus gave us a little shade, and prickly oak and thorn bushes caught at our clothes if, attracted by some flower, we ventured off the road. Vines grew thinly on shallow terraces; there were occasional fields of maize and near a small shuttered house, a group of pomegranate trees.

Occasionally I looked back and saw the Sisters—the Green and the Dark—like two prehistoric animals petrified by a million years, and caught between them, the two villas, Argus and Marathon.

As we walked, Elaine would stop and pick up something—a leaf, a stone—and put it in her mouth. The stones alarmed me at first until I discovered that she had no intention of trying to swallow them. She tasted them like a child picking blackberries in an English hedgerow, who, finding them sour, tossed them away.

Occasionally, without any apparent reason, Elaine paused and stared ahead of her. I wondered whether a sudden thought struck her or if it was an impression made by something she saw which puzzled her, although she could not name it even to herself. What happened behind that sweet, blank mask? Did she have flashes of another dimension, a different world from mine? Or, by wondering that, was I playing with a fantasy? Most of those who knew her would say that I was—that Elaine's mind had neither logic nor reason. Yet I believed that no mind could be a complete wasteland.

When we neared the village Elaine began to drag her feet, but I was quite certain it was from boredom rather than tiredness. After all, what could walking be to someone who did not know what it was all about? Besides, I was a stranger to her and I could not hope for the slightest affinity as yet.

"Come," I said, "let's have a race." It was the last thing I felt like doing in the growing heat of the morning, but amusing her as well as trying to understand her impulses was part of the challenge I was undertaking.

7

AS we ran together past a grove of pale acacias and a mule cart whose driver first stared at us and then laughed and called a greeting, I wondered whether anyone had ever tried to teach Elaine to jump or race for the sheer joy of her own movement. Her passivity seemed natural enough for her, but it was too adult. And I could not believe that the inherent vitality of a fourteen-year-old was completely sapped.

We came to the village, and I saw a jumble of children and hens and thin cats moving in the center of a small square surrounded by dusty shuttered houses and pepper trees.

The children had stopped running after one another and were staring at us. One or two called out to us, and from their shy smiles, I knew it must have been a greeting.

Elaine had taken my hand, and one little girl with a huge red scarf tied round her middle and a string of blue beads round her neck, came up to us, reached out a tentative hand and touched Elaine. As soon as she had done so, she ran away and a boy of about five with a finger in his mouth moved forward as if he also wanted to touch her. But he stopped a few steps away, and without taking his eyes off her, put his hand quickly to his chest. I had an odd feeling that he was mentally crossing himself.

Elaine looked back at the children entirely without recognition. Yet she had lived on the island for some years. Did she recognize nobody from one day to the next, or had Matt kept her so closely guarded at Marathon that she had never seen any of the village people before? I intended to find out.

Beyond the group of children, women stood about talking to one another in their swift, strident voices. They were large women who walked with a natural queenly arrogance, a pride of Grecian race. The islanders were a black-haired people with bold noses, and their dress seemed to be almost uniform—black skirt and embroidered, if somewhat tattered, blouses.

Many of the women we saw were clutching clothes which I guessed they were taking to wash. I noticed that the fountain was dried up and green with clusters of maidenhair fern;

had it not been, it would probably have served as their communal laundry.

A few bicycles were propped against crusty white walls; tasseled bags swung on hooks outside shuttered shops. The *tavernas* were not planned to tempt tourists and the men who sat at the tables had obviously come straight from the fields. A charcoal brazier burned outside one shop, and fish was being fried on it by an old man with wrinkles like black paint on his brown face.

I peered into a darkened shop, and the man inside, seated on a crate, saw Elaine and leapt to his feet, stabbing a little pile of wrapped Turkish Delight. "*Loukoúmi.*" He beamed at me.

Elaine held out her hand and I realized that Kate or Ludmilla or Matt must have come to the shop regularly to buy that particular sweetmeat for her. I bought two bars and slid them into my purse for her to eat later.

Outside, a battered car had drawn up opposite a shop where some kind of fish was laid out on racks to dry in the sun, the wind teasing their thin tentacles.

"That stuff looking for all the world like a tangle of string is octopus," said a little gnome of a man with stiff white hair, shrewd

111

eyes and a shirt that was brighter than any geranium I had ever seen. "You're Miss Charles, aren't you?"

"I am. But—"

"How did I know? Everyone knows everything here, and having answered your question, I'll answer one you haven't asked. Who am I? I'm Jock Anderson, once a doctor in London and now a retired lay-about. I treat any of the islanders who can't get into Hagharos to see the Greek doctor who calls there twice a week, or isn't ill enough to be flown to Hydra." He turned to Elaine. "Child, I know what you would like to drink, and I hope Miss Charles will enjoy a coffee with me. Come and sit down."

We followed him to one of the small tables outside a *taverna* at the corner of a row of shops in front of which was a well-worn but still recognizable pebble mosaic of a woman.

"Aphaia," Jock said. "The island of Aegina claims her temple; we claim her portrait in stone. Aegina has a great peak; we have two, called the Sisters." He laughed. "You see how jealously we vie with each other to guard our sights. We are all a little drunk with our own particular gods. And, to drop to mundane things, if you should come to the village

112

on your own, choose Turkish coffee and preferably have it at this place. The owner's name is Constantine Stephanides and he has a wife, Ismene, who will tell you every legend there is about the island and steal a few dozen from other places just for the hell of it."

Constantine Stephanides, who had seen us and was hovering by my chair, had a face like a medieval brigand. He brought us tiny coffee cups which could not possibly hold more than four sips, and a cold drink for Elaine.

"Orange," Anderson explained. "It's made here from the natural fruit."

Our brigand returned with a dish in which lay a bunch of grapes glowing with the cool patina of green marble. He spoke some words and I looked helplessly at Jock Anderson for a translation.

"Constantine says, 'Eat with pleasure.' So enjoy them, Miss Charles. The Greeks are generous."

"Thank you," I said in English and registered the fact that I would need to learn the Greek phrase for that.

The grin on the man's face had broadened into delight as if I had conferrerd a favor on him by eating his grapes. When he had left to serve two men who had sat down at another

113

table, Jock Anderson leaned across and put the mug in Elaine's hand. He picked a grape from the bunch, took out the pips and handed it to her. She seemed to hesitate until he touched his mouth and then she ate it, cautiously tasting as if she had never eaten a grape before, her hands fumbling.

"I don't understand," I said. "She eats awkwardly as if she didn't know what to do with her fingers, yet she makes her marvelous shadow pictures."

"If I could answer all the questions of normal and subnormal behavior in human beings I'd be a millionaire." He chuckled. "And I'm not. The one thing that seems to be general in all these children is that the critical time is between the ages of fifteen and nineteen—and Elaine is fourteen. So, that's when Matt will find his guardianship most testing to his patience—and he has precious little, anyway." His eyes rested, full of interest, on me. "I heard you're going to marry Louis d'Arrancourt."

"Your village grapevine hasn't quite got the facts, Dr. Anderson. We *might* marry—we don't know yet."

"Are you a cautious girl by nature?"

"I don't think so, but marriage isn't something to be impulsive over."

"You've come to the island together and that's quite enough for the people here. A man and a girl have only to blink at each other for the church bells to ring."

I said lightly, "Then you can tell anyone who is interested that we came here on holiday in order to get to know one another better. It's as simple as that." I broke off, ate a grape and asked, "Are you married?"

He roared with laughter. "Good God, no! I'm a cynic, but not a misogynist. I love women in small doses, but I love them even better when I have shut the door on them and can sprawl in a chair with a Brahms symphony and a bottle of Scotch—or perhaps I should put the bottle first." He felt in his pocket and brought out a string of small yellow beads with a tassel hanging from them. "Fidget beads," he said in explanation. "Here they call them *koumbologi*, and I've caught the habit from the locals. These that I have are carved amber." He leaned back, fingering them and watching Elaine. "You know, Miss Charles, there's something to be said for having a brain that has never developed beyond the age when a child lives

115

for the moment. The tragedy for Elaine is that she lost the power of speech, otherwise I think I envy her."

"They say she lost it when her mother died. Shock—"

"That's right. Shock. But not that of being told about it. Instead, of seeing something."

"That's what Kate told me."

"And what the island thinks." He was suddenly grave, his hands lying quietly over the beads. "It was talked about and whispered about for months afterwards and the shadow is still hanging over those concerned." He jerked his head over my shoulder towards the distant Dark Sister and the sea.

"An accident?"

He opened his eyes wide and I realized that even for him, the mystery of Helen Braddon was still of absorbing interest. "A sophisticate like Matt's sister wouldn't climb what's little more than a goat track just for a pleasant exercise at midnight."

"Why necessarily midnight? It could have happened early in the evening."

"They say she was seen at Marathon at eleven o'clock. Oh, well, 'They say: what say they? Let them say.' " He chuckled and fingered his beads again. "What do the islanders care, anyway? They had no love for Helen—the village women locked up their young sons when she came by."

"But one of them could have attacked her."

"They wouldn't have dared."

"You said—a shadow still hangs over those concerned."

"That's right. Not the Greeks, but the English, or rather, one Englishman—Matt. You've met him, I know."

"But it's horrible—I mean, if you think—"

"Oh, I've stopped conjecturing. What's done is done. Somebody must have had a reason for tipping her off the cliff—Helen was a bitch."

I stared out at the small square, busy with women and children, hens and dogs; the wind tossing the branches of the trees, sweeping down the few narrow-arched streets, playing with the geranium heads that hung over old, crooked balconies.

"Do you know Matt well?"

"I know him," Anderson said steadily. "But *well?* Who does? In so many ways he's like Kipling's cat that walked by itself. Whether by desire or necessity I've no idea.

He doesn't tell. But it's an odd life for a comparatively young man."

By our side Elaine was interested in a bee which hovered, honey-laden, over the tables. I was afraid she might try to catch it and get stung, but Anderson saw my anxiety and laughed. "Don't worry. Something, or someone, looks after that child. She never comes to harm."

"She seems to love everything that moves."

"I'd put it that she loves everything . . . full stop! I'm not a psychiatrist, but although we don't perhaps realize it, I'm certain that each retarded child has within itself something which is as whole and sound as that of a normal child. At the same time, it would be useless to put Elaine in a place run by people who are trained in these matters, because she will never learn and Matt was told she'd be happier with a home life than in an institution."

"So I heard, but it must be a dreadful strain for him."

"He has willing helpers"—Anderson grinned—"Ludmilla and Kate d'Arrancourt. It's not a very great headache for him, shut away most of the day with his writing and away in London for weeks at a time. The two

118

women are the ones who bear most."

"Last night she wandered out when she was supposed to be in bed and came to the Paradise Garden."

He gave me a long shrewd look over his cup, drinking his coffee noisily. "I'm not surprised. You saw her, I believe, earlier that evening—oh, you see, I even know that Kate's car was in the garage being serviced and Matt and Elaine met you. These subnormal children are not so stupid that they don't instinctively go where they trust, and I'll lay a bet that without even knowing what she was doing, she came to look for you. And found you—" He threw back his head and roared with laughter. "I'll bet also that that maddened Louis."

I thought: *That gossip-loving grapevine on Chrysolakis has a strong stem in you, Jock Anderson.*

I switched the focus of the conversation. "Louis has gone over to Palacanthus this morning to see Costos Machelevos."

He said in surprise, "Well, that's something we've missed in the village. So he's being taken up by our bachelor millionaire, is he?"

"It's business."

"And I may not ask what it is?"

"No, that's for Louis to tell—if the project comes off."

He said without rancour, "All right, Miss Charles. What is your Christian name?"

"Justine."

"Then I shall call you Justine. It's a beautiful name."

"Since *you* are dispensing with formalities, do *I* call you Dr. Anderson?"

"Jock. It's Scottish but I'm half Irish, too. That's a combination for the books!"

I looked at my watch, saying reluctantly, since I liked this quizzical man playing with his amber beads, "I'll have to go. Louis is expected back soon after midday and I have to see Elaine safely home first."

He rose and took my hand. "Take advice from me, will you, Justine? I'm a disinterested spectator, but, as such, I see most of the game."

"Advice on what?"

"Be careful. That's all I can say at the moment."

"It isn't. You can't tell me to be careful without explaining what, or whom, I have to be careful of."

His face was built more for impish humor

120

than seriousness, but he continued gravely, "You are on a strange island among people you don't—and can't—understand in the space of a few weeks."

Elaine had finished her drink and I drew her to her feet without taking my eyes from Jock Anderson's face. "You could still be more explicit."

"The hell of it is, I can't. I just know—like those potholers who climb blind into subterranean caves—that there's something here I don't understand and which troubles me. A danger for the unwary, and I can't be more explicit than that. It probably doesn't concern you at all, so don't let me scare you. All I can do is to wish you well. I like you. I think you have courage and also moral strength . . . Oh, what the hell am I trying to say?" He turned away abruptly, stopped, and then turned back. "Can I drive you back to Argus?"

"I'd rather like to walk, but Elaine might be tired."

He glanced at her with a practiced eye and laughed, saying, "She's strong. I'll make a bet she could outwalk you. It's probably nature's compensation for what it has withheld from her."

"Then we'll walk," I said. "But thank you, Jock."

He grinned at me. "There are none more energetic than those who come as visitors. Oh well, don't get sunstroke."

I watched his broad back slide into the dilapidated car. The exhaust burst out in choking fumes, the engine roared and he was away. Jock Anderson's old car was probably the noisiest thing in the whole of Chrysolaki. Through the din I could hear our kind brigand's voice calling, *"Adió. Adió. Sto Kaló,"* and lifting a hand as though he were blessing us.

8

AS Elaine and I made our way through the square, children stopped again to look at us. I greeted them, using the phrase of greeting from Kate's pad, "*Yássas Pediá*," and as they stared uncomprehendingly at me, I realized how appalling my accent must be.

There were some broken steps that led to one of the narrow, archwayed streets and a lemon tree shaded one side.

"Shall we ask them to join us, Elaine?"

She gave me her incurious look and I took her hand and led her to the shallow steps.

I patted the stones, calling to the children in English, "Come and sit down."

A hen ran past me, neck outstretched, paused and pecked nastily at my sandal. I drew in my foot and laughed. The watching children laughed too and came nearer.

I held out the pad Kate had given me and pointed to a phrase. Two of the children peered at it without understanding. Then a third, older child pushed forward, read the paper and nodded. The words had read in Greek, "I do not speak your language."

The girl spoke to the others, and they came nearer, walking close together, and sat round us, on the steps and on the dusty road. Polite, shy, very curious, they looked me over. But it was Elaine who held their attention.

I pointed to some words on the pad. "What are your names?"

They told me. Thanas and Christo, Nerina and Dyna.

I said, "This is Elaine. El-ai-ne. And I am Justine Charles."

Their lips formed the names slowly, very seriously, and trying to establish contact, I pointed to other phrases Kate had written on the pad, only to realize that even the eldest was limited in her capacity to read. At the same time they seemed happy to sit with us, and although I was the stranger, it was Elaine at whom they looked longest. The smallest child, with a thick cloud of blue-black hair, picked up some fallen lemon leaves and laid them in Elaine's lap. I thanked them in English.

A bell sounded from across the street and they got up like a tiny army obedient to a command, gave us a last stare and then ran off. They were halfway across the dusty square when little Dyna came running back. She went straight up to Elaine, her hair flying, the blue beads of her necklace bright in the sunlight. When she reached us, she paused and touched Elaine's hand, her face grave and wondering; then she turned and raced back to join the rest.

It was a small thing, a child trying to make contact with another, and yet there had been in the gesture a curious element of reverence like that of religious adoration.

Elaine hadn't moved. I wondered if, sensing their shyness with us, she herself became shy. It hurt, as it hurt to see a wounded animal, to feel her gentle aloofness as her hands played with the lemon leaves and watched the children run off.

There are people who would marvel at that small gesture Dyna had made. They might say, "That is adoration," and think it wonderful. I did not. It was a troubling revelation of how these children saw this beautiful, dumb child: the very reverence of Dyna's movement isolated Elaine, separating her from what might have been gay and human between them.

The children disappeared down a narrow

street, their motley clothes of red and green and black merging with the shadows.

I took Elaine's arm. "If we don't start back home, they'll think I have kidnapped you."

I was hustling her and she came, dragging her feet again in the reluctant way which seemed the only sign of rebellion of which she was capable. A small cavalcade of donkeys laden with a family's belongings passed from one arched street across the square towards another and immediately Elaine's interest was switched. She ran from me to the animals and put her hands on the back of the last one in the line. Its ears twitched; it flicked its tail and stopped. The man driving them carried a staff which he whipped lightly round the donkey's hooves. Elaine swung round, lifting her hands, looking at her fingers as if it were they which had been struck.

I went quickly to her. "It's all right, darling. The man hasn't hurt the donkey."

As if some intuition told him what this foreign woman was saying, the driver gave the donkey two hefty pats and grinned at us. The bells set up a light jingle as the animal cavalcade moved on, delicate hooves clattering. A few passers-by smiled at us and called,

"*Yássas . . . Yássas . . .*" The tops of the pines swung in the wind; the Green Sister rose out of the azure sky, its flanks softened by distance, its topknot of gray boulders poised as if waiting for an affronted Zeus to step from Olympus and hurl them down upon us in anger at our rejection of his existence. The sea swung gently, ruffled by the *meltemi*, so that a caïque looked like a rocking toy laid on blue silk.

A child ran out of an isolated cottage. She was enveloped in a huge dark-blue cloak that was heavily embroidered with green and scarlet braid. She kept tripping over it and laughing back at someone inside the cottage. Then, when she turned and saw us she stopped dead, her eyes on Elaine, shy and wondering and watchful.

"Well, look," I cried. "Now we have fancy dress!" I turned to Elaine.

She had drawn away, her face suddenly tight with fear. Her hand went out to clutch something, found nothing, shook and fell to her side. Even the small, mechanical smile that was part of her lip formation was gone.

"Darling," I said. "It's only a little girl dressed up." I had seen cloaks like the one the child was wearing in photographs Louis had once shown me. He had told me that in the old days the villagers used to wear them in winter but now few did, although cloaks still hung behind kitchen doors in the cottages. The people of Chrysolaki used the old Cretan word for them, "*Kapa.*"

Elaine's fingers were working as if pushing something away and I saw how her wrists trembled. But her fear was uncommunicable.

I put my arm round her. "It's pretty, isn't it, with all that bright color on it?"

I knew she wouldn't understand, but I had achieved what I had hoped for. The tone of my voice had soothed her, and her fingers stopped their violent working and she stood quietly, looking at me, waiting for whatever I chose to do with her.

The child had disappeared indoors and there was a crash, as if she had fallen, and a loud wail and then a voice scolding her.

The small scene was over in a minute, but as we walked on, I was puzzled. If Elaine had no conscious memory, then why had she been afraid?

"Elaine is perfectly happy because she doesn't understand that life can hurt," they said.

But did "they" know more? They did, of

course. The mundane things like whether her meat had to be cut up for her; butter spread on the crisp bread baked in ovens hundreds of years old. Had she a normal appetite? Those were the things they knew. What *I* knew was that she was capable of sudden fear.

I glanced at her as we walked on. Her face was serene, the upward curve of her lips was there again, giving her that sweet, remote smile. But I knew that whatever they said to the contrary, there was somewhere inside her a place as vulnerable as any in a normal child, a corner open to fear and perhaps to pain.

Matt was sitting in the shade leafing through some typewritten sheets and he looked up as our footsteps sounded on the stone slabs of the path.

"We've had a lovely morning," I said. "At least I have and I hope Elaine has, too."

"Let's go and sit in the patio and have a drink." He led us under the thick vine. "What would you like?"

"Something long, please, with ice. What does Elaine have?"

"Oh, orange or lemon or *Sarizá*, which I doubt if you'd care for, because it is soda water. It's an odd taste drinking it neat, but the people of the island like it and so does Elaine. Don't you?" He ruffled her hair lightly as he passed her.

Elaine copied me and sat down, leaning her head back and watching me, her hands restless in her lap. I knew that my interest in her was both a challenge and a form of conceit, for I wanted to be the one to penetrate the barrier and find a contact that would break her isolation. I wanted to be able to say, "I know what she feels, what she thinks." But I had no idea as I sat with her in silence under the living green canopy.

When Matt returned with the tray of drinks, I told him that we had walked to the village and had met Jock Anderson.

He said, amused, "He's quite a personality on the island."

"And we met some of the village children and tried to talk to them. They thought my accent very odd."

Matt took a long deep drink before he replied. "I don't think that was wise."

"What wasn't?"

"Letting Elaine meet the children. Of course, if you want to get to know them, that's one thing. But I'd rather you didn't involve her."

"She enjoyed it. I'm sure she did."

"Perhaps. But if I, who live with her, don't know, how can you?"

"Matt, if you had seen the way she looked after them when a bell rang and they left us." I waited, watching Siphi in the distance, forefeet in the air, nibbling at a branch of a tree.

"Let's start from the beginning, shall we?" Matt said.

"If I'm to understand, I suppose that's the best way."

"We are living on an island the tourists have passed by and the people here are centuries behind Rhodes and Patmos and the rest. They are simple and superstitious; Christianity and paganism is all mixed up in them."

"I thought when I was in the village that the women walked like goddesses. Perhaps they think they are—"

"It amuses you. I'm not surprised, because you can't understand the power and mystique attached to pagan superstitions by simple people. The Chrysolakians believe utterly in their folklore, in magic, in charms to keep off the evil eye. Didn't some of the children you met wear necklaces of blue beads?"

"As a matter of fact, they did."

131

"And you'll find them occasionally around some animals' necks, too. That is indicative of life here, Justine."

"At least," I said, "it makes for a change from too much civilization."

"That's all right so long as you don't defy what you don't understand. For instance, if you can't remember the Greek word for five, don't—here on Chrysolaki at any rate—hold up your hand with fingers spread and palm facing outwards. It indicates that you're casting a spell."

"In this day and age?"

"The things you are learning about the people here seem to amuse you."

"Oh, Matt, I'm sorry! It's a sign of ignorance to laugh at what you don't understand, isn't it? But it's all so—so incredible."

He ignored both my apology and my comment. "All of which brings me back to Elaine. Because she can't speak, is so very fair, and, to them, has an unearthly beauty, they've endowed her with some peculiar mixture of young pagan goddess and saint. It is the women who cling to these beliefs—the men trade with the other islands and are more sophisticated. But never underrate the power of the woman here." He looked across at me.

"When you were with the children I'm perfectly certain that some of them touched Elaine. Ah yes, I thought so. 'For luck,' Justine, as you'd touch a talisman. Nonsense to you, but I have learned to respect strange ways."

"It disturbed me," I admitted. "I wanted the children to accept Elaine as someone they can mix with, whatever the difference between them—"

"*You* want!"

"I don't mean to sound high-handed, but I'm sure Elaine loved being with the children—they're nearer her age, anyway. When they ran away I felt she longed for them to have stayed."

"And if they had? And if it became a habit, while you're here, for her to join them, what do you think would happen when you'd left and the children still tried to see her?"

"They would all know one another by then and there would be a kind of friendship."

"Good God!" he exploded. "Who are you that you think you can move mountains?"

I may sound blundering to you, but I'm just trying to help. Please understand!"

"It's the village children who wouldn't. And by trying to mix them, you'd be destroying without constructing something to take its place—the barrier is too great. The children would expect Elaine to be like themselves and that will always be impossible."

He was so arbitrary, so final in his opinion that it was hard to check my sudden anger with him. "Matt, can't you see? I'd be trying to *give*, not to destroy." I glanced at Elaine and saw that her hands had stopped their weaving; she was sensing anger and was looking from Matt to me and back to Matt again. I continued more quietly, "First, I would learn enough Greek words to make the children grasp that Elaine can never be like them, and then I'd teach them to accept her as she is—that would be the first step."

"You say 'as she is.' How *do* you see her?" His eyes were cold.

"As a retarded child—"

"Like any other layman," he said impatiently, "you use words that generalize. Elaine is not just a casebook child; she's an individual, gifted in her own way. Perhaps, in spite of that part of her brain that has never developed, she has something to teach us . . . You look surprised."

"I'm not. Kate says that Elaine is always happy—that's important, that's something that she has and most of us haven't."

"But you leave it there. You don't ask why this child—who hasn't your mind, your abilities—is a completely happy person."

"What do you mean?"

"That people see only surfaces. Elaine is happy because she has no prejudices, no hatreds."

"And so," I said eagerly, "the children should be taught to love her. At least I could start by helping them to understand a little and to be kind."

He said quietly, "Maybe you enjoy the idea of taking on an impossible task, but thank you, I have no intention of letting you."

The momentary silence was filled with a polite enmity. Elaine, looking out into the garden, saw the gray cat, and ran out to him. We watched her kneel as he settled, sprawling in the sunlight, and rest her bright head close to his gray velvet body.

"Why do you isolate yourself as well as Elaine?"

He gave me a long, startled look, then he threw back his head and laughed. "No one could ever say that you were afraid to come out with a question, however difficult it might be to ask—*and* to answer."

"I'm sorry. I scarcely know you. I had no right—"

"No, you hadn't. And we'll let it go. My reason for living on Chrysolaki is my own affair. But let's not quarrel about it. I don't ask you why—"

"Why what?"

He gave me a steady, direct look. "Why you are engaged to marry Louis d'Arrancourt."

"Oh, it's not settled. Our holiday here is a kind of testing time."

"Do you have to put it to the test?"

"There are so many ways of loving," I said, "and we want to be sure ours is the right one." I knew as I spoke that I should have said that *I* wanted to be sure—Louis had no doubts.

"And from your definition what is the right way?" He was watching me, his eyes alert and faintly amused.

"That we could bear one another's conversation for the rest of our lives; that we feel friendship as well as—as—"

"As physical desire."

"Yes."

He was aloof as if he had been my doctor listening quietly for my symptoms.

"Sometimes," I said, "You love someone and don't really like them—it's not that way with Louis. With us it's just that it happened so quickly. I think love is many-sided and it has to be the right one for marriage."

"Have you experienced all the facets of love or are you philosophizing? No, don't answer; I think we're getting into rather deep water." He moved to take my glass.

I covered it with my hand but he slid it adeptly from me and went into the house. I wondered if one ever got the better of an argument with him. But another long cool drink on a hot afternoon was too pleasant a thing to be marred by a duel of wills.

I turned and watched Elaine lying very still and quiet by the side of the cat. I had been so certain that I had found a way in which I could ease her isolation, and Matt was determined to stop me. It could be that he didn't know me well enough yet to be sure he could trust me; or it could be, again, the quiet arrogance of his self-will. Whatever it was, our conversation had disturbed me. I watched the wind tearing at the treetops and swinging the tendrils of the plants on the low walls on either side of the patio. Under the vine, I felt none of the fret of the wind, only the cooling breath of green shadow and the smooth marble slabs under my feet.

Looking up, I could catch glimpses of the house between the branches and I wondered which was the room where Helen's portrait hung . . . the empty, discarded room in the beautiful house.

Matt returned trailing an inflated yellow balloon. He set down the drinks tray and then went to where Elaine lay and gave her the balloon. She took hold of it for a moment and then let it go. The wind seized it and tossed it into a tree.

"She enjoys freeing things," he said. "She has no sense of clinging to possessions. It's odd, isn't it?" Then, without the slightest pause, he said, "You know, Justine, you are very strong. But then you're perfectly aware of that, aren't you? You're also very vulnerable. It's a dangerous mixture. You have the power to stand as a buffer between someone weaker than you and the rest of the world. But you also have the capacity to let those people hurt you."

It was a shatteringly accurate assessment of my character and I challenged it with laughter. "Do you always dissect your guests?"

"Only when they interest me."

"Thank you. Or *do* I thank you? Is it a compliment?"

He smiled, shrugged and picked up his drink. "We'll have to find out, won't we?"

I glanced at my watch and saw that it was half past twelve. "Louis is probably home by now." I finished my drink quickly and got up. "Please may I take Elaine out again?"

"You defeat through sheer persistence, don't you? All right, yes." He reached out and brushed a strand of my hair from my shoulders. "In the sunlight it has a red gleam. It's very beautiful." His hand dropped to his side. "Goodbye, Justine. And thank you for being kind to Elaine."

I hid my triumph and said, "Thank you for letting me."

Matt came to the gate with me, and as she saw us moving down the drive, Elaine ran to me, resting her forehead briefly and lightly against my shoulder. I said, "We'll meet again tomorrow."

She wanted to come with me but Matt held her back: "Not now." He had an arm round her, but as I turned left towards the d'Arrancourt villa, I looked back twice and saw that she was resisting his attempts to steer her towards the house. She was watching me, her fingers held out in front of her, making shadows on the ground, as if using the only way she could to bid me goodbye. Or to tell me something.

She was forever out of reach, and yet, in her way, she was trying to make contact. It was a challenge to me to try to breach that wall between her and the people in the world around her. Since she did not know the way, I must be her medium.

9

I SHOULD have been hurrying back to Argus but the noonday was too hot. I sauntered under the trees in the olive grove knowing that it would take me less than seven minutes to reach the villa.

As I drew near the narrow strip of grassland between the orchard and the side gate of Kate's house, the sun glinted on a metal object. It was Jock Anderson's old car drawn up in the shadow of the trees, the hood catching the light only when the *meltemi* blew the leaves of the olive trees apart.

The small white gate was open and I went through to the path which led to the terace at the back of the house. Kate's oleander and hibiscus made a wall on either side so that only someone very tall could be seen approaching.

Kate and Louis were sitting under the awning on the terrace, and as I quickened my pace towards the house, something moved, or rather, someone crept along, keeping close to the white wall. The man's hair was crisp and white, his face nut-brown against the spider-crawl of cracks in Argus's gray wall.

Jock Anderson . . . I nearly called his name aloud, and then suddenly I stopped as I realized that he had no intention of going up the terrace steps to make himself known. His head was tilted so that one ear was thrust forward towards the terrace. He was standing there blatantly listening. I stood for a full minute watching him. That, then, was how he knew the gossip of the village: he eaves-dropped. Perhaps for a man who had spent most of his life listening to his patients telling him their troubles, to come to an island where there were few people to confide any-thing was like having a well only a quarter full of water. Perhaps he was parched for personal involvement and this was the way he had to satiate a natural curiosity about people.

Behind me the wind suddenly crashed the gate shut and I leapt round as if I were being stalked by an enemy. When I turned towards the house again, Jock had vanished. The noise must have alerted him to someone's approach.

I had no idea what Kate and Louis had been talking about because as I rounded the bend in the path, Louis saw me and rose and came to meet me.

"I was just about to send all Kentulakis out looking for you." He swept me up and kissed me. "When I return home, my girl, I like to find you here. Where have you been?"

"Looking round the village." I glanced in the direction where I had seen Jock's car, but the place was hidden from the terrace by a group of pepper trees. "I also met Dr. Anderson," I said.

"Well, that was nice for you. And did he tell you the history of everyone within miles around?"

"No. But we talked quite a bit and then he left and we walked back—"

"We?"

"I took Elaine with me and I delivered her to Matt and had a drink with him. But never mind all that. Tell me about your morning."

"Everything is perfect." Bronzed and golden, he hurried me, laughing, onto the terrace. "I've just been telling Kate. I've got the commission, all signed and sealed. About fifty full-page color photographs of the house, the grounds, the island and any of the house guests whom he wants included—but I'll have to take hundreds of pictures for him to choose from. The book is to be bound in cream goatskin, edge-gilded in gold leaf, and each volume will be presented in a carved cedarwood box. How's that for splendor? Machelevos is behaving like a child promised a fabulous toy. The fact that he is paying for it is a mere detail.

Kate said, "Oh, successful businessmen are often either very sentimental or childishly excited over small things."

"It's a superb island." Louis still had on his face the wonder at what he had seen. "The house is built like an Italian palazzo, the gardens are formal and loaded with flowers—even your favorites, my darling, are massed there prolific as daisies in our fields."

"Crown imperials?" I said. "How lovely to see them growing."

"When I've been to the island a few times, I want to suggest that you come over with me. I'll explain that I need an assistant."

"But you don't."

"Don't I? We'll see." He turned to Kate, his whole manner that of triumph. "Justine doesn't really know me yet, does she? But she'll learn."

"Tell me," I said, "so that I'll be spared that lesson later."

144

He leaned over me as I sat down in one of the rattan chairs. "I intend to work it so that you come over to the island with me each day, but I can't do it immediately."

"And what am I supposed to infer from that?" I lifted up my arms and caught his head as he bent over me. "Darling, what?"

"That you must always be near me, come hell, hail or high water. From now until the end of our lives, you'll never be far from me."

Kate protested, "Louis, don't be so extravagant in your demands."

He went to the table where the drinks stood and he laughed. "But I *am* extravagant and you know it—and now so does Justine." He paused, looking across at me. "Why did I leave both my cameras on the island? There are so many studies I want to take of you."

"You'd be disappointed. You once told me I can't pose."

"That's just it, you're natural. And against the trees at the foot of the Green Sister, you'd look like a naiad."

"Hallo, everyone," said a new voice.

Hand raised in an airy salute, Jock Anderson was coming along the garden path with the casual nonchalance of one who has just arrived.

"Jock!" Kate jumped up and went, both hands outstretched, to greet him. "What brings you this way?"

"I had to call at Marathon. Old Ludmilla has rheumatism again—how that woman manages it in a dry climate is a mystery, but I took her a bottle of liniment and looked in on Matt."

Louis handed me the long iced gin and lime I had asked for. "Justine was there, too, so you must have met."

"No, we didn't." I looked straight into Jock's bright watchful eyes.

"Oh," he said, "you'd been there and gone. Matt told me. You'd taken Elaine out. But I knew that already, didn't I?" He turned to Kate. "We met in Kentulakis."

"That's right." I tried to outstare him, but he won. *You're a consummate liar, Jock*, I told him silently while he and Kate talked. *If you went near Marathon, which you may have done, you certainly didn't see Matt.* There hadn't been time in between my returning Elaine and finding him pressed against the wall of Argus, listening.

"I thought I'd collect the clock," he said. "It's time I started on it."

"Oh, Jock, would you?"

146

"I promised, didn't I?"

Louis, sprawled by my side in one of the long rattan chairs, lifted his glass to the light and studied it, twirling it round, so that diamond lights flashed in the fizzy tonic water. "Kate, tell Justine. And for heaven's sake, sit down, Jock. You make me feel hot just to see you hopping about there in the sun. But pour yourself out a drink. There's *ouzo* there."

Jock went to the table and chose his favorite Greek drink.

"You really must go in and look at the clocks," Kate said to me. "They represent four hundred years of d'Arrancourts. It's fabulous, isn't it? And each generation, and each family within it—sometimes ten separate family lines—has had its portrait painted on a panel fixed to some part of the clock so you can see the unbroken line of our history. Some are painted by great artists. I'm afraid I can't afford to employ a good professional, so Jock is going to paint our portraits on the panel of the clock I have bought. He's a very good amateur and I'm sure we're going to be delighted with the work he does. It's terribly kind of him."

"Kate dear," Jock said, "In all the years

I've known you, surely you're aware that I do what I do to stem boredom. It'll be a joy to me to get down to doing something for posterity. Oh dear God, my work preserved on a clock for a thousand years! Louis," he called across, "promise me that if ever you can afford a really top-class artist for the job, scrap my painting and use him. I won't be in the least offended."

Kate said, "But you are a very good portrait painter, Jock. I'll never forget that painting you did of Ismene Stephanides. It's quite superb."

"She's a superb subject," he said. "Unfortunately Justine didn't see her this morning, she only met her husband."

"You mean she's beautiful?" I asked.

"As a Greek dragon, if there are such things. She's strong-boned and a tyrant among women. Blazing power, fanatically superstitious and the leader of all the trouble there's ever been at Kentulakis!"

"Trouble?"

"Oh—" Jock waved a vague hand. "It's over now and done with"

"Yes," Kate said softly. "It's over."

By a flash of instinct I knew that they were thinking of Helen's death and the whispers of

Matt's involvement. For a moment or two there was a silence so strange that I felt everything—trees and flowers, insects and birds—was waiting and listening.

"I'll get the clock, if I may," Jock said, "and go. I need my siesta and then I'll drive into Hagharos for the paints I ordered from Athens. They must have come by now. Dear heaven, what I'd give for a daily delivery such as I had in London."

It was I who said, "Why don't you go back?"

He looked at me in amazement. "My dear, when you reach my age you'll learn what things are really important and what are not. My old bones like this dry climate; my naturally idle disposition enjoys doing nothing at all."

And, I thought as he gave me his slightly secretive grin, you can indulge your love of gossip here in ways you never could in an enormous, impersonal city.

"I'll get the clock for you," Kate said.

"No, I'll fetch it. That is, if I may."

"Oh, Jock, you know you're free to come and go here," Kate said warmly. "I'm very grateful to you, anyway. Artists can be expensive people."

"I'm no artist, but I'll do my best."

"I really can go and get it for you." Kate fussed.

"Oh, for heaven's sake, let Jock go! The clock weighs a ton. And take Justine with you. I suppose"—Louis turned to his sister—"you haven't got around to showing her that room yet?"

"I'm afraid not."

I wanted to protest: But I've heard the clocks and that's quite enough! Instead, I murmured, "Thank you, I'd love to see them."

"Go along with Jock then. He knows the way. And I'll collect those English Newspapers he wants." Kate laughed. "He's much too lazy to bother to order them himself, so I save him the week's batch."

At the top of the stairs, Jock paused. "I suppose you're sleeping in that guest room next to the clocks."

"I am," I said.

"Of course Kate would put you in that room. The only other spare room is Louis's and has almost his lifetime possessions in it. This family hoards like squirrels stoking up for a millennium." He flung the door open. "But I wonder you don't go nutty with all

150

those clocks raising a hullabaloo every hour."

"I've only had one night—"

"Well, don't let them get you down. Just tell Louis he must change rooms with you. They don't even hear them, you know! But there's no reason why you should spend weeks of jangled nerves and have to come to me for a sedative."

"I won't," I promised. "I'll get used to them."

"If you don't, just be firm about them." He flicked on the light and urged me in front of him into the room.

Room? It was a museum. Long and narrow, I had a sensation that it was permanently shuttered as if the two long rows of clocks standing on shelves in velvet-lined niches must not be exposed to air. Nearest the door were empty spaces.

"For future generations of clocks," Jock said. "If, that is, future generations keep up the d'Arrancourt tradition. Will *you?*"

"I don't know."

He chuckled, laid a heavy hand across my shoulders and propelled me along the aisle between the clocks.

They were all shapes and sizes—some of them extravaganzas of past craftsmen's dreams. Marble and gilt and rose quartz, plain and ormolu, they stood facing the aisle down which we moved. Some, obviously Victorian, were solid and unimaginative; others were so elaborate that I had to search for the clock itself. There was a ship with the face on its mast; a bronze clock shaped like an ancient Egyptian headdress with an asp curling above it, emeralds for eyes. A genial lion held a timepiece within its paws: French clocks, garlanded with roses held by cupids, were fashioned in tinted porcelain. Brass pendulums swung; ornate hands pointed to a few minutes to midday, to noon, to a few minutes past the hour. Kate had been fairly conscientious in syncronizing the clocks.

It was like watching the petrified progress of a dynasty. Every d'Arrancourt son and daughter and their families must have been portrayed on those special bases beneath the clock faces: bewigged and powdered men; women wearing snoods or feathers or Gainsborough hats, they looked with unseeing eyes as we walked by.

Time passing . . . time, the enemy . . .

I must have given an involuntary shudder, for Jock said, "Stuffy sort of place, isn't it?"

"And depressing. Though I don't really know why."

"The end of a long family line, such as we see here, is like seeing a garden full of plants you know will never flower again. Though, of course, there's Louis to revive the d'Arrancourts."

I avoided the glance he gave me.

"Poor Kate," he said. "These clocks must remind her, every time she comes into the room to wind them, of the way her family squandered their fortunes."

"Then why keep them?"

"Hasn't Louis told you?"

"Told me what?"

He stroked the small gilded stomach of a cupid. " 'Fear not, till Birnam Wood do come to Dunsinane.' " He looked at me.

"I know," I said, "Macbeth. But I don't get the connection."

"A superstition, Justine. There used to be a silly belief in England—your great-grandmother might have known about it—that if a picture 'jumped the rail,' as they called it, then it denoted a death in the family very soon after."

"What is 'jumping the rail'?"

"In Victorian and Edwardian days, there

used to be a molding round the walls of the rooms on which the pictures were hung. Sometimes, for some odd reason, a picture leapt off the hook hanging from this rail without the cord breaking, and if that happened the whole family would speculate on who was going to die a sudden death. All so silly, but they believed. And like the d'Arrancourts before her, Kate believes it applies to the clocks. If they stop ticking—then watch out!"

"I'll lie awake all night listening."

He shook his head at me. "You laugh! But don't exist on too practical a level, my dear, at least not here on Chrysolaki." He picked up the alabaster clock fixed on its clumsy wooden base and held it up. "It's the best Kate can afford. I only hope I do justice to her and to Louis and"—he looked down at me—"to you?"

"*Me?*"

"Painted for posterity, Justine. That is, if you're going to marry Louis."

The thought of future generations coming to look at my likeness on a clock face was strangely uncanny. I went quickly into the passage and heard Jock switch off the light and close the door.

The sun streaming in through an unshuttered window dazzled me, and for a moment or two I saw stars dancing. But the room had so depressed me that I was grateful for the light.

Kate's bright, affectionate voice called from the sitting room where she was tying string round a small pile of newspapers. "They're in the right order, Jock, so mind you read them that way. Ah, Justine, did you enjoy looking at my clocks?"

"They're fascinating," I said truthfully, "and some of the names on them are beautiful."

"Many of them are Old English. It would be so lovely if you and Louis could resurrect the most charming for your children—Arabella, Hereward, Ninian—"

"My dear Kate, don't wish a loadful of responsibilities on us before we've had time to have fun together," Louis said, laughing and impatient. "All I can think of is having Justine entirely to myself and no children clinging to her pretty legs."

A silence fell. Jock fidgeted, downed his drink and said, "I'll have to be off. Did you look out the photographs of yourself and Louis for me to copy from?"

"They're on top of the newspapers. Louis dear, help Jock out with all that stuff—take the clock, you're younger and stronger than he is and it's rather heavy, I'm afraid."

Louis unfolded his long legs, picked up the clock and said, "It's pretty hideous, Kate. Where in the world did you get it?"

"In Athens and it was cheap."

"I'll bet it was. Well, never mind, our faces will brighten it up. Where's your car, Jock?"

"I parked it under some trees so that it won't be quite so oven-hot when I get into it. Your drive isn't very shady at this time of day."

Under some trees, while you creep up to the house and listen. To what? What did you learn that you could tap out on the village grapevine, you old gossip? *And had it been Jock who had listened outside the walls of Marathon on the night that Helen died?* For someone had spread the story Louis had told me about the quarrel that night between Matt and his sister.

Each morning a launch was sent to bring Louis to Palacanthus. He told me that Machelevos had suggested he leave all his equipment on the island, and Louis had

156

agreed. He once told me that wherever he was, his favorite Rolleiflex had to be under the same roof all the time or he would not sleep easily. He said, "It has a being of its own; it knows what I want it to do." But he had no fears about leaving it at Palacanthus.

When I saw the mass of film he had brought with him to the island, I knew he had pinned his hopes in advance on the letter written from London to Costos Machelevos. Someone had once accused him of wasting far more film than he actually needed and he had retorted, "Right! I do. I snap and snap until I find just the model's pose I want or just the right reflection of light. I know as soon as a model comes to the studio what I want from her—a movement of a few inches this way or that will make all the difference to the play of light, the angle."

Although he assured me that he would be back at Argus by four o'clock each afternoon, I knew that this was a far too optimistic calculation. Louis was a perfectionist, and I had watched him too many times at the Yacht Club—photographing people and water scenes, taking endless trouble, endless time—to be the least surprised to find that it was always nearer six o'clock when the launch from Palacanthus throbbed towards the little jetty on the beach below Argus.

The pattern of our meetings when he returned home was always the same. He would come and look for me and, over a drink, would tell me about his day. He had an envy and a grudging admiration for Costos Machelevos; he told me about the magnificence of the house, described the guests who were known to me only as politicians, stage personalities, or members of the jet set. In different circumstances, he would have looked on his work at the island as a more exciting way of spending his time than staying with Kate at Argus, but the conversation, begun with his excited report on his day at Palacanthus, would turn into a demand for reassurance that I had missed him.

At first I would say, "You must know that I have," and the feeling in my voice would convince him. After a few days, my reply had been diminished to "Yes, yes, of course." I was learning, though, that nothing satisfied Louis but a vehement protest that I hated his absences and longed for the commission on the island to be over. He wanted my total absorption in him, and one evening, when I

158

had told him about a long walk I had taken, finding an old Byzantine church some miles from Argus, he said, "You seem to have enjoyed your walk."

"I did. It was all wonderful."

"So you found it fun, even though I wasn't there?"

"You know it will all be more fun when you are."

He said vehemently, "I want you to hate the island when I'm not with you."

"That's something I can't do."

"Then you must, darling. You see, I have to teach you never to be happy without me."

I had thought it was just an impulsive exaggeration and I had laughed. To my amazement, Louis had said violently, "I mean every word of that, Justine. Don't ever enjoy anything or anyone more than me."

It was, of course, just one of those lovers' extravaganzas and I accepted it as such. But I was learning that his love for me was far more demanding than mine for him and I must tread warily on his swift, highly charged emotions.

We were together even less than I had thought at the time he accepted the Palacanthus commission, for every night

Louis had to develop what he had done that day for Machelevos to look over the following morning and decide to accept or reject. Quite often Louis himself wasn't satisfied with his own work, and then there would be a violent tearing up of pictures that I considered beautiful.

He had fixed up a darkroom in a huge cupboard under the stairs at Argus and spent about two hours after dinner shut in, developing the day's work.

In the evening I usually sat with Kate on the terrace. She would talk to me about her life before she came to Chrysolaki, about the great house on Chelsea Embankment where once Henry VIII had rested on his way to Hampton Court and summoned Sir Thomas More to meet him in the d'Arrancourts' drawing room. "And George the Third once slept in our splendid main guest room, and Clive of India . . ."

I suspected that many of her stories were embroidered, but I didn't mind. With so little in her life, she had to have her dreams and they hurt no one. So far, our only evening visitor had been Jock, who came, exchanged local gossip, drank *ouzo* and drove off again in a cloud of dust.

It surprised me that Kate was content with a life that was so circumscribed, bounded by her part-time work for Matt, her gentle care for Elaine when Ludmilla was busy, her constant first-aid services to the villagers, and her garden. Had she been older, I would have supposed that she had enjoyed a full and exciting youth and was satiated. There was only three years' difference between Louis and herself, yet her manner was more that of a mother to him.

She never suggested in the late afternoon that we go for a walk together, nor when I returned to the house did she show much interest. Her world was enclosed in the small area in which she lived.

Life for Matt at Marathon was very different. He had his absorbing creative work and the journeys to London. He also, Kate told me, received visitors from the United States and England, some of them friends and some who came with letters of introduction just to look at a great writer.

Louis had once said, "Matt will eventually start a colony of writers and artists here. And he'll be the Grand Panjandrum at whose feet they'll sit, drinking in his words as though he had the gift of angels—or the devil." And then he had laughed.

When Louis finished his work in the darkroom, we would sometimes go into Hagharos, driving fast in Kate's car along the bumpy road. Among the high-spirited, noisy Greeks, Louis shook off the mood that seemed to surround him after his day at Palacanthus and away from me, and was gay again. At such times I was certain that it was only Louis I wanted in all the world; at other times I began to doubt, and something deep inside myself withdrew from this man who wanted me to have no happiness except when I was with him.

10

SINCE my arrival at Argus, I had looked longingly at Kate's blue-and-white cabin cruiser moored against the tiny jetty. Although smaller, in design she was like the boat on which my father and I had spent so many weekends, and I knew that I could handle her.

One morning, on an impulse, as Kate was getting into her car to drive to Marathon, I said, "If I were very careful and hugged the coast as much as possible, would you let me take *Persephone* out? I'd love to get the feel of a wheel in my hands again."

"Of course. She's very small and easy to handle and Louis has told me how good you are with boats—well tutored by your father."

"I was," I said, remembering those long, windy, racing-cloud days.

"Louis bought the boat for us to use here—we had a beautiful one once, but that was in the days before I speculated and lost my money." She got into the car, saying, "I'm afraid *Persephone* doesn't get used much these days. Occasionally Jock takes her out, or Matt, but I really only keep her so that Louis can use her on his holidays. There hasn't been any chance on this one, has there?"

"We'll make up for it when Louis is free."

"Have a short trial run in her this morning. You'll find everything in order because Jock was going to take her out and had everything including her engine checked, and then changed his mind about going."

"I might be able to find a small bay where I can swim."

Kate said unhappily, "You don't like our beach? Oh, I understand. It's our fault; we should never have told you that terrible story about Helen, it has spoiled our strip of sand for you."

"No—" I began, and then gave up trying a polite protest. Kate was right. The Dark Sister hung its tragedy like a black wing over the sunny bay, so that I could not help but be haunted by it.

I waited until Kate had driven away and then went down the path between the brilliant flower beds, through the tamarisk hedge to the beach. The little boat rocked gently on the clear, mint-green water in the shallows. I entered the wheelhouse, noting

164

that the chart was in place on its board. Nothing was quite as immaculate as on our own English boat, but when I looked into the tiny cabin there were neat yellow curtains and striped buttercup-and-white cushions. The galley was tidy and the crockery stacked away.

Back in the wheelhouse, I gave another cursory glance at the chart. I was quite certain the coast was safe or Kate would never have allowed me in the boat. The coast to the east seemed absolutely clear of rocks and the sea was like bright fingers beckoning me. I could have started the engine and been away, skimming past the Dark Sister into some brighter bay. But I remembered Elaine and knew that I had to take her with me.

They said she had no memory, but from her small, charming greeting each time I saw her—forehead laid swiftly and lightly against my shoulder—I had begun to believe that she knew me and was pleased to see me. If that were true, then she would be waiting and watching for me as usual that morning and I could not go without her.

I left the boat and took the path that led past the small field to Marathon. Ludmilla was peering out of an upstairs window; I called a greeting and then, going nearer, said I would like to take Elaine out in the boat. Was that all right?"

She nodded in the direction of the field. "She over there. You see?"

I saw Elaine with Siphi at the opposite end of the field I had passed on my way from the beach. As soon as she saw me, she put her fingers round the goat's single horn, laid her face for a moment against its pagan head, and then rose and came towards me.

"I've got something different for us this morning," I said. "I hope you like the sea, but if you don't we'll come back."

She let me take her hand, and I saw that she wore a little bracelet of plaited grass.

"That's pretty," I said, and she looked at it with interest. She obviously had no desire to destroy it, and I wondered who had made it for her.

Elaine was in a dawdling mood, pausing to touch a flower, to watch a bird. She went ahead of me, wandering up the path that led to the main road and Kentulakis. She didn't seem to understand that we were going down to the beach and for a few minutes a curious obstinacy seized her. Then, just as I had decided to give up the whole idea, she came willingly, almost running down to the shore.

It wasn't easy to steady her so that she stepped and did not jump from the jetty into the boat, but, puzzled by its persistent rocking, she eventually let me help her down.

Beyond the shelter of the bay, the sea was lashed by the *meltemi*, but we kept close, hugging the shore. I wasn't certain how Elaine would enjoy being on the sea and I tried to keep her interested, pointing out to her the tiny arrows of marine life that jerked away from us as the boat's moving shadow disturbed them.

But Elaine sat as quietly in the boat as she did in Matt's garden, and I saw that her eyes watched the horizon more than the under-water life that played around us. Her head was lifted, and it was as if she were listening to something far outside my hearing, beyond my understanding—for all I knew as she sat there so still and so serene, she might have been in tune with the infinite.

There was another bay beyond the Dark Sister, but the beach was narrow and too exposed to the *meltemi*. Beyond it again was a line of jagged cliffs, not nearly so high as the one which shadowed the piece of coast at Argus. The boulders were scattered as if,

167

some while ago—perhaps at the time of the earthquake—part of some greater cliff had collapsed.

The wind had increased, blowing strongly from the land, and I looked towards the angry sea pounding the rocks and then consulted the chart. As I had noticed when I had looked over the boat earlier, it showed no rocks, no possible hazards for at least another ten miles. Puzzled, I traced the line west towards Hagharos. The name didn't even appear on the chart. Yet it was the little port for the island. I even looked to see if the Dark Sister was marked, but even if it had been, I could not read Greek. The chart had been well used, and the name Chrysolaki, ringed in an ornate scroll, was written in ink in capital letters. But I saw, underneath, scratched and almost obliterated, the original printing of a name I could just trace with my fingers.

Spetsai . . .

Too alarmed at any unknown danger to wonder who had superimposed the island's name on the chart, I knew that I must turn back. The sea foamed over the rocks and heaven knew what worse hazards might lie ahead. Looking down I could see that I had already driven the boat too close inshore.

I stopped the engine, looking to see which was my safest way out of the mass of underwater hazard. And as I did so, I remembered how Kate had said, "You'll find everything in order."

It was, except for the one vital thing—that wrong chart.

Jock, Kate had said, had been going to take the boat out. To Spetsai? And had he pinned his own chart there in readiness and then, perhaps having drunk too much *ouzo*, started scribbling over the name, filling in the letters as children did, idle and bored, listening to lessons or adults talking. Then, familiar with the Aegean waters around his group of islands, had he left the chart there, knowing that it was for Spetsai?

And I? Why should I have looked closer? I had taken it for granted that the name Chrysolaki, although heavily inked in, was the correct one.

My relief that I had found out the mistake in time to clear *Persephone* from the rocks was stillborn. On the first turn of the wheel, the boat resisted me and rocked wildly as if caught in a strong crosscurrent. I steadied her and then slowly reversed the engine to avoid the current and, instead, make a left arc turning to the coast. The engine purred and we left a clean trail of foam like a half-moon behind us. But suddenly there was a scraping noise and a shudder ran the length of the little boat. Then she stopped.

I knew immediately what had happened. We had come too close to the shore and had been caught between submerged rocks. I had been too relieved to escape from the danger further out, where the wind was playing havoc with the sea, to think of danger beneath us. But the rocks had lain in wait for us just below the surface of the water. I looked down and saw them, like crocodiles awaiting prey.

I had cut the engine immediately, knowing that I dare not move until I had found out exactly how the boat lay. The water was so clear that it was all too easy to see that we were caught fast in a cleft between two ridges that were not visible above the water line.

The old saying that when one is drowning the past is relived in a matter of seconds did not apply to me. For one thing, we were nowhere near drowning, for another it was my future, not my past, that hit me. I lived the prelude to all the furies that would be heaped upon my head.

From Louis: "You're supposed to steer a

boat, not smash it" . . . From Matt, since he had a temper (and the fact that I was a comparative stranger would count for nothing) "You bloody little fool!" . . . From Kate, wide-eyed with horror at the things that might have been, "Oh, Justine, you could have drowned Elaine!" Could have? I still might, at that.

The thought brought me out of the immediate shock which had plunged me into a state of numb inactivity. Staring down into that emerald water laced with foam was doing nobody any good. I measured the distance across the rocks that could be clearly seen at each rhythmic ebb of water. It would be just possible to wade to the shore from where we were. Elaine was physically strong and she was fairly tall. A drenching in sea water would not hurt her, and the hot sun would dry us as we walked back to Marathon.

Walked back! I looked along the way we had come. Two miles would be an under-estimate, and would Elaine, frightened perhaps by the experience of having to make her way over the rocks, be able to walk that distance? If she were not, how could I cope with someone who had no understanding of the situation and, as her calm, blank face seemed to indicate, no fear? It appeared impossible to hope for help. I could see neither cottage nor any sign of cultivation along the wild shore.

Persephone shifted slightly, settling herself more comfortably between the two boulders.

"We're going to have to walk through the water," I said. "Can you?"

She turned her face to me, trusting, unafraid, the sunlight in her violet eyes, entirely without understanding.

"Come," I said and settled a kind of "We're-going-to-have-fun" look on my face, since expression was all that she could interpret, and I didn't dare show alarm. "Let's take off our shoes and wade ashore." I bent and slid out of mine and she watched me. I pointed to her white sandals but she didn't understand and I took them off for her. I made her hold them, and then picking up my shoulder bag, I climbed cautiously out of the boat onto a wet, slippery rock. Then I leaned forward and took her hands.

It was difficult enough getting myself out of a slightly listing boat; it was a major operation to get Elaine to climb out.

I held out my arms to her and she just sat and looked at me. I urged her with words and she knelt on the seat smiling at me.

"Darling, I'm not some sort of monster fish," I pleaded. "Do *please* get out. I can't lift you. *Elaine* . . ." I reached, almost over-balancing, my toes clinging to the jagged rocks, and seized her hands. "Out!" I pulled. "Oh, do try to help yourself!"

Suddenly, she either understood or was afraid I would leave her alone in the thing I called a boat, and she grasped my hands and scrambled over the side of *Persephone*, landing uncertainly, one leg on a smooth rock, the other in the water. The hem of her skirt splayed out in the ruffled waves, and she watched fascinated as it moved with the swinging water. I tried to pull her onto the boulder on which I stood, but she resisted me and stepped down so that she was in the sea up to her thighs and quite happy about it.

Fear ripped through me. *Oh God, what now? If she falls* . . . I need not have worried. She kept her balance, one hand in mine, and together we waded towards a shore that seemed too far away. It was lucky for us that the bay was sheltered from the wind that whipped the waves beyond the protection of the land.

I didn't dare let go of Elaine's hand in case

she slipped or, having no idea of the depth or danger of the water, decided on some illogical impulse to sit down. So I kept her moving, and with the sun blazing on us, we waded through the waves to the shore. For me, it was a terrifying test of any acting skill I might have. If I showed fear, Elaine might panic—how certain could I be that they were right in saying she was never afraid? Hadn't I seen it when the child in the cloak had run towards us? And if fear struck her, I had no idea how she would react.

Fortunately she seemed far more sure-footed than I among the rocks we had to scramble over, and was perfectly happy splashing and slithering, plunging into pools and scattering the tiny wriggling life in them. The little grass bracelet had long since been sucked off her wrist by the waves as, every so often, she would bend down and hit the water with the flat of her hand, half drowning us both in the splash.

We had almost reached the beach when a jagged rock scraped the ball of my foot. Pain shot momentarily up my leg, then I felt the sharp astringency of salt water on what, although I dared not pause to look, was obviously a line of torn skin.

174

We plunged on until we emerged, like wet Venuses, from the deeper water to the shallows where the waves merely licked our feet. After that, it was only a few steps to the hot, dry sand.

I stopped and lifted my foot and saw blood trickling from the wound the sea had cleaned. But it seemed too superficial to bother about and I urged Elaine forward.

The beach was deserted, which was fortunate since our dresses clung to us in a way far more revealing than any wet swim-suit. Even my white shoulder bag dripped water, and when I opened it to get out some tissues, they were a sodden mass.

"We'll have to put our shoes on wet feet," I said.

But Elaine didn't want to wear her sandals, and remembering how unworried Matt had been about her wandering barefoot on our first night, I decided to carry them. I stuffed a tissue in my shoe to cover the place where the jagged rock had cut me and put on my own sandals.

From where we stood I could see the stark outlines of the two Sisters, and my spirits sank as I made a guess at the distance between us. But they were my only guides back to

Marathon, and their outlines taunted me in the gilded light.

The track we followed wound inland; the sun was very hot but the *meltemi* was blowing strongly and keeping the temperature down. Elaine stopped and picked continuously at her clinging dress, holding it from her legs and making little dismissing gestures.

"I know it's uncomfortable, but we'll soon be home," I said, aware that I was only lying to myself, since she could not understand—or so everyone told me. How right or wrong they were was something I had yet to discover.

Our walk led us through a deserted world. I saw no houses, no farms, only wild scrub-land, occasional oases of trees giving us a few minutes of welcome shade and a ruin that was three broken walls and a piece of vaulted archway hanging perilously over the road.

Someone would have to be sent to get *Persephone* off the rocks. I doubted if the boat was damaged, except for her paint-work, but my anxiety must be kept hidden until we reached home. While we trekked back, I had to keep Elaine happy.

I began to sing jingles dredged up from my childhood to amuse her, but while they came mechanically to me, a question hung at the back of my mind. Where was the chart that should have warned me against going too close inshore beyond that second bay?

It was at that point of puzzlement that I saw a man working on a small plot of land. He was picking delicately at the leaves of a row of lettuces.

"*Parakaló.*"

He straightened himself and looked with utter amazement at us, his dark-brown eyes first incredulous, then amused, then alarmed. In the brief time it took him to leave his plot and come towards us. I realized how bizarre we must look in our wet clinging clothes.

On such a tiny island no one was a stranger, and he would surely recognize Elaine. I tried by signs to explain what had happened. He scratched his head and grinned. I held out the wet phrase pad Kate had given me; the writing was smudged by sea water but clear enough to understand. There was, however, no phrase there for "We have been shipwrecked," which, although it had more diplomatic implications, was in a way true.

I pointed to one question: "*Boríta na mou dixte ton dromo sto Argus?*" Then, in case he couldn't read, I seized his arm and forced him

177

to come with me along the track to a bend where we could see *Persephone* snuggled between the rocks like a blue-and-white whale sunning itself. Then, "Marathon," I said, and pointed to Elaine.

Immediately he seemed to understand, and a finger tapped Elaine on the shoulder, then he waved his arms and began to talk rapidly and delightedly as if two very wet females were just the diversion he needed from his chore of tending lettuces.

"Takis," he said, thumping his chest. I grasped that he was introducing himself. He pointed to an ochre-colored cottage almost hidden by trees.

Perhaps he had a wife who would let us stay in her cottage until the sun dried our clothes. He might even have a bicycle and ride to Marathon or Argus for help.

Still smiling broadly, Takis again jabbed a finger, this time at the spot on the ground where we stood, pointed to himself and then into the distance. It was easy to interpret that we were to wait where we were and he would come back after—after what? I had a picture of a startled wife emerging from the trees that hid the cottage, to look us over.

Elaine had wandered into the shade, and I

brought her back to the sun. The heat of the morning was one thing, the cooling wind was quite another and I didn't know how robust she was.

I was beginning to wonder if we had just been left to sit in the sun and dry off, when Takis appeared with a donkey harnessed to a small cart.

Swooping down, he picked up Elaine and sat her among large baskets of tomatoes, dark-green olives and a broken mandolin. Then he bent to pick me up; I gave him a delighted smile and jumped up unaided beside her.

The cut on my foot burned in my damp shoes, and I slipped off my sandal and sat barefoot.

Three of us—a brawny, black-haired man who couldn't speak a word of our language and we, who sat in his brightly painted, smelly cart—bounced and rocked along the rutted track. The donkey trotted with a spring as if his load were thistledown, the man sang at the top of his voice.

Our wet clothes were drying in the heat of the day, and as we passed two men sitting by the wayside, our driver shouted, "*Yássas*." The men looked at us and laughed as kindly as if we were all good friends.

In our situation, dignity was ludicrous and I laughed back. Elaine sat by my side, her fingers picking at her dress, which was drying quickly.

After half an hour's rough riding in the painted cart, the donkey swung round a corner, and as Takis pulled it to a halt, it gave a small impudent kick with its back heels which tipped us forward like peas out of a pod, and then stopped. We had come by a route unfamiliar to me to the gates of Marathon. While Elaine was being helped down, I looked out to the sea. It stretched from the earth's sandy rim to the sky's edge, so rich and empty that I longed to be in it or on it—anywhere but within a second or two of a storm that would hit me from all directions.

11

MATT was in the garden talking to Niko. Takis reached out his arms to me, looking me up and down with approval, then remembering that *Kýrie* Braddon might be watching, strode towards him and began what was obviously a voluble account of how he came to be driving two wet girls home. I saw Matt feel in his pocket for money. Takis spread the coins in his palm and grinned with obvious pleasure. Then, as he returned to his cart, Matt came to where we stood, his expression unfathomable, his voice very quiet. "Go inside, both of you."

I had never felt more like a juvenile culprit, listening with a plunging heart to the rattle of the cart and the happy clatter of the donkey's hooves going home.

Someone had to speak first. "I'm sorry," I said, and turned and faced Matt as we reached the shade of the patio. "I couldn't help it. I suppose I shouldn't have taken Elaine with me, but I do know how to steer boats."

"I don't doubt it. But you obviously have no knowledge of reading charts. Or perhaps you think you know more than those who had surveyed the seacoast in this area, and so don't need their advice."

"The chart in the wheelhouse was for Spetsai," I said, "but the name was almost obliterated by . . . by doodles."

"Doodles?" He stared at me as if the word meant nothing to him.

"Those marks people make sometimes when they're thinking—you know, they just seize a pen and scribble. I never dreamed the chart wasn't one for Chrysolaki. It even had that name printed in ink over the Spetsai name."

Matt was staring over my head. "If Kate ever uses the boat, she only hugs the coast, so there must have been our island chart there."

"Did *you* ever take the boat to Spetsai?"

His eyes moved swiftly from the distance to my face. "No. I'm not that much of a sailor."

"But why should anyone print one name over the other? Why have that chart there, anyway? Kate said I would find everything in order."

He made no comment.

"Matt!" I was wet and cross and beginning

to be frightened about the fate of *Persephone*. "What'll—what'll happen now? I mean . . . the boat . . ."

"I'll send someone to get her. I should think you know enough about small boats to be able to tell if you've done much damage."

"If the correct chart had been there—" I was talking to the empty air. Matt had taken Elaine into the house and I heard him calling Ludmilla.

I walked restlessly the length of the patio, brushed my hand across an oleander that grew at the foot of a thin stone column. Some petals dropped to the ground and I scooped them up, crushing them in my fingers. I was puzzled and damp and becoming scared at the possibility that I might have damaged *Persephone* more than I knew. It was enough to have to face Kate eventually, without having to cope with Matt Braddon's ice-cold anger.

I flung down the bruised oleander petals. Escape was ignoble, but I cared nothing for courage as I ran out into the garden, the hot sun striking my face, the scent of herbs and roses heavy on the air. I was going to take the quickest way to Argus to face a more kindly Kate.

"And where are you rushing off to?"

I jerked to a stop and wheeled round. "Home," I said to Matt.

"Ludmilla has a bathrobe for you. Go and put it on and lay that dress and anything else you're wearing out to dry in the sun. Well, go on . . . And then come back to the patio for a drink."

"I don't want—"

He made the short distance between us seem like a single stride. "It'll take you ten minutes to walk to Argus. You've got a charming figure, and for that reason alone I wouldn't say that, as you are, you're a sight for Greek eyes. Now, go and find Ludmilla."

For some utterly unaccountable reason, I obeyed.

When I had undressed and rubbed myself dry, I put on the white bathrobe. Ludmilla fussed round me, all the time keeping an eye on Elaine, who wore a blue robe with frills at her elbows.

I combed my hair, which was still damp from Elaine's powerful splashings, and Ludmilla watched me, nodding furiously.

"You nearly drown, Missa Justine . . . Ugh!" She made a short, sharp sound like an

184

irritated mother. "You young; boats for men."

"I can handle them, too." I used a lipstick and looked at my improved reflection. "And you did give me permission to take Elaine out with me."

"On boat? Never!"

"I called up to you when you were at the window."

"You say you take Elaine out. That good. You take out every day. But not boat."

I realized that she had either not heard me mention *Persephone* or had not understood, and I said no more. If I could have escaped the house in nothing but the bathrobe I would have done so. But I didn't trust Matt not to be one step ahead of me whichever way I went.

"Now," he said when I appeared in the patio. "Here's a drink for you. Sit down. You know, you look rather nice in that get-up."

"Does that compliment mean that you've thought better of being angry with me?"

"Not really, except that I suppose I shouldn't have expected you to realize the dangers of having to cope with a retarded child in a crisis. She could easily have drowned."

"Not with me," I said. "I'm a very strong swimmer, and I hugged the coast because I thought it was safe." His expression didn't soften. "Matt, I'm telling the truth! The chart for this coast wasn't there."

"Then we'll have to ask Kate about it. In the meantime I've telephoned Hagharos and two men are already on their way to salvage the boat. And I also called Kate."

"Oh, dear!"

"She's much more concerned about you and Elaine than *Persephone*."

"At least I haven't holed it. All that's wrong is probably some scratched paint-work."

"And, I gather, two pieces of rock gripping her like pincers. I only hope the salvage operation doesn't damage her hull. It's often more tricky freeing a boat than entangling her."

"I've thought of that, too," I said miserably.

Matt leaned back, crossed his legs and took time to speak. When he did, his voice was very quiet. "In the future, Justine, if you want to take the boat out—"

"I doubt if Kate would ever let me do it

again. I wouldn't, if someone had run a boat of mine on the rocks."

He ignored my interruption. "Just remember, you have free will; Elaine hasn't, and you endangered her life."

"But, Matt—"

"Wait till I've finished. You *did* endanger her life. No one can ever know how sub-normal children will react to strange situations, or how sensitive they are to fear in others."

"I wasn't afraid and I was careful to let her see that I wasn't. Don't you understand? I didn't do something idiotically impulsive. I've managed boats most of my adult life, and I knew that although we were stuck, we were in no danger. Anyway, I was trying to bring a breath of change into Elaine's life. Even retarded children need stimulus. And what does she ever do but exist here, in . . . in this . . . this ivory tower of a place . . ." My voice had risen again, and I hesitated at the last few words because honesty had crept in and I knew that fright and a sense of guilt were turning my defense into an attack. "I'm sorry." I sank into the yellow cushions of the patio chair, longing to be invisible or to be able to get up and run, but forced to face, now that need for action was over and I could stop and think, that I *had* been impulsive in taking her with me. "You're right. I should have taken the boat out by myself the first time."

"It seems unnatural to you that I guard Elaine so closely, doesn't it?"

"She's your responsibility. I can't criticize."

His laughter was unexpected. "I've a feeling you do a lot of things that you shouldn't. Don't we all?"

I snatched up my glass, drained it and rose. "Thank you for the drink. I'm sure my dress is dry by now and I must go and see Kate." I ran from him and found Ludmilla. My clothes were stretched on a patch of grass at the side of the house. They looked like cutouts ready for dressing a child's outsized cardboard doll, stiff and unreal. I snatched them up and went into the kitchen. Ludmilla was there chattering to Elaine in her queer English. She turned from making a salad as I rushed in, and said, "You put clothes on? They dry?"

"Yes, thank you." I peered through a half-open door.

Ludmilla nodded. "You put clothes on in

there, Missa Justine. I guard. No one come."

I found myself in a cool tiled pantry and dressed with clumsy haste, then thanked Ludmilla again for drying my clothes, kissed Elaine's cheek lightly and ran down the hall to the front door.

"Not that way," Matt said from the living room. "The car is round the other side of the house in the shade."

"I can walk."

"I'm quite certain you can, but you aren't going to. Don't you ever do as you're told without argument?"

He was taller and far stronger than I, and his grip on my arm was viselike.

One thing that I dreaded was that he should think I was trying to be arch in my resistance to him. I wasn't, and so I said quietly, "I'm trying to consider you, so please let me walk home. I'm keeping you from your work."

"Yes, you are."

"Then why don't you go back to your study?"

"I don't know," he said with amusement. The car stood in the shade of some yew trees. I got in, and after we started down the drive, he glanced at me and then reached over and pulled down the visor.

"Thank you," I said, relieved to be shaded from the relentless light on the windshield.

We drove in silence to Argus, but as we reached the gates I said, "Matt, I really am sorry."

"What for, now?"

"The whole damned morning. The boat—"

"You probably weren't going fast enough to do much damage. Let's hope not, anyway. And Dinos and his son are already on their way to rescue it."

"And your morning's work."

"Ah yes, that's different. You really have ruined about an hour of that. I was trying to think out a difficult chapter."

"So, if that particular chapter isn't successful, you'd better blame me."

He threw back his head, laughing, lifting his hands momentarily from the steering wheel, so that the little car did a sideways swerve.

I said humbly, "You think me irresponsible for taking Elaine with me. But I don't know what you call lifting your hands from the wheel of a car in motion. There's a deep ditch on my side of this unspeakable road and any moment now—"

Without a word, he turned the wheel.

The silence between us wasn't a particularly easy one and I said, making conversation, "I'm afraid Elaine lost her little grass bracelet, or perhaps you didn't know she had one. When we got ashore she kept looking at her wrist as if wondering where it was. The sea had washed it away."

"Niko makes them for her," he said.

"It's odd. She doesn't tear at them."

"Why should she? Do you think all retarded children are destructive?"

"I'm sorry. I didn't know."

"Niko will make her another one," he said, "and she'll wear it until the goat decides to eat it."

We had reached the dark avenue that led to Argus. "Don't go right up to the house," I said. "But thank you for bringing me home."

"Think nothing of it! I have to live on the island and I don't want it said that you caught pneumonia because I let you walk home."

As I got out of the car, my foot sank into one of the potholes which pitted the drive up to Argus. I lost my balance and fell, my sandal went flying and I sprawled for a moment in the thick dust.

Matt shot round the car, held me against

191

him and reached down. "Your foot . . ."

"It's nothing. I cut it on a piece of jagged rock."

"You've really gashed it, haven't you? And now you propose to walk on it."

"It doesn't hurt. I took off my sandal and gave it a good airing in Takis's cart."

"You did *what*?" He still held me. "No, don't bother—I heard. Now, get back in the car."

"I'm all right." I broke away from him and hopped on one foot over to retrieve my sandal.

He was behind me immediately and took the sandal from me, lifted me up and dumped me in the car. "Now, stay where you are until we get to Jock's place."

"What for?"

"I'm not risking a case of tetanus, my dear."

"But I won't—"

"You don't know what's been carried in Takis Sikelianos's cart. *I* can guess! Let's only hope Jock will be at home. If he isn't, we do a round of the *tavernas* until we find him."

"I shan't get tetanus."

"You're right, you won't if I can help it."

He handed me his handkerchief. "Tie that round your foot—it's clean, which is more than I can say for your shoe."

"We walked for ages along that dusty road."

"I know, since you got as far as Takis's cottage."

"If Jock is with friends somewhere and we rout him out, I won't be very popular."

"Jock knows the hazards of a primitive Greek island. Now, suppose for once you restrain that will of yours and just stop protesting."

12

JOCK ANDERSON'S house was two-storied, its ochre plaster peeling, its shutters faded and it garden overrun.

The door was opened by a middle-aged man startlingly formal to be in the service of someone like Jock. I felt that when he answered the telephone he would announce, "Dr. Anderson's residence. This is the butler speaking."

But if he was alien to the façade of Jock's house, he most certainly was not out of place in the interior. The hall and the huge room into which we were shown were full of expensive comfort; the windows looked out onto a garden quite different from the one which showed its face to the world. There was a small fountain, a lovely little stone figure of a mermaid and well-trimmed flowering bushes.

Jock did not take long to give me an injection and bind up my ankle. Then he opened a drink cupboard. "Now let's enjoy ourselves. I'm not giving you alcohol,

Justine. Which will you have—an orange or lemon drink? They're both chilled." He raised his voice and bellowed. "Manos?"

The man came at once and then disappeared to fetch ice. Our visit was brief because I was anxious to get back and have news of *Persephone*.

"Come again," Jock said, "but next time without a bloody foot."

Argus seemed deserted. We could not find either Kate or Ruth. I limped to a chair on the terrace, but Matt reached it before me and turned it round towards the sun. "I'm getting to know so well what you like, aren't I? Even at high noon when you are wise enough to sit in the shade, you still like to face the sun."

He leaned against the stone balustrade, his head bent, looking at me strangely, as if a thought had struck him and he didn't much like the idea. "How many times have we met, Justine?"

I counted on my fingers from the day I arrived. "About twelve. All those times when I've brought Elaine back and we've sat in your garden . . . I've enjoyed them."

He half turned from me, "There have been too many times—"

"I've wasted your time. I'm sorry—"

"I've told you before to stop apologizing. It's out of character."

"You know me so well."

He leaned forward and touched my cheek. "So well, I'm afraid—and that last word is the operative one."

"That's too subtle for me—"

"I'm glad. Forget it. And I must go. Where food is concerned, I'm utterly controlled by Ludmilla. Don't get up, there's no need to stand on ceremony."

But I came and stood with him at the terrace edge and stretched my arms wide to the shimmering morning and the dazzle of flowers. "Oh, this lovely island."

"Justine Charles—a romantic for all her practical arguments with me at Marathon!" His laughter was brief and a swift intensity crept into his voice. "When I first met you I thought you were a managing little realist, but I was wrong. Oh, you're strong, but you have a soft center, so soft, so vulnerable—that's the devil of it! You give too much—and God help you!"

"Why do you say that?"

He was remote again. "You're young, but in time you'll understand. Life isn't in the least like its surface appearance, so guard your impulses, Justine. They can lead you to be badly hurt."

I leaned over the terrace and touched the tendrils of the morning glory. "That sounds very like a warning."

"Are you or are you not engaged to Louis?"

"No."

"Then go back to England." There was a sudden intensity in his voice; his eyes flashed at me and then looked away.

Before I could question and protest at the arrogant order, he said quietly, "I'm sorry. It's my turn to apologize. It's none of my business whether you go or stay. Only I'm selfish, and peace of mind is the one thing I must try to find. And I can't—God in heaven, I can't!"

He left me so swiftly that when I turned he was already disappearing round the house.

He talks in riddles . . . Let him go . . . let him go . . .

But I couldn't. Something strange and frightening had crept into the atmosphere and I disliked being left with a mystery I couldn't solve by myself. The mystery that,

197

after all, might be nothing more than a mood of Matt's. Some instinct told me differently.

As soon as his car drove away, I heard Kate's firm, matter-of-fact footsteps crossing the hall. I went to meet her, and found her laden with bread and a basket full of peaches and figs.

"Let me help you—"

"No, thank you." She swerved away from my outstretched hand. "I'll get rid of all this in the kitchen and then we'll talk."

I waited unhappily for her on the terrace and when she appeared, I said, "Kate, I'm so sorry . . . about *Persephone*."

She sat down in one of the rattan chairs, laid her hands on her knees and looked up at me, shaking her head. "I was wrong to let you go out alone."

"The boat . . ."

"Oh, Dinos and his son have gone to fetch it. They couldn't leave immediately because they had urgent repairs to do on one of the fishing boats. But, Justine, when Matt called me he said that you had found the wrong chart in the wheelhouse . . . Sit down, sit down . . . What have you done to your foot?"

"It's nothing. Matt took me to Jock for a

tetanus injection. And Elaine is all right, that's the most important—"

"Elaine?"

"Yes. I took her with me. Didn't you know?"

"*You—took—that—child—with—you?*"

"She enjoyed it."

"Justine, how could you? How—" Words seemed to fail her. She put her hand to her neck and swallowed as if she had a sore throat. "You must have been mad! A subnormal child—she could have climbed over the side of the boat, jumped over—and if she had, what could you have done?"

"I watched her carefully."

"And in doing so, ran the boat onto the rocks."

"It wasn't like that at all. The chart—"

"Before we discuss that, I want to know why you did such an irresponsible thing as to take Elaine."

"I always spend my mornings with her and I thought it would be a change for her. She enjoyed it—I know she did. It was something new—"

"She doesn't want newness, she wants the security of habit."

I longed to say, How do you know? How

can you know? But according to Kate I was guilty of irresponsibility, and from her point of view there was no argument.

"I'm sorry. It's over now and I'll never do it again."

"No, Justine, I'm afraid you won't."

I repeated my apologies but I couldn't calm her. She sat, tense and distressed, watching me as if I were a stranger. "What induced you? Elaine . . ."

"I've told you, she's fine." Then I added, "And I think Matt has forgiven me—"

"Oh, Matt . . . !"

"Why do you say it like that?"

She gave me a strange look. "When a man is dedicated to his work, human beings often come second."

"I don't believe it with Matt."

"Very well, then you must *dis*believe me, mustn't you, Justine? Never mind."

"I'm worried about the boat. I can't have damaged it badly, can I?"

She brushed my question aside with a wave of her hand. "It's the chart that puzzles me. I know the one of Chrysolaki was there a few days ago, and neither Matt nor Jock has used the boat—"

"The one there now is of Spetsai," I said,

200

and told her of the heavy ink scrawl and the name Chysolaki super-imposed, and as I spoke a sudden terrible thought struck me. "It was as though someone wanted me to take it for granted it was Chrysolaki and not to look too closely."

Her lips tried to form words that she could speak only with shocked difficulty. "Justine, what *do* you mean?"

I had shocked myself as well. "I don't really believe what I'm saying—it's too incredible. But—but the chart *was* the wrong one."

She sat biting her lips so fiercely that they became cherry-red, and watching me with stunned, startled eyes. "You're my guest, you're loved by Louis, the villagers here like you because they are generous and kindly people. There *can't* be anything sinister in what happened. There *must* be some simple explanation. We'll go down together and look when the men bring the boat back. But, Justine, don't ever again take Elaine on the sea. You can never be sure what her reactions will be."

She got up and walked up and down the terrace, her fingers to her temples. "I blame myself most of all; I should have realized that you're young, and the young don't think. But then I had no idea you intended to take Elaine with you; you didn't tell me."

"When I went to fetch her, I saw Ludmilla and told her. She agreed, though I realize now that she can't have understood what I said. I knew you were busy and I didn't want to interrupt."

Kate stopped in front of me. "All right! All right! It's over, so let's forget it. Louis will see Dinos about any damage there may be to the boat. The thing you and I have to do when *Persephone* is brought back is to look at that chart." She paused, stared over my head and exclaimed, "But, of course, the children!" She peered at me. "Did you see any of them on the beach?"

"No."

"But they must have been somewhere there. I think I begin to understand what happened. As I told you, Jock was going to take the boat to Spetsai and he must have had the chart for that island somewhere around. Did you go and look over *Persephone* before you went to fetch Elaine?"

"Yes."

"That's it, then. The children watched you and then, the little devils, they went on deck and scrawled over the chart and wrote Chrysolaki."

"In English lettering?"

"That's just what they would do because I've taught them to write a few names in English—their village, Kentulakis, for instance, and Athens and Greece. They know perfectly well the boat belongs to us. This is something I intend to find out. I can guess the boys are at the bottom of the affair, but they egg the girls on. Now we've talked it out, let's relax." She threw herself back into her chair. "That foot of yours—"

"It's only a slight cut. Matt fussed—"

"Ah yes . . ." Her eyes took on a queer, glazed look as if she had forgotten me and was thrust into some personal memory. "I wonder how long he will be able to stand it . . . a subnormal child and a healthy man . . . Perhaps one day . . . one—day—" She broke off, and her body jerked tense and upright. "What am I thinking of? It's not my affair, anyway. It's no one's but Matt's."

"What isn't?"

She shook her head. "We all have to cope with the situations we make for ourselves . . . Let's have a nice, cool drink."

After lunch I lay in my shaded room wanting to sleep, to wipe out for a few hours the anxiety I felt over *Persephone*. But now, lying with the shutters closed and the house still and airless, the clocks took over, seeming to beat a terrible tattoo against the wall of my room. If I could only ask Kate to stop them—but long-standing superstitions in ancient families died hard, if they ever died at all.

As I lay there, memories of the morning rolled backwards and forwards across my mind, and each time they stopped at a moment when Kate had said, "I wonder how long he will be able to stand it . . . a sub-normal child and a healthy man . . . She knew Matt far better than I did; she knew all the village gossip, the whispers and the suspicions. I rolled over onto my back and stared up at the shadowy gray patina of the ceiling. A terrible thought had struck me. Why had Matt taken on the responsibility of Elaine? Why? And, as if he were there and I asked my question of him aloud, I heard his possible reply. *I have a secret I can share with nobody and for the rest of my life I must live with it. Looking after Elaine is my atonement . . .*

I sprang off the bed as if the words had

been attackers, and ran across the room, slid my feet into sandals, ignoring the pain of the one I had forced on my bandaged foot, and went downstairs through the garden and into the olive grove. There, on the hard earth in the shade of the crooked trees, I slept.

At some time during that sleep, Dinos and his son must have gone out to rescue *Persephone*, for, when I awoke and was on my way back to the house, I caught sight, through the high tamarisks, of the little blue-and-white cruiser at its mooring post. I limped as hurriedly as I could into the house, and hearing the rattle of teatime cups and saucers from the kitchen, went to look for Kate. She was coming out of her room, stifling a yawn. "How I want my tea!"

"The boat," I said. "It's back."

She ran in front of me down the stairs and out along the garden path to the beach. I followed, asking, "They brought it back without telling you?"

"You don't understand. To have come up to the house would have delayed them. The siesta is almost a religion with the island people. Besides, they wouldn't dream of disturbing my siesta, either." Her voice came back to me as I followed her happily, as if the last anxiety had been overcome.

We walked over the sand to the boat and climbed down. The chart was on the board. Kate peered at it and I looked over her shoulder.

"Chrysolaki," was printed there, and there were no scribbles and scrawls.

She straightened and turned and looked at me. "I don't understand."

"Nor do I."

"The children . . . the children, of course, must have heard that Dinos was going out to bring the boat back and they waited here to replace the charts. That is . . ."—she gave me a sudden, sharp glance—"that is, if you weren't mistaken."

"Kate, I *know* I wasn't! Someone, as you say, must have been watching and replaced the chart. But why—"

"Mischief, of course. There's no other explanation."

I went out on deck and stared at the deserted beach. Children could have hidden in the waving tamarisks and watched me, and children everywhere often did stupid and dangerous things when they were bored. Yet I could not remember ever having seen the

206

village people on Kate's beach. A fear shivered through me that the explanation might not be as simple as we were supposing. But what was the alternative? Who would want me to drive the boat on rocks and risk Elaine's life and my own?

I turned and found Kate behind me. "I don't understand . . . I can't think that the children . . ." Her face was twisted with doubts. Then she shook herself visibly. "Of course, I must go down to the village after tea and get to the bottom of this. Oh, Justine, you could both have been killed."

"But we weren't. And there'll be no more risk," I said, "because if I go out into the boat again, it'll be with Louis."

"How wise . . . how wise," she cried with relief and kissed my cheek.

13

I WAS in my room changing into something fresh and cool when Louis arrived home an hour early. I heard him talking to Kate and I waited, letting her give him the version of what happened that morning.

I was sitting in front of the ornate dressing table when Louis stormed in without knocking, and as I turned I scarcely recognized him. His face was suffused with anger and he slammed the door after him and stood leaning against the wall.

"So I'm home early. So what did you imagine you were going to do this late afternoon? Pretty yourself up to slip secretly back to Marathon on the pretext of inquiring how Elaine was after her ordeal and in reality to spend an hour with Matt before I came home?"

For one moment I thought that he was playing some ridiculous stagy game of the jealous lover. But then I remembered something I had learned from a wise friend of my father's. He had said, "A man's breathing is always light in relaxation, but heavy in tension." Louis was breathing as if he had been running a hard race. His anger was real.

I said quietly. "Kate has told you everything about this morning. I'm sorry, Louis, about the boat."

"Damn the boat."

"Then—?"

"Matt," he said. "Matthew Bloody Braddon visited every morning and even in the afternoons. Good God, can't you keep away from the man while I'm working?"

"I wasn't aware that I'd ever made an effort to meet him."

"Facts, Justine. It seems it's the talk of the village."

"Who told you that?"

"You forget I can understand Greek—even some of the islanders here seem to forget it, too! Or maybe they find it amusing to let me overhear bits of gossip. 'What's that foreign girl up to? Playing one man against the other?' Small islands are hotbeds of gossip." He stormed across the room and stood looking down at me, his eyes blazing. "Don't tell me you and Matt sit and talk about the weather every day!"

"I take Elaine out and return her safely. That's all there is to it."

"But always making sure that Matt is there—or is it he who makes sure that he's around when you return? Whichever way, it makes no difference; the result is the same. You and Matt whiling away the hot, pretty hours."

"I spend twenty minutes, at the most, at Marathon—just long enough to have a drink and a rest. It's hot work walking in the sun and I can't take Elaine to the beach in case she runs into the sea; you must know that she has no fear—or so they tell me. But I enjoy my mornings and I think I am helping Elaine."

"You should know well enough that no one can do anything for that subnormal kid. She's unteachable."

"I didn't say I could teach her; I said 'help.'"

"And you think I believe that's the reason you go to Marathon?" He seized my shoulders, dragged me to my feet and shook me.

"Don't!" I tore at his hands.

"You're not going there again, do you hear? If you do I'll make such hell for that man on this island that he'll have to run for his life. And I mean that literally."

It was as if I were seeing a stranger—a man enjoying his hate. "I hope I don't understand you; I hope I'm mistaken. You see, Louis, I don't like threats."

"But I'm in a position to do just that, darling—to threaten. And Matt knows it. So I suggest for his sake, if not for your own, you stop going to Marathon."

"No."

Had Louis not stood between the door of the room and me, I would have walked out and left him to cool off. As it was, I was caught.

This violent unrecognizable Louis frightened me and I didn't know how to deal with him—whether to keep silent or laugh his mood out of him.

"Are you in love with Matt Braddon?"

"You could just as reasonably ask me if I'm in love with every man I meet."

"That's no answer."

"Then, I scarcely know him. Is that an answer?"

"I'd say it's the understatement of the day! You've seen him at least every morning for nearly three weeks and I've more than a

211

suspicion that when you pretend to go out for a walk alone, you really slip up to that house."

"If that were so, how could I tell you and Kate about the Byzantine church I'd seen and the monastery over at Amkavalla and the ruins—"

"Matt himself could tell you about them."

"Dear heaven, what a devious mind you have!" Then suddenly I blazed at him. "But I'll tell you the truth. In spite of seeing Matt briefly every day, I may know and understand him more than I know and understand *you* after this piece of blind, idiotic jealousy."

Losing my temper with Louis was the last thing I should have done. He took hold of me again, swung me round and flung me across the bed. He lay over me, his body heavy on mine, his eyes fiercely antagonistic, without a flicker of tenderness. "You are most certainly going to know me, my darling—and better and better—so well, indeed, that in the end we will really be one. You will want no one but me, you will *have* no one but me. Do you understand?"

I shut my eyes against his closeness, which, for the first time, I hated.

"Justine . . ."

"Yes." My eyes remained closed.

"You will marry me, here on this island. Do you know that?"

"I won't."

"It's your only hope," he said, and his voice was suddenly soft. "Don't you understand? This is what it's all about between us—the complete possession of both of us of the other. I've talked to Kate—"

"You've discussed all this with her . . . downstairs . . . just now?"

"She always sees my point of view in the end. She's a doting sister." His voice held mockery. " 'My brother right or wrong!' "

"Then *you're* wrong, Louis, because love can't be ordered. I've no intention of marrying you here on Chrysolaki. And now, please let me go."

"You can't see, can you, what you're letting yourself in for with Matt Braddon? Someone has to protect you physically, since you're such a little fool."

"I'm in no danger . . ."

"I'll bet Helen said that once, too!"

I jerked my head up. He put his hand to my forehead and pressed me back onto the silk coverlet. "Lie still and let me do the talking—unless, that is . . ."—his voice took

213

on the well-known, well-loved tenderness again—"unless, here, in the quiet, we make love. Darling, I love you."

I lay tense and rigid, pushing his hands away. "No . . . Louis, no quarrels with me will lead to grand reconciliations, so please don't try. Tell me, why should I be in danger from anyone on the island?"

"I didn't say '*anyone*,' I said 'Matt.'"

"What is he going to do? Carve me up in little pieces?" The words were flippant, but it was a mask over the strange pain deep inside.

"Justine, listen. Please listen to me." He laid his face against mine, speaking against my cheek. "Don't you understand yet why the wrong chart was there on *Persephone* . . ."

"Children."

"Or Matt. Now, listen, before you start another protest. When Kate, with that innocent chattering of hers, told me that you had been seen by some woman in the fields with Elaine this morning, some way from the beach, I realized that you didn't go straight there and that Matt had time to nip down to the boat and change the charts."

"He couldn't . . . he didn't. Anyway, he works all morning."

"You called to Ludmilla that you were

taking Elaine to the boat. She didn't understand, but Matt could have heard what you said from his study."

"Please get up, you're hurting me."

He put up his fingers and caressed my throat, shifting his weight only slightly. "Take off that dress, Justine."

"You've just insinuated something terrible about Matt. Does that excite you to want to make love to me?"

"*Yes!*" He began to tear furiously at my clothes. I fought, shouting at him that violence and argument didn't excite me, and at that moment I had no love for him.

Quite suddenly the door opened. "*Louis!*" Kate stared at him.

He had risen and was smoothing his hair. I got off the bed and went to the window, and said with my back to them, "I think the best thing I can do is to leave Chrysolaki. I hate scenes."

"No!" Kate cried. "Justine dear, please don't go. I don't know, Louis, what you've been saying to her or how you've been behaving, but you can apologize right away. I'm not having a shouting match in my house."

She left the room. I stood by the balcony,

and Louis was at the dressing-table mirror.

"I'm sorry. Kate was right; that was unforgivable of me. Please—" He turned and held out his hand. He looked so sure of himself, of forgiveness . . .

I rubbed the red marks on my sun-tanned arms where Louis had gripped me. "Some women enjoy a man's jealousy; it flatters their vanity. I want to be trusted. Marriage—if I ever marry you—won't mean imprisonment for me; I have no intention of being in purdah for any man . . ." I turned and walked out onto the balcony.

"Love itself is an imprisonment and that's what I have to teach you."

"You never will!"

He was behind me, drawing me back against him. "That's an argument for tomorrow. For today, for now . . . darling, please try to understand, I'm thinking of—oh, of myself, but mostly of you. I've got to make you face the truth."

"About—?"

"Matt killed his sister. That isn't something which is just in my imagination—everyone on the island knows it. Helen had a black temper; Matt has it, too. And once you

216

commit a desperate thing like murder; it's easier the second time."

I broke away from him. "You terrify me!"

"Because I warn you of your own probable danger?"

"Because you talk as you do."

"Listen. Do you hear me, Justine. Stay here and listen." He put out a hand and stopped me from escaping into the room. The sun beat down on my head and Siphi's bell jingled like a gay summons to a pagan rite.

"I believe that Elaine is becoming too much of a responsibility for Matt, he needs to be free of her—hell, I can understand that!—but he doesn't want fingers all over the world pointing at him, the great novelist, and saying that he banished her to some home for retarded children. Something must happen to relieve him of her without his seeming to have any hand in it."

"You're trying to say that it was Matt who put the wrong chart in the wheelhouse of *Persephone*? That he was prepared for me to smash the boat on the rocks and kill . . . and kill both Elaine and me? I think you must be mad!"

"Unfortunately, I'm too sane. He may not

217

have intended to harm you. He probably knows you're a good swimmer."

He did, because I had told him one lovely morning in his green garden.

"Have you told this—this outrageous theory to Kate?"

"She will never accept the truth about Matt. She's too afraid—after all, a lot of her living expenses here depends on the salary Matt pays her."

"Louis!" Kate was calling. "Louis . . . Justine . . ."

"Go," I said. "Please, just go and let me be."

The door closed and I was alone.

Jealousy discolored life, possessiveness insulted individualism. I stood silent and shaken by the sudden harsh light flung across my relationship with Louis as a result of the morning's accident. I told myself that if Matt had had any hand in Helen's death, it didn't concern me and I pushed the horror of such a thought away from me. I was concerned with the present—with Elaine and a disfigured chart on a boat.

Separate events took place that seemed complete in themselves—a boat stuck fast between rocks, an accident . . . But it was not like that at all. Repercussions were flung out, unleashing unexpected emotions in people who were not directly concerned. Like some ghastly earthquake, where the burning lava flowed and consumed everything in sight, what I had done that morning had, by showing me a different man, shown me also a frightening aspect of my own fate with him. I did not want to be completely possessed; I wanted to be myself, not a shadow of a man who had put a ring on my finger.

I said aloud to that bright empty garden, "I love Louis."

And swiftly on hearing my own voice, I thought: This is it! This is what drives two people apart—the disagreement on a principle, the insistence on absolute belonging, the one-sided fight for dominance . . . intangible things that people break their lives upon . . .

I leaned against the balcony and turned my face from the lowering sun.

A recollection came of something read, registered and forgotten, only to appear now on the rolls of memory: "Infatuation is a passion of the imagination." Was that it for me? I didn't want to believe it. I wanted to love Louis, to acknowledge his faults and accept them as he accepted mine. Not to forgive was arrogance and I hated to think of myself that way. Yet strangely, I felt that something had died inside me, something that had nothing to do with Louis, but with me. We had come together through a mutual need and for a few weeks we had existed in a no man's land of fantasy, until a few minutes ago, when a crisis had shown each of us another side of the other.

And now, what? Should I leave Chrysolaki or should I keep my promise to stay seven weeks and give us both a chance to understand and compromise? It would be the fairest thing to do for both our sakes—no love could die swiftly on a first quarrel.

Whatever my problem with Louis, the incident in *Persephone* troubled me. A mischievous act by children or one far more sinister? I had to believe Kate's simple theory, and yet Louis's suspicion lurked behind it black and hideous as a vulture's wing.

In fleeing from the room and my own turmoil, I nearly fell headlong down the stairs and landed in a breathless rush in the living room where Kate and Louis sat.

"My dear . . ." Kate came quickly to me.

"I thought I heard you fall. Have you hurt yourself? Is it your foot?"

"I'm all right, thank you."

Louis said, "She's shaken by what I told her."

"What *did* you tell her?"

"Precisely what I told you—about Matt and the chart and—"

"Louis, how *dare* you!"

"My dear Kate, nothing is sacrosanct between members of a small, close-knit family like ours. We tell our suspicions."

"You can keep that one to yourself. It's evil—it's . . ."

"You're at a loss for words, Kate, so let's change the subect. Is it too early for a drink?"

"Yes, it is," Kate said, and walked to the terrace. "Justine, come and talk to me while I water the flower beds."

14

KATE watched us anxiously over dinner that night, but she had nothing to fear. It was as if the scene in my bedroom had never happened. Louis was gay and over affectionate to both of us.

Persephone was mentioned only once, and that was when Dinos telephoned to announce that the only damage the boat had suffered was scratched paint.

Kate said, "I wouldn't really care if she was a total wreck now that Elaine and Justine are safe."

After dinner Louis told us that he had no intention of spending the whole evening in his darkroom.

"I'm taking time off, and if Machelevos is waiting to see all the proofs of the photographs I took today, then he'll be unlucky tomorrow morning. I'll finish off one or two and that's all. You and I, Justine, are going to Hagharos. This is the night the folk dancers come from all the surrounding villages. It's

222

quite an occasion. You'll come too, won't you, Kate?"

"I've seen them so many times. No, thank you. But I'm sure Justine would enjoy them." She looked longingly at me as if to plead, *Forgive him, please forgive him* . . .

"I'd love to see the dancers," I said.

We left Argus an hour and a half later in Kate's old car, and when we drove into the main square of Hagharos the dancing had already begun.

Looking round after we had been shown to a table, I doubted if there were any tourists watching. The dancers gathered, so Louis told me, once a month, not to give a show for foreigners but for the sheer joy of dancing.

They wore the traditional Chrysolakian costume—the women in full purple skirts banded with white, little red pillbox hats and embroidered boleros; the men in baggy brown trousers, wide-striped cummerbunds and blue sleeveless jackets over white shirts with wide bell sleeves.

First the men, then the women danced in front of the fountain to music that had a touch of the Oriental in its plaintive rhythm—violins and guitars and lutes in a medley of enchanting sound that set the watchers' feet tapping. A man near us started up, shouting, "Ho! Ho! Ho!" like the demon in a pantomime, and then, lifting up a wine pot, he threw back his head and poured the wine into his mouth like a single squirt from a fountain.

Louis said, "I tried that once and ruined a perfectly good shirt."

Flowers cascaded from the balconies and everywhere the shutters were flung wide and the twanging of guitars was background music for a hundred nonstop voices.

Jock Anderson came by, paused and joined us. A lamplight over the trailing vine shot onto his white hair making it look like a cap of bearskin. He asked me how I felt after my morning's adventure.

I said, "Fine!"

"Odd about the chart."

"Yes."

"And the Chrysolakian one showing up like that!"

"I suppose," Louis said, "the whole place is speculating on the why and the how and the who of it."

Jock laughed. "Of course. What else do you think we live by? Gossip and whispers, superstitions and old legends, with a few mad

English to liven up the mixture. You and Louis and Kate and the man at Marathon." He gave me a deliberate leer. "I hear you looked very pretty in his bathrobe."

Louis sat up. "What are you talking about?"

"Justine had to wear something while her dress dried. So Matt offered her his bathrobe."

Louis's face went tight with anger and I sat tensely waiting for another outburst. But he only said quietly, "I hope it smelt of shaving soap."

I did what I was not meant to do. I giggled, but Jock fanned the flame of Louis's annoyance. "Oh, come! Doesn't a little heathy competition make the prize all the sweeter?"

"There's no competition, and you can tell that to the prying islanders."

"Human nature, laddie!" Jock suddenly became very Scottish. "Ye can't stop it; it's the master of us all." He had pulled out a chair and sat down. Louis fixed his eyes on the dancers and did not ask him to have a drink.

The old doctor was watching me. "There's a lot to be said for living in a small place. For one thing, you're never among strangers as you are in a big city." He glanced at Louis. "Were you here the night, two years ago, when, after the folk dancers had finished, Helen Braddon called out from her table that she wanted some sort of dancing where she could join in and the band struck up a fox trot and she dragged some beautiful young man—I believe he was a shepherd from the hills—to dance with her? He hadn't an idea in hell what it was all about, but she was wild with *ouzo*, and some of the women were scandalized and dragged her away. I believe there was quite a fight. Helen was a tigress when she was roused."

Louis laughed. "That would have been quite something to watch! If Matt was with her, I guess he was mad."

"He was. He had his fingers curled round his wine glass as if he wished it was her neck he was squeezing. I think he could have cheerfully killed her for making an exhibition of herself." He paused, then he asked softly, "Do you think, in the end, he did?"

Louis sat staring at the women, dancing round one another, white handkerchiefs waving. "I've got my theories, but for the moment I keep them to myself."

I had a feeling that the remark was addressed to me, that behind the obscurity, there was a warning. *Stay away from Marathon, Justine, or there's no guessing what I might tell . . .*

Jock turned to me, his eyes twinkling. "You mustn't mind what you hear: We who live on remote islands express what, in polite society, would be inexpressible because there's no one to censure us. You see, we all need touches of melodrama to keep our minds alert. People in the cities have international problems to make headlines; we have our occasional tragedies and because they are few and far between, we flog them until they're in shreds. Helen was not only our island tragedy but also our mystery."

Louis sat smiling in quiet triumph, as if he had achieved what he wanted by bringing Matt into the conversation. He had probably hoped that Jock would add his own censure of Matt, but the old doctor was not to be drawn into discussing personalities. The drink he had ordered for himself came and he raised his glass. "Here's to crime!" he called, and tossed the *ouzo* down with a loud gulp.

Suddenly Louis said, "Look!"

I followed the forward jerk of his head and

saw, through the dancers' weaving skirts, Matt sitting at a café table with a handsome dark girl in a tangerine dress.

Louis said, "So now he imports them!"

Jock answered, "Why not? He's a virile man, but he's not the type who can take a masculine interest in simple village girls. He has to have intelligence mixed somewhere in the ingredients. And, by God, that girl looks as if she has brains. I wonder who she is?"

Louis said softly to me, "Now you know, darling."

"What do I know?"

"That you use the well-worn cliché about safety in numbers when you think of Matt Braddon and women."

"That's fine by me. He can have a harem if he wants one." I spoke lightly, but I watched the girl with the gilt bracelets gleaming on her wrists, her hair piled high like a crown of jet.

Capriciously, since we had only arrived half an hour earlier, I wanted to leave. The evening was young from the point of view of the Greeks, who, as Kate said, never seemed to sleep, but I decided that so much sun and air was suddenly taking its toll of my energy and that the whirling and the deafening noise was just too much to take. It could possibly have been those things, or even a mood, although I was not given to them. I knew only that I wanted to go back to Argus, and I said so, apologizing to Jock. "Perhaps I've had too much sun today."

"And an experience you'd better not repeat, or you may drown next time, and you're far too pretty to die."

"Next time," Louis said, "she goes out in a boat, she goes with me. Come on, if you want to go, then let's." He began to chant, "'There sleeps Titania some time of the night/Lulled in these flowers with dances and delight.' Only there won't be any dancing where I'm taking you, darling. I hope you're impressed by my quotation. We did that Shakespeare play at school and I was Oberon. Do you get the message of it?"

I did. There was only one place for a Midsummer Night's Dream and that was the Paradise Garden. But like the crowded, noisy square at Hagharos, that was another place I did not want to be on this star-filled night.

Jock took my hand and kissed it with exaggerated gallantry.

"I'm sorry," I said, "leaving you like this."

"Think nothing of it. I know almost everyone here. I shan't be alone. Off you go, and be young together."

When I had gone a few steps, I turned and looked back. Jock was already squeezed in at a table for six, roaring with laughter and waving violently for more drink.

On our way to the car we had to pass the table at which Matt sat with his elegant companion. As we reached it he rose and stood in the aisle, blocking our way. "Come and join us and meet Clytia." As he introduced us I saw that she looked at Louis as all women looked at him, but his acknowledgment of the introduction was brief. "We're on our way home. Justine is tired."

As he spoke the music stopped, and the dancers disbanded. Then with the briefest pause, the small orchesta started up music for modern dancing.

Matt was saying, "You must stay for one drink with us; Greek hospitality demands acceptance—even if it is only a sip of Turkish coffee."

I looked quickly at Louis and saw that the girl Clytia had caught his attention. I already knew that his artist's eye could not resist a cool feasting on beauty, and Clytia had that strong, classical loveliness that was characteristic of so many Greek women.

At the same time, as Louis drew out a chair for me, I wondered how he could, in one day, attack Matt as a murderer and then sit and drink with him. A small suspicion leapt to my mind that he was setting a trap for me, watching to see Matt's and my reactions to one another. Well, then, let him discover the truth, that we were casual acquaintances and there were no tensions or emotions that we had to fight hard to hide.

Clytia was saying in her deep, slightly harsh voice, "Matt and I are old friends. The first book I ever tried to read in English was his first novel, and that is something we have to celebrate occasionally."

Matt asked us what we would drink and we chose coffee. While we waited for it, I learned that Clytia Kouvakis ran a bookshop in Athens.

Matt said lightly, "She's so efficient that if I didn't know her well, she'd scare me."

Clytia laughed. "That's a fallacy. Nothing frightens Matt. He is one of those men who can cope with any situation. I suppose having imagination prepares people for all contingencies." She turned to me. "Are you enjoying your stay here?"

Louis answered for me. "At the moment I doubt it. I'm tied up at Palacanthus every day, photographing for a book Costos Machelevos is bringing out, even working weekends, would you believe it? But I'll soon be free now." He touched my cheek, adding, "You see, this is really a kind of premarriage holiday. When I've finished work, we'll be having almost a honeymoon, won't we, darling?"

Clytia smiled, making no comment. Then she turned to me. "Matt's new book will be published next week. I hope you'll let me send you a copy for him to autograph."

"Thank you, I would love that."

Coffee came, and after a pause while it was served, the pattern remained the same. Each time Clytia spoke to me, Louis interrupted, drawing attention back to us as a pair, as belonging. I had no idea whether it was in order to hold Clytia's interest in a man already unavailable or whether it was meant as a warning to Matt. As if Matt cared; as if, with his ability to be both friendly and remote, it mattered to him that Louis was intent on his absolute possession of me . . .

The music played by the four guitarists under the trees changed its pace. Clytia's haughty eyes grew brilliant as she looked at Matt.

"Oh, no!" He pressed himself back in his chair. "I'm no dancer and I'm not being dragged out there."

Louis said, "I know this tune. It's played for the only Chrysolakian folk dance where men and women join up. I learned it years ago. I wonder if I remember?"

"Come and try." Clytia's eyes challenged him.

He turned and looked at me with mockery, asking, "Shall I?"

"Of course."

With a swirl of skirt and a release of sandalwood scent, Clytia leapt up and dragged Louis with her. I watched them run and join the dancers.

On their way Louis looked back twice and I knew why. While he danced he would watch Matt and me, alert to our reactions at being left alone together. He wouldn't be able to help himself because jealousy was innate in him and, with it, came the helpless urge to watch and perhaps hurt himself as a result.

Left together, Matt and I made no effort at conversation. There was a complete unself-consciousness about his silence; he sat back in his chair, relaxed, because there was no more risk of his being borne off to dance, and seemed only faintly interested in all the speeded-up animation. He had probably seen this wild vitality letting itself go so often in his life on a Greek island that it no longer had power to quicken his blood.

I broke the silence between us. "I've done something for the first time in my life."

He turned to me so sharply that I felt I had disturbed thoughts far removed from the Square at Hagharos. "Is this a confession, or a boast?" He was laughing.

"Neither. It concerns you."

He waited, looking wary.

"I've read your book *Not Without Honour* through twice," I said.

"That does sound as if your stock of fiction is low. I'm afraid Kate doesn't read much except magazines. You can come any time you like and choose from my shelves. They're in my living room, so you won't be disturbing me."

"Thank you."

Under cover of the table top, I opened my purse and took a swift look at my face. My small jeweled pencil fell out and rolled onto the floor. Matt dived for it, and before handing it back to me, sat looking at it.

"Turquoise, the Eastern stone, the old Oriental riders' talisman, and—"

"Garnets," I said.

"Not garnets—rubies, deep and rich as the color of a damask rose."

"You know a lot about gems."

He was fingering the large red stone at the tip of the pencil. "I know a bit about a lot of things, but nothing much about anything. Mogok—"

I waited for an explanation of the odd word. None came, so I asked, "What's Mogok?"

He took so long answering me that I thought he hadn't heard my question in the din around us. His head was bent, his lean fingers tracing the lines of the stones in their chased gold setting.

"Mogok," he said at last. "In Upper Burma, where rubies come from. Here, take it . . ." He thrust the pencil at me, his manner suddenly harsh. I saw him glance towards the dancers, his eyes brilliant and enigmatic. I turned to look, too, and knew that he was more aware of Louis and Clytia than of me. I was just the girl left to sit with him while the two danced.

Because I was suddenly uneasy I began to talk, to fill the silence. "Louis gave me the pencil. It belonged to his grandmother and you can just see the initials in that tiny engraving." I leaned across the table to show him. "H.C.L. I believe it originally came from Kashmir."

He glanced at me, and for that moment either a mask covered his face or had been thrown aside, so that I saw the real man. I didn't know which. All I did know was that suddenly I saw the violence that Louis had discredited him with only a few hours earlier in my room at Argus.

It shook me so much that I turned my face away and watched the dancers. Clytia and Louis were facing one another, heads thrown back, laughing into each other's eyes, moving voluptuously to the loud rhythm of the music. And Matt was in the throes of some controlled black emotion.

To distract him, I asked the most innocuous question I could think of. "Your next book, the one that comes after the one Clytia is giving me—is it nearly finished?"

"No."

"It tires you? Writing?"

"Yes."

"A love-hate relationship," I said.

His tenseness eased. He said, "You are perceptive," and then he spoiled it by adding, "or perhaps you aren't. For if you were, you'd have less blind courage."

The atmosphere at the little table was unaccountably tuned to disharmony. I felt that perhaps I understood. "About this morning, Matt, I really am sorry. I hoped—"

"What in the world are you apologizing for?"

"I thought that by 'blind courage' you really meant 'stupidity' . . . in taking Elaine out with me this morning, I mean."

"I meant nothing of the kind. A thousand waves have come and gone over those rocks since then. Forget it."

"But I thought—"

"Yes," he said. "*Think*, Justine, it might save you great unhappiness; even more—even perhaps—"

Perhaps what? It could be that he had intended to stop there to intrigue me, but he made it seem that Clytia and Louis's return checked his words, for he looked up as they came, flushed with their hectic, violent dancing, and flung themselves into their chairs.

"She's marvelous," Louis said. "To think that a sophisticated Athenian can dance like that!"

She laughed. "We're born to it. Before we can even walk, we dance with our fingers in our cradles."

"Like Elaine," I said. "She talks with her hands." I looked about me as if expecting her to materialize at my side. "By the way, where is she?"

"At home."

"Oh, Matt, she'd have loved this!"

"The crowds and the noise would have upset her."

"Not if she were with people with whom she felt safe."

Under the table Louis kicked me none too gently, and Clytia said quickly, "There's a most marvelous animal book just published in America which I think would interest Elaine."

"Charge my account with a copy," Matt said, but his tone was unduly fierce, as if, in his mind, he were saying something quite different.

Under cover of loud voices from the next table arguing about something that was making everyone there extremely heated, I

238

whispered to Louis, "I want to go home."

"Good." He flashed me a smile. "I'll dance you across the Square." Then he said in a voice that held triumph, "Matt, Justine wants to go. There's a hell of a lot of noise here."

"The Greeks are an ebullient people," Matt said, and stood up, hands at his side, and didn't try to stop us. "Goodnight," he said. His voice was quiet, but I sensed an anger that would explode when Louis and I had gone.

Louis had his arm round me, leading me through the stream of people. Once, rounding a table, I glanced back. Matt and Clytia were sitting watching us, and the Greek girl raised her hand in a small salute. Louis waved back "Matt has a beauty there," he said.

We left the Square, and passing near Jock's table, we heard his *ouzo* laughter ring out. The night was young in Hagharos and the dance was wild.

15

WE stopped once on the way home and Louis tried to make love to me. The surroundings, the blue-black night, the stillness, the scents of Chrysolaki—herbs and pine and roses—floated in and about us like champagne in our blood.

But exciting and sensuous though it was, I felt the stronger pull of bewilderment touched with fear. The strange, dark question mark of Helen's death and of Louis's compulsion to denigrate Matt in my eyes had quickened—probably because of our meeting that night with Matt in Hagharos and his strange, subdued violence when Clytia and Louis had danced together.

The atmosphere affected me and I could not shake it off. I had no more desire to make love among the pines than I had had to dance in Hagharos.

Of course, Louis didn't understand. I hadn't expected him to. I even said I was sorry because I was disappointing him; I took

240

the blame because I *was* to blame. Or was I? Could I help my strong reactions to the undercurrents that seemed to run like hidden roots under the surface of this lovely island?

"I'm restless and there's something about this place that makes me nervous. I can't explain—"

"I can," Louis said. "Love in the open air is fine for some, but not for you. You want closed doors . . ."

I didn't. But I was relieved that he restarted the car, although I dreaded more argument when we arrived at Argus.

There was a light in the sitting room when we reached home. Kate was there and, between a lamp and the wall, sat Elaine. There was a large illustrated book on the table, and her hands wove, making beautiful recognizable shapes of animals on the white walls. Her fingers bent and splayed with the same fluid grace I had seen once before but which was missing when she held a cup or used her hands for any small normal act.

She looked over her shoulder as we entered and gave me her sweet, blank look.

"Don't stop," I said and pointed to the wall.

She understood and began again, the

shadow likeness of the camel in the picture before her taking shape, supercilious head poised.

"Lovely. Now show me a bear."

"Justine, she can't!" Kate cried. "Don't you understand? She can only copy what's set before her; she has no memory of things she can't see at the moment."

I turned the pages of the book and pointed to a frog. Immediately her hands reproduced its squat body, and the fingers that formed its shadow throat undulated like a frog's when it croaks.

I turned to Kate in triumph. "And you say she has no memory! Then how does she know that a frog's throat moves like that? She must have seen them here on the island and remembered. The picture in the book isn't animated."

Kate looked up slowly and stared at me. "I never thought . . . Justine, you could be right. Sometime or other she *must* have seen a bullfrog *and remembered*. It's extraordinary that Matt has never realized this, either."

"Perhaps he has. And chosen not to mention it." Louis, who had followed me into the room, moved back to the door, waving a mocking hand. "Let the charade go on! But not for me. I'm not interested in children's playtime."

"Elaine's shadow pictures are exceedingly clever," Kate said indignantly. "There's nothing childish about them."

"All right, enjoy them. Justine and I have our own fun ideas, though she doesn't look particularly bright at the moment, does she? What's the matter?"

Nothing, I thought, and everything . . . Something had turned the evening sour. Matt . . . Louis . . . I . . . or perhaps all of us had been touched by some devil of irascibility. I had a feeling that Louis was in a mood to quarrel as easily as he might become loving. There was only one thing to do: to say goodnight and call it a day.

"I'm going to bed."

"But you can't. Not at eleven o'clock in Greece."

Kate said, "Why have you come home so early? The dancing goes on for hours."

"Oh, Justine didn't want to dance—"

"She couldn't with that bandaged foot—"

"—and so we were leaving. Then we saw Matt and he practically shanghaied us to his table. We had a coffee together and I danced with Clytia, Matt's girl of the moment. I

243

don't know what went on between Justine
and him while we were dancing."

"We talked," I said serenely.

"And then said goodnight, when you
should have said goodbye, because you aren't
seeing him any more."

"Oh, don't quarrel again!" Kate cried.
"Louis dear, why don't you go and do a little
more work? You'll be sorry in the morning if
you haven't got any of today's studies to show
Machelevos. What did you work on today,
the garden or the house?"

"Rooms full of treasures that would keep
this whole island in luxury for its life. But—"

"Go along, dear . . . go along . . ." Kate was
steering him away from us with little urgent
flapping gestures of her hands.

I was certain, though, that it wasn't her
persuasion that tipped the scales in favor of
the darkroom; it was the thought of dis-
pleasing Costos Machelevos. A word from
him could make Louis professionally and he
was too anxious to succeed to risk failure.

He said sullenly, "I'll be through in an
hour. And don't dare pretend you're tired
and go to bed, Justine."

Elaine had dropped her hands in her lap
and was watching us. Kate went over to the

table where the candles burned and snuffed them out. "Come, darling, I'm taking you back to Ludmilla now. She'll put you to bed."

Elaine's hands lifted once more, shadowing the wall just before the last candle was extinguished. I had seen that movement before, the hunched hand, the finger thrust out. I watched the heavy effort at a concentration impossible for her as she twisted and contorted her fingers, which had no difficulty with camels and tigers or rabbits. But this curious, almost frantic effort to convey something that was in her mind was beyond her. I saw Kate gently lower her hands, holding them still for a moment. "No more. It's time I took you home."

The obvious distress while she was fighting to convey something beyond her vanished, and she let Kate lead her to the door. There, however, she turned and ran back to me and made her usual little farewell gesture, forehead against my shoulder.

Louis looked after them. "The way Kate behaves with that child! I suppose it's a kind of suppressed motherhood!"

"She should have married. But perhaps she will if she can only meet people."

"Jock was keen on her once."

"Jock?"

"Uh-huh. And she on him, I think. But somehow it all went lukewarm and now they're friendly enough, but that's all." He folded me to him. "Do I really have to work now?"

"Darling, it's as well to remember that you don't displease millionaires!"

"The things I do for our future! But the more I do now the sooner we'll be free to be together. Kiss me."

Footsteps crossed the hall and Louis said furiously, "Damn this house, it's never empty. That's Ruth, hovering."

"I think we disrupt her life. She and Kate must be so used to living quietly."

"She'd be shocked to see me make love to you on that settee, wouldn't she?"

"Go and work." I gave him a push.

Left alone, I wandered onto the terrace. In the drive, Kate's car started up and she drove off to Marathon.

The night was breathless, and the curious tension that I had felt in Hagharos seemed to have followed me back to the house. I had to breathe clearer air than the heavy cloying flower scents of Kate's garden. It was very different from the clean, perfumed gardens of England at night.

I crossed the terrace and walked through the tamarisk hedge and across the soft sand to the water's edge. The waves, exhausted by the winds of the day, lapped gently at my feet. To my right, in the far distance, I saw the lights of Hagharos stretched, crescent-shaped, round the bay. To my left, the Dark Sister rose like a jagged wing, heavy and matte-surfaced. I had no fear of it; Helen Braddon's tragedy was no part of my life and I stood breathing with relief Chrysolaki's faintly spiced air.

"Justine."

I leapt round.

Matt stood behind me. "I'm sorry. I didn't mean to scare you."

"But we left you in Hagharos. How—?"

"How did I get back? The same way as you did, by car. Clytia caught the special night ferry to Athens which is run once a month when the dancing takes place here. Can we sit down, or would you rather I went away?"

The low rocks made excellent seats, and I sat on one carved by the sea and by age into the shape of an old straight-backed English settle. Matt sat by my side.

"Do you see, far over to your right, the boats starting for the fishing grounds?" Before I could answer, he said in the same casual voice, "I followed you here. Did you know that?'"

"How could I? And why did you?"

"An impulse," he said vaguely. Then, "Why are you alone?"

The question was so unexpected that I took a moment to find a cautious answer. "Louis is doing some more work and . . . I like being alone sometimes."

"Then we have that in common."

The moon had shifted imperceptibly, but sufficiently for a half-beam to fall upon the tip of the Dark Sister.

Tell me about Helen . . .

"And are you waiting for Louis here?"

The question cut across my silent demand. "No."

"So you came out on your own—and troubled."

"Why should anything be troubling me?"

"All right. It's not for me to ask. But you react too sharply for me not to suppose that something is." He got up and went to the edge of the sea, looking into the waves.

What happened next was pure impulse on

248

my part. I crossed to the Dark Sister and looked up at the path that wound steeply and narrowly upwards. From the top there would be a magnificent starry view of the island. I began to climb, and because the path was so narrow I was able to hold on to the rocks on either side, helping myself over the steep places. The sea broke on the boulders below, but while I hung on to the rocks as I climbed, I was in no danger of slipping. Yet Helen had fallen . . .

"What the hell do you think you're doing?" Matt's voice came, loud and furious, from close behind me. I had no idea he was there, and as he grabbed my shoulder, I stumbled against an arm of rock.

"There must be a very fine view from the top," I said.

"There is, but you're not going to see it."

"I've climbed more dangerous cliffs in England."

"If you want to play at being a goat, do it there, not here."

"I enjoy climbing."

"With a bandaged foot?"

"It scarcely hurts."

"It'll hurt a hell of a lot if you fall."

"Like Helen . . ."

I could have bitten off my tonue; but the words were out and nothing could erase them. The silence was unbearable.

"I'm sorry, Matt. I shouldn't have said that. I didn't mean to remind you—"

"I'm reminded all the time."

Of course, Elaine . . .

He turned and climbed the few yards down to the beach and I followed. The desire to get to the top of the Dark Sister was gone. Anyway, I would see nothing in the darkness.

Tomorrow, in daylight, I might try and perhaps find caves—a cave—where Helen might have gone to meet someone and had found instead—who? Her brother waiting for her? Oh, no, it mustn't be Matt . . .

Standing on the fine sand, I shivered. I knew I wouldn't climb the Dark Sister the next day. I knew for one thing I had aggravated the pain in my foot, and that had served me right . . .

"And now, " he said, "you'd better go back to Argus."

"Why?"

"Because you're not the kind of person to like anticlimaxes. And that's what this is, the two of us standing here feeling rather tame after a tussle neither of us really won. So—"

"So, 'Go home, Justine.'" I turned on him. "I came down to the beach because I wanted to, and I want to stay. *You* go home. I'm not trespassing here and I happen to love looking at the sea."

"Very well then, I'll go."

"I'd have thought there was enough space for two."

"I wasn't thinking of space," Matt said, and kicked at a stone and turned away.

"Goodnight," I called after him, "and tomorrow I'll come and take Elaine out for a while."

He turned and faced me, saying slowly, "I don't know that I want you to. Elaine is not to be anyone's five days' wonder girl. To give and take away is worse than not giving at all."

"I've *told* you, I'll try to make her happy, and when I leave here, I'll have given her something that I hope will last. It isn't my companionship that is important to her, Matt. It's—it's youth she wants."

He asked almost sadly, "Will there always be a lost dog for you to help, Justine?"

"You have the wrong impression of me. I'm not made of missionary material. Elaine interests me."

"That doesn't mean that what you do for

251

her will be the wise thing." I thought I heard him sigh. "It's against my better judgment—and why you should be able to impose your will on mine, I've no idea—but very well, take Elaine out. And when you call for her, Ludmilla will be able to tell you where you can find her."

Again the same oblique warning. *Don't come and ask me . . . Don't disturb me . . .*

As soon as Matt had disappeared through the trees that guarded Marathon, I no longer wanted to stay on the beach. I went back along the path to Argus, dragging my feet, reluctant to return, equally reluctant to remain. It was as if something had gone wrong with my encounter with Matt: a wrong not struck, a mistaken reaction, an aching regret.

Somewhere near me, leaves rustled. But I had not touched the bushes and there was no wind. I stopped and listened and the sound came again.

"Louis?"

There was a deep silence, and I supposed that I had disturbed some nocturnal animal that had shot into its burrow. But some sense told me that it was no animal that had stirred the leaves. On an island like Chrysolaki, the smallest event was of interest and someone could be watching me without the least intention of harming me. I need have no fear, I told myself—but I ran as fast as I could towards the lamplit windows of the Villa Argus.

There was a light in Kate's room and Louis was on the terrace.

"Where have you been?"

"Down to the beach."

"You scare the daylights out of me when you disappear like that. Don't do it again on your own. Wait for me."

"Why? What on earth could happen to me on a short walk to the sea?"

"I don't know, but I don't like you out of my sight. I like to feel when I'm in the darkroom that you're near me; the terrace is the farthest I like you to go. Damn it, it's midnight."

As if on cue, the clocks in the room above began to crash and jangle, beating out the hours.

"They make such a noise!"

"What do?"

"The clocks."

"Oh, those! I never even hear them. You should have got used to them too, by now."

I never would. A single clock chiming could be a kindly sound, but whole centuries of clocks assembled in an airless room was a merciless reminder of time passing—haunting and inexorable.

If I married Louis, those clocks would be stopped. I would not hand on to my children the fearful legacy that held Kate guardian of a ridiculous superstition.

If I married Louis.

16

I SAT in the garden for some time the following morning knowing that later I would go and find Elaine. I was not certain what we would do that morning, since I could not walk far with my bandaged foot. Elaine was not allowed on the beach because waves had a fascination for her, as had all moving things, and she would run into the sea with no more fear of it than she had of people.

Beyond the tamarisk hedge, the shimmering blue arc of the sky met the water in a haze like a mirage. I could see the vague outline of Costos Machelevos's great yacht and beyond and around, the Aegean Islands beckoned and lured—though I would have to wait to see them until Louis was free from his work on Palacanthus. Then we would visit them together.

When, eventually, I went to fetch Elaine, I took the shortcut that led to the side gate of Marathon. Between the garden and the path that wound to the sea, was a little field where Niko kept his donkey. Oleander bushes made a familiar thick, bright-pink splurge on either side of the gate, and as I neared it I heard rustling beyond the bushes. I saw children's dark heads bouncing up and down among the blossom-laden branches. I checked my normal walk, curious as to why they were there and a little alarmed by the obvious secrecy of their watch on the house. They were jostling one another so that there was a waving of bare legs, bare arms, bare feet—two boys and three girls, and none of them more than seven years old.

Children could be cruel to those unlike themselves, to the young outsiders. When I had brought Elaine into contact with them earlier, they had been shy, polite, watching her with a curious reverence. But I had been with her then and I would have had a steadying influence.

Did they sometimes come to Marathon and watch for her to be brought into the garden to play? I had seen the yellow rubber ball and the little bunch of bells. But play? It had taken me three days to teach Elaine how to pick flowers by their stems and not drag at them by their petals, and the next day she had forgotten how to do it.

Of what use were toys to her? Only the

great picture books of animals and birds were important. But at that moment, the children's watchfulness made me curious; they crouched, fidgeting, sometimes jerking away from one another, rustling the leaves, scattering flower petals. If they had come in order to mock Elaine while Kate and Matt and Ludmilla were at work in their various ways, then—language difficulties or no language difficulties—I'd dare them to scoff and they would understand. I'd see to it that they did.

So far, the children had not seen me and I crept nearer.

Ludmilla appeared with Elaine from the side of the house and they crossed the neat lawn towards the field. Ludmilla said something to Elaine, who stood quietly as if considering where she was. Her hair was like corn-colored feathers and her sleeveless dress was the color of the sky. After a moment or two of stillness, she ran across the field and put her arms round Niko's donkey, her face resting against its rough coat. The animal's ears twitched, and his neck twisted so that his head came round, nuzzling one of her hands.

The watching children in the oleander bushes were so quiet that I moved round to where I could see them. Their expressions were like those of children I had seen the previous year in a Spanish church when they had stood looking up at a gilded Madonna.

Reverence? It was too innocent for that. Wonder, then?

I wanted to cry to them: *Elaine is human and she needs companionship. Talk to her, although she can never talk back to you. Treat her gently; love her. But don't stand in this awed wonder as if she were something apart from you . . .*

I moved out of the shadow of the bushes and called her name loudly, "Elaine . . . Elaine . . ."

She heard me, looked round and then came towards me. The children ducked, but before they could escape I greeted them. In atrocious Greek, I said. "*Yássas pediá.*"

I recognized them as some of the children who had been in the group I had tried to talk to in the village square some days earlier, and they recognized me. But I was merely an ordinary adult who was a stranger to them, and though they smiled, their eyes were wary, their lean little bodies poised, ready to run.

I waved to them and took Elaine with me back to the house, not knowing how to ask them to wait but hoping they might still be there when we came out again.

I left Elaine in the hall and went to find Ludmilla.

"I can't walk far today, so I thought I'd let Elaine make some of her shadow pictures. Could I, please, have some candles and matches?"

Ludmilla nodded, reached in a cupboard and handed me four white candles and a small red matchbox.

"And a book for her to copy from?"

"In sitting room. On table. You find?"

"Thank you, yes, I'll find it."

I collected the book and returned to the hall. Elaine was kneeling by the door watching an insect with bright-blue wings swinging on the stem of a crimson flower.

There was a flicker of pleasure in her violet eyes as she saw the book and the candles I was carrying. These were the things she understood, the things that connected in her mysterious mind.

I led her down the path to a hut that stood near the main gates of the house. Once, passing it, I had glanced in. It contained Niko's garden tools and various discarded objects—a wardrobe, a fine old cottage dresser, odd chairs and a slab of marble that looked as if it had once been a tabletop. It would be a perfect place for Elaine's shadow play, and as we neared it, I saw that the children were still half hidden, watching as if in a crowd waiting for the arrival of a queen.

I held up the candles. "We're going to make shadow pictures. Come and see."

They edged away, nervous as colts, but I was determined to bring them together. I walked casually to the door of the hut and pushed it open. Then I turned and beckoned them.

They held small, whispered consultations and kept looking first at us and then over their shoulders, as if fearing their mothers would appear and issue slaps at their trespassing on Matt's forbidden territory.

They would understand nothing I might say, but my voice would reassure them. "It's all right. You can come into the hut. Come . . . Come . . ."

Elaine had been holding on limply to my hand, but suddenly she let go and moved towards the group of children. Her action was like a magician's touch, the concerted poise for escape was checked, and they looked from

Elaine to me and back to Elaine again.

The contact had to be made somehow and I reached out and took her hand, leading her into the hut. The children crept closer, eyes curious as they watched me strike matches and light the candles I had set on the marble tabletop, steadying them with blobs of their own hot wax.

Flames, however small, have a fascination. The children came, step by step, closer. I found the one good chair and pulled it into the space between the candles and the white wall. Then I opened the book at a page of four animals—a panther and a giraffe, a cat and an elephant.

That was what Elaine understood and loved. She stared for a moment or two at the animals, and then, raising her hands, became absorbed and forgot those who watched her. On the wall, pale gray against uncertain white, came the shadow likeness of a giraffe.

The children were already at the door, and Dyna, the smallest and the bravest, crept inside. The others followed. One by one, pattering in their bare feet across the stone floor, they came and, finding a place among the litter of discarded furniture, sat down, crouching on their heels, and watched the shadow play.

I had closed the door in order to strengthen the shadows, and animal after animal came to gray life on the wall, the flow of Elaine's fingers never ceasing—lines curling and snaking into abstract designs in between her changes from one likeness to another—disciplining her marvelous fingers into the shapes she saw in the book.

Illumined by the candles' glow, the wild little faces with tossed hair and huge, brilliant eyes were absorbed in Elaine's magic. In their gypsy clothes, red and magenta, and many wearing the string of blue beads—their talisman against the evil eye—they sat: the enchanted children watching an enchanting child.

This could be the real beginning of Elaine's escape from her isolation into the world of children, and I was the one achieving it. I, the stranger.

Time had no importance and I had no idea how many pages of the huge book I turned or how many shadow animals and birds appeared on the wall of the hut. I was so absorbed that when the door burst open, I leapt from the table on which I was perched and felt the sharp pain from the cut on my foot shoot up my leg like a spear of fire.

Voices from the doorway screamed and shouted at me; the candles flickered in the draft as a group of women rushed at us. In their perpetual black clothes, they were like huge bats descending on us, arms waving, feet thudding the floor, hurling unintelligible words at us . . . at me.

The children had sprung to their feet and were huddled together against parental onslaught, but the women's focus seemed to be the candles. They seized them and dashed them to the ground, stamping on them and uttering some strange invocation either to their saints or their old gods.

Moving like the Furies, they crushed the candles and the smell of burning wax clogged the air. Then, the flames extinguished, they turned to their children. One woman tore off her necklace of blue beads and flung it at a child while she made a grab for another, who was younger.

"What, in the name of all that's crazy, is going on?" They couldn't understand my words, but my meaning must have been clear; they screamed something at me and continued to drag at their frightened, protesting children. The battle raged through the hut, the children not understanding, the women shouting in their strident voices, and I, at whom they hurled their crazed sentences, standing untouched, my arm round Elaine.

One of the women crossed to where we stood and spoke softly to Elaine, trying to take her arm without touching me. Elaine drew sharply back and looked at me, sensing the urgency and the violence, puzzled rather than afraid.

"It's all right, darling. They don't understand . . . nor do I." I hit out at another woman who tried to drag Elaine away. The woman leapt from me as if I were a raging fire.

Fear could rivet me; common sense told me that these women would understand neither an attempt by words or gestures to explain why we were in the hut. Temper, on the other hand, ignored both fear and common sense.

I turned on them, my eyes blazing. "You stupid women! What harm do you think I'm doing? Get out . . ."

But they had broken the shackles that made them subservient to their menfolk who were off now either fishing or tending some plot of land. The women were on their own, mistresses of themselves, and they whirled round me, their hair loosened from the pins in the struggle with their frightened children. I gave a swift thought to them. At least they had spirit, resisting their mothers, small, brown arms flailing, voices raised in sobs and shrieks.

And I had caused all this . . .

"What are you afraid of?" I cut across the noise. "We were all happy until you came along. What's wrong with a few innocent candles? *And don't look at me like that!* I'm no more a monster than any of you . . . Oh, what's the use? Damn ignorance, damn superstition, if it's that which is making you act like crazed animals, scaring your own children." My voice, ringing loud and harsh round the hut, didn't seem to be mine at all, but it checked them and they backed away from me as if I were placing curses on them.

Gripping their children, clutching one another, their bold faces touched with an almost masculine handsomeness, their eyes on me, fixed and staring, they held their ground.

But suddenly one of them shouted something, and it must have been either a command or a warning, for the momentary silence which had followed my outburst was charged again with frantic sound. Pushing and fighting one another, enfolding their cringing children in their black skirts, they squeezed through the narrow doorway, elbowing each other so that the hut door crashed and banged back against the wall, the ancient hinges straining with the women's weight.

Then, when they were all in a mass outside in the sunlight, their courage returned. Crammed together in the doorway, their faces were like those of a frenzied medieval mob in a film set. They stood in a bunch hurling one word at me.

"*Kakoríziki . . . Kakoríziki.*"

Children's faces peered from the women's funereal skirts, and then suddenly Dyna broke away from her mother and ran towards us. She seemed to be scarcely aware of me. Her eyes were fixed on Elaine, her face alight with something very near to religious adoration—a thin, tanned little face with great eyes and a big mouth slightly open as if in awe. When she was near enough, but carefully avoiding me, she reached out and touched Elaine.

"Dyna . . . Dyna . . ." The mother's voice was a wail of fear, but the child took no notice. Tears welled up in her eyes and trickled down her cheeks.

"Please, don't cry." I put out my hand to her.

The effect was electric. Her mother sprang from the crowd of women at the door and came at us. Trapped in a corner of the hut by this great Amazon of a woman, I shielded Elaine. For one moment I thought the woman was going to strike me, but her hand fell to her side and I could guess why the impulse to attack me had been checked.

Don't touch her; it will bring evil to you. Don't touch her . . .

Lucifer's daughter, Justine Charles from London.

Elaine had her face on my shoulder and I held her close, telling her that there was nothing to be afraid of; these people would never harm her. I was surprised that she wasn't trembling, nor even clinging to me. She wasn't in the least frightened, only bewildered.

"Go, all of you." I hoped the tone of my voice would translate my words. "You've made your point. Now let us be."

The woman with Dyna backed to the door and out. Did one, I wondered on a small note of hysterical amusement, treat the daughter of the devil as royalty and back from her presence?

I moved to the center of the hut and did not for a moment take my eyes off the women. I had an instinctive feeling that in their violent mood I had to treat them as wild animals and must hold their gaze or they would assume power over me. It was a horrifying, hypnotic experience.

I didn't see the first stone. It landed with a thud a foot or so away from me. A second followed, and a third.

I had witnessed mob hysteria; now it was insanity. I pushed Elaine into a corner and shielded her with my body. Couldn't anyone in the house hear what was going on? Didn't the shouts and screams reach anyone there? But the drive at Marathon was long and the trees would muffle the sounds. I was cornered in the hut, and the women, brave now that they were out in the sunlight with their children, were going to stone me.

And the child behind me?

"You're mad! You really are mad . . . all of you . . ."

268

But it wasn't my wild accusations that stopped them, hands groping for more stones—it was another voice shouting at them in Greek. I saw them hesitate and look over their shoulders; I saw the doubt that crept over their faces as they broke up, making way for someone.

Matt? Kate? Ludmilla?

Whoever was coming had broken their attack. I heard the crunch of gravel and rushed to the door, keeping Elaine carefully behind me.

"I'm in the hut. Help me."

Sunlight poured onto Niko's black, curly head and he strode in, took one look at the mashed candles and said, "You come with me. Come."

I hesitated at the door and Niko understood. "They will not hurt you. See—" He stepped out into emptiness. "They have gone. You will be safe with me."

As swift as native hunters in an African jungle, the women had vanished and the gilded, fragrant world was empty. Or so it seemed. They could not have gone far in so short a time, and I guessed that they were hiding in the bushes beyond the gates of Marathon.

"You saw, Niko, you did see, didn't you? They came here and they attacked me."

"What you did—" He waved his hands, trying to find the English word he wanted and ending lamely, "It was wrong."

"That much I guessed. But *what* did I do wrong?"

"They are not bad, but you made them fear."

"*What? What?*"

"You burned candles."

"Of course, so that I could let the children see Elaine's shadow pictures."

For once he forgot to try and impress me with his masculine charm. He said gravely, "You lit candles and you closed the door."

"To keep out the daylight."

"To them that was—wrong."

I knew that he could not find words for a clearer explanation and I said, to his obvious relief, "I shall ask *Kyrie* Braddon."

"Yes. Yes. Ask *Kyrie* Braddon."

We walked the rest of the way to the house in silence. The sunlight was gay and clear on the wind-swept trees, and the green shutters made cool oblongs across the windows of the white walls.

If I wrote and told the story of that morning

270

to my friends in England they would think that the Greek sun had overheated my imagination. Realists, all of them, they would never believe a frantic pagan fear.

Elaine let go of my hand and went to an oleander hedge. A normal child would have retained the memory of what had happened in the hut and would have kept fearfully at my side. Elaine moved as if in an untroubled dream, pulling awkwardly at the oleanders, and from a bloom she had broken off, some petals fluttered to the ground.

I took the mangled flower she held out to me. "It's lovely, darling. But come along, let's hurry." *Hurry away from this fear that is clouding the crystal light, chilling the hot, sweet earth. Let's get indoors and hide. Strong? Who said I was strong?*

I walked towards the patio feeling crushed and weak, and aware at last that Matt was right and I wrong. He knew that Elaine was safer kept away from a world where opportunities might approach and then be torn away, where misunderstandings would leave her bereft. I thought of the two women whom Matt had employed to be her companions. Had similar things happened to them—had they, too, been hunted and hated? I doubted it, since they had probably not dared to try, as I had, to work a miracle—a miracle which had produced a medieval curse in my optimistic hands.

Kate was coming through the patio, and the vine flung cool shadows over her.

"What have you been doing this morning, Justine? You know, you really shouldn't be walking on that foot. You must give it a chance to heal."

"I haven't been walking much."

"You've come this far, and it's quite a little distance. Oh, Niko"—she turned to him—"I believe Ludmilla wants some fruit fetched. Will you go and see what it is she needs, please?"

Having delivered me safely to someone who talked my language, he was eager to be gone.

"Now," Kate said. "Elaine dear, stay in the garden like a good girl until Ludmilla comes for you. We must be getting home. I've got the car over in the shade."

"I think Elaine should be with someone," I said. "Could I take her into the kitchen to be with Ludmilla? We've had a frightening morning and I can't really tell if it's upset her or not."

"What do you mean, 'frightening'?" Her face sharpened. "What happened? Sit down—it's all right. Matt is out, lunching with Jock, and we're alone. But tell me."

I gave her a pretty graphic account and she listened with horror. "But this is terrible! I heard nothing, but then my office is on the other side of the house and Matt left quite early, obviously before it all happened. If only I'd known what you were going to do, I would have stopped you."

"Why? I was only showing the children. Elaine's shadow pictures."

"The candles—and the closed door."

"Without electricity in Kentulakis, a lot of the villagers must use candles in their homes."

"You are a stranger here, so how could you know? But you took the children into a dark place in *daylight*. You closed the door and burned candles when the sun was shining. You were, according to the women, glorifying the forces of darkness and you took the children with you."

"To try to bring them together—with Elaine."

"Elaine, yes. That was part of it too, I have no doubt." She nodded, as grave as Niko had

273

been. "You see, Justine, Elaine is their—oh, what shall I call it—"

"You once told me. Their saint-child—or their goddess, according to which religion it suits them to acknowledge."

"You sound derisive and I can understand. But it's true that that is how they feel about her. The fact that she never speaks increases their reverence for her."

"This is the twentieth century, Kate!"

"Here, on Chrysolaki? I wonder." She brushed her hand across her forehead. "You must remember, too, the accident you had on *Persephone*. The people of the Aegean respect the sea and the wild winds so much that the men cross themselves before they go out fishing. I think that, to them, you risked Elaine's life by taking her in the boat."

"So I'm the evil—"

"Dear, don't use such a word!" she interrupted me. "But the islanders have never forgotten the story of the time when the stones rang out from the Green Sister. The men laughed at the women's fear, but the next day a great storm blew up and their men were drowned."

"So they fasten on an ancient coincidence. Do they think that the stones must have rung

274

out last night to warn them that I was going to cause Elaine's death this morning? Only they hadn't heard that warning? Do they think their gods are pointing a finger at me?" I demanded in bitter derision.

"I wish I could make you see, Justine. But how can you understand? I couldn't when I first arrived. Coming from the sophistication of a large city, it makes little sense."

"And the chart?" I brought her back sharply to the vital question.

"Children—I'm sure of it. Up to mischief. But I can't find out which of them did it because they cling together like one family."

"And when I got them into the hut, what was I supposed to do with them?"

She spread out her square hands and looked at them. "In the second century, Greek witches used burning torches for their spells behind locked doors in a dark room."

I calculated quickly. "Eighteen hundred years ago!"

"But you know, Justine, there are even remote villages in England where people still cling to superstitions. So who are we to judge a more innocent—"

"Innocent! What in heaven's name was I

supposed to be? A kind of Pied Piper of Hamelin?"

"In a way."

"Then the sooner I get off this island, the better!"

"Justine dear, please, don't talk like that! I'll speak to them—of course I will. Ismene Stephanides is the one behind it all, I'm certain of that. She's like the uncrowned queen of the village. The only person who ever dares to defy her is her own small daughter, Dyna. But it'll blow over, I'll see that it does. Then, soon, Louis will be free and there'll be no more village nonsense. He understands their language and they won't make difficulties for you when he's around." She rose. "Now, let's go back to Argus and have a long cool drink and lunch."

Elaine was in the kitchen with Ludmilla, eating biscuits made of almonds and semolina, which I had tried and disliked. She looked up at me; her eyes had no shadows in them and I knew that the incident in the hut had no lasting place in her strange mind.

I left her, feeling relieved, and joined Kate in her car. For a moment before she started the engine, she laid a hand over mine. "Don't let what happened worry you too much. I'm sure the women would never have really harmed you."

Wouldn't they? A stone, aimed a little higher, a little further, would have struck my head.

The car moved forward. I sat by Kate's side, hands gripped together, looking carefully straight ahead of me. I had a feeling that the women had still not dispersed, that the bushes hid them. And, had I walked alone back to Argus, would they have attacked me? I knew no answer.

The brilliant afternoon lay ahead of me and I dreaded it. I dreaded the evening, the night. I was supposed to be self-contained and independent and I felt neither. I was quite certain that Kate had never seen the women in the mood that I had seen them and that her imagination did not stretch to visualize the horror of that morning to me.

While we sat under the pepper trees and drank iced lime and while we were at lunch, Kate filled the time with inconsequential chatter. I knew that she was trying to be kind but it didn't help. Only time—and a long time, at that—away from the island could erase the memory of the morning.

277

After lunch I was urged to go and rest in my room. I went upstairs, closed my door and sat down at the dressing table. I was almost surprised to find that I had a reflection in the mirror; witches, I believed, and ghosts, did not. But there I was: long dark hair, sun-tanned skin, green eyes . . . witches' eyes . . .

I started up, and my elbow knocked my small hand mirror off the dressing table. It crashed to the floor, face downwards, and there was a crunch of breaking glass. I picked it up, turned it over and saw my face, distorted by cracks, disintegrated.

And then, suddenly, as if they were laughing at me, the clocks began to chime, falling over one another like people shrieking to make their voices heard above the din . . . like the women at the door of the hut.

"Kakoríziki!"

I had forgotten to ask Kate what it meant.

I turned, flung open my door and fled from the house into the gray-green quiet and the stony soil of the olive grove.

17

LOUIS'S laughter rang out and he hugged me, as if I had just told him the joke of a century.

I had changed into a fresh dress for dinner and was slipping into shoes when he walked in—again without knocking—swept me up and said, "What's this I hear about you having a fight with the villagers?"

"Fights are usually with fists or knives. They didn't touch me."

"Tell me the whole story," he said with delight. "I hope you got the best of it! I couldn't get any real sense out of Kate—she's so emotional about it. But you"—he held me at arm's length—"you look fine. No bruises, no broken bones . . ."

"They didn't touch me," I repeated, "because they didn't dare."

"Of course not!"

"I'm Satan's daughter."

He sat down beside me on the edge of the bed. "I'll settle for you, with the devil for a father-in-law and all." He slid an arm round me and began kissing my cheek, my throat.

"It was serious, Louis."

"About as serious as a row in a school kid's dormitory. You and Kate are really making a lot about nothing, aren't you? Well, it's understandable. So little happens here that if someone scowls it makes a page of history. Darling, don't look so tight-faced. It's over and I'm here with you and, by the way, I'm getting very tired of this platonic arrangement."

I got up and went to the balcony. "Have you ever seen a witch hunt?"

"Burnings at the stake, darling, died out in—I believe—the seventeenth century."

"They began to stone me."

"Oh, come off it! All you experienced was a lot of silly women shouting at you. I'm quite certain you were capable of coping with them."

"I was afraid."

"Of what, for Pete's sake?"

"Of the thing you said they were incapable of. Violence."

He laughed and held out his arms to me. "Come here, sweet, and stop making such a fuss. It would have been interesting to have watched—you against the women!"

"You would have—watched?"

"Men don't interfere in women's quarrels; they're usually capable of looking after themselves."

It was his tone rather than his actual words that hit me like a heavy depression, as if something were cracking inside me, leaving a void. "I'm only just beginning to understand you." My voice came out in a whisper.

But Louis heard. "That's fine. *I* understand *you*. You're strong and I'm quite certain you'd never expect me to fight your battles for you. You're no clinging vine, darling."

I had a feeling that he was treating what had happened that horrible morning like a brawl in an English public house but when he gave me a quick sideways look, sliding his eyes round at me, I knew that he had been given the facts frankly and frighteningly by Kate but was choosing not to take them seriously. I had said I was learning fast about both Louis and myself—I learned a little faster about Louis in that moment. If I were in trouble, I would be on my own.

"Louis . . ." Kate called from below.

He laughed. "She knows I'm up here and she's thinking the worst. She's a prude, you

281

know. I've always thought that she was born in the wrong century."

"Louis . . ."

He went to the door. "I'm here in Justine's room, as you well know. What is it?"

"The wine for dinner. Neither Ruth nor I can open the bottle. I think we've broken the cork."

"Oh, damn the wine!" His eyes mocked as he turned back to me. "That's a feeble excuse for keeping us from making love on your bed! 'The wine . . . we must have the wine!'" He struck an attitude, and then held out his arms to me. "Take off that dress. There's half an hour before dinner."

"No."

"And don't be provocative. You're not the type."

"I've had a shattering day."

"That's all the more reason to forget it in the best possible way." Then, as I tried to part his arms from round me, he said impatiently, "Justine, stop playing hard to get. We've been here three weeks and I've been damned patient. Darling, I know that bed, it's beautifully soft . . . take off your dress or I'll do it for you."

"*Louis!*"

282

"I'm not coming," he shouted back at Kate.

"Oh, yes, you are." My voice was as loud as his. I called down to her, "I'm just pushing him out of my room."

"Oh, for God's sake, two of you!" He caught at the neck of my dress, then suddenly let go, and without a word, turned and went out of the room.

I had noticed so many times before how, in the end, he always obeyed Kate. For all her sweetness and her fussy kindness, she was the stronger character of the two.

"One of these days"—Louis stood just outside my room—"you're not going to order me out of your sight or out of your life, my darling. I'm going to have you utterly and completely and no one else will ever share you, not even children, because we won't be having any. But then, I doubt if you're very maternal. And if you are, you can mother *me*. That's what most men want, a sister and a mother and a mistress all rolled into one."

I turned my back on him and picked up my broken hand mirror. Louis was running down the stairs—to open the wine or to prove to Kate that he and I were not lying on my bed making love.

It was strange that I had been on Chrysolaki nearly three weeks, yet when we were together, Louis and I had talked of everything except ourselves. I realized, looking back, that it had always been he who had led the conversation, talking to me of his day at Palacanthus, the guests at the great villa, of the more splendid boat he would be buying when the studio began to make a profit. And when he was not talking of his plans we were swimming or sunbathing or driving into Hagharos for coffee or a walk round the enchanting little port.

Did Kate know how Louis felt about having a family? I doubted it, or she would not have been so blissfully happy at the thought of our marriage. She wanted, above all things, the continuance of the line: a resurgence through Louis and me of a strong and splendid d'Arrancourt dynasty. Kate was the kind to have great and unpractical dreams.

And I? A thought crossed my mind that perhaps Louis had chosen me because I had no parents, no brothers or sisters who would demand a little of my love. Or perhaps I was making too much of the things he was saying in anger. Louis might, as many men did, change after marriage and become a proud and spoiling father.

I should be able to shrug off that part of our conversation, and yet I could not. It lingered like a cloying scent and became linked with our earlier talk when Louis had laughed at the thought of the village women's fury towards me.

From those two brushes with him had emerged a sharp insight into a quirk in his character. For all his love of beauty through the eye of a camera, Louis was particularly insensitive where the feelings of others were concerned. It was not that he was callous, but just that he was temperamentally incapable of putting himself in another's place; of seeing anything except through his own eyes, or the eye of his camera.

I walked about the room, touching things, readjusting the marigolds in the yellow bowl on the heavy carved chest of drawers, putting away my sandals, wiping spilled powder with a tissue. And, as I did so, it occurred to me that Louis had never once asked me, on his return from Palacanthus, whether I had enjoyed my day. The fact that the holiday, so far, was entirely different from what we had planned, and that there was little to do on the

285

island except swim and sunbathe on my own, did not cross his mind—or rather, it crossed it with delighted knowledge that the whole of my day was probably spent missing him.

Yet, perhaps because of the unexpected work on Palacanthus, we had achieved our aim of knowing one another in circumstances that were more realistic than ideal, and that was salutary.

18

I WAS in the garden after tea helping Kate snip off the dead heads of flowers. In all that dry heat the petals of the bougainvillaea and the stocks were warm to my touch. Lower on the ground were the dwarf marigolds with their little heads like tiny orange umbrellas.

Ruth never raised her voice. She came walking down the path looking almost Greek in her black dress and dark hair.

"Mr. Louis is on the telephone. He wants to speak to you."

"Oh, no!" Kate raised her head, her face flushed. "He's not going to be late again, surely! I must say, nice as they tell me Costos Machelevos is, he really does expect people to work all hours!"

Louis's message, however, was quite different. Costos Machelevos had heard about me and he wondered if I would like to go over early that evening and have drinks with him and his guests. And also, would I like to bring Elaine? He had met her two or three times through Matt and he felt that a change of scene might be pleasant for her. "Will you come, Justine?"

It would be fun to see how a millionaire lived, and my curiosity about beautiful houses and gardens was irrestistible. "I'd love to. But I don't know about Elaine."

"Don't worry. I've already rung Matt and he agrees, so long as she stays with you. O.K?"

"Fine."

"The launch will be with you in half an hour. Put on your most expensive dress—"

"I have none."

"Then that yellow one that clings to you so maddeningly," he said and laughed.

I laughed, too. It was an invitation I would probably dine out on in London for a long time. "I had drinks with a millionaire. He showed me round his fabulous villa . . ."

"I'll fetch Elaine—" I said.

"No, let Kate do that. Darling," he added as I began to protest, "that's her life, running round after other people. Besides, the less you see of Marathon, the better I'll like it. You go and put on that yellow dress. Don't wear any jewelry. You see, the people here have all the money in the world and you couldn't compete that way—you can only be outstanding by looking different. Just the yellow dress. Right?"

"Right," I said, and as I went through the house to the garden to tell Kate, I realized that it was this kind of touch that made Louis an artist. "If you can't beat them, then be totally different."

I remembered the story of one of the mistresses of a French king who, when attending a function at which all the famous courtesans were to be present, wearing their fabulous finery, came herself in a simple black dress, her maid behind her carrying a tray on which were piled her jewels.

I was still laughing when I joined Kate. I told her of the invitation to visit Palacanthus and she was delighted.

"But that's wonderful! I hoped Louis would arrange some way in which you two could meet, so that you would be welcome to spend your days there with Louis. You see, I *know* Machelevos will like you. He couldn't help himself. So it'll work out marvelously."

The thought that this was the prelude to my being invited to go over every day and "help Louis in his work" was sobering. But I decided that no bridge should be crossed before one came to it.

Kate herself suggested that since she had the car, she would go and fetch Elaine.

"If Matt has given his consent, then that's fine. It'll do the child good to walk round a beautiful place like that."

I put on the yellow dress. It was three-quarter length and of chiffon, and I had felt at the time I bought it that I had paid far too much for it. Now it had its use. I piled my heavy hair up on top of my head, decided that I didn't like it and let it flow again round my shoulders.

Elaine arrived in a dress of white silky cotton, and Kate fussed happily, making us stay on the beach side of the house and wait for the launch to come for us.

When it came, the Greek boatman in the white blue-braided uniform got out and lifted Elaine into the boat. He obviously knew all about her, for he settled her carefully, almost lovingly, in the cabin while he came back to help me in.

It was the sort of small cruiser my father would have loved. My thoughts of him made the first part of the journey across to

Palacanthus, with Kate waving from the beach, a nostalgic one.

But Elaine took my attention again. She was fascinated by the waves, and I led her outside to the stern of the boat so that she could watch the dancing white foam that followed in the wake of the launch.

At first, the island of Palacanthus was just a blur of mauve in the distance, but as we came nearer I saw tall cypresses and a hillock on which stood what I supposed was a pavilion, very white and classically built, like a miniature Acropolis.

The boatman must have known that I wouldn't understand even if he tried to speak to me, and so the only sounds were the purr of the engine and the slap of the water against the side of the boat. When we came near Machelevos' great white yacht, the boatman pointed to it and I nodded and said how beautiful it was, hoping he would get my meaning. He seemed to, and grinned and nodded back at me.

Once past the yacht, the island became clear. I saw the landing stage and some small, flower-enclosed villas, beyond which were thick woods, the plumed tops of the trees waving in the last of the wind before sunset.

291

Louis was waiting for us, and after the boatman had lifted Elaine on to the immaculate landing stage, Louis helped me out.

"They're charming," I said, looking at the little shuttered villas.

"Oh, you've seen nothing. Those are the homes of the men who patrol the island. There are lookouts also on the other side. It's a fortress, but then, it needs to be with all the treasures it contains. Come along . . . oh, Justine, don't let that child dawdle!"

Elaine had found a pale fawn Pekingese. It was standing looking at her, its snub face curious, and once again, as with the donkey in the field, I felt that they were communicating in a strange, silent way.

"Come *on!*" Louis shouted.

I went back for her and took her hand and led her along the path that ran between the tall trees. And all the way, Elaine kept looking back as if she had been dragged away from a newfound friend in the little dog.

We came quite suddenly into the open, and before us, beyond the perfect perspective of gardens and trees, was the Villa Palacanthus.

Millionaires' houses can be of any shape or size according to their tastes. Costos Machelevos had borrowed from the Palladian architecture for his. Its façade was impressive. Two flights of steps converged at the top onto a columned terrace, and above it, gleaming in the low sunlight, was a great dome. As we approached I felt a sudden nervous regret that I had come. I didn't belong in a setting like this, not even for a few hours. But Louis walked by my side as if he had been used to such places all his life.

We didn't climb the steps to the vast double doors but went round the house, passing an ornamental lake where the water lilies were as pale as primroses, their great petals spread out to catch the sun's rays. Statues stood among the ilex trees and the lawns were as green as peridots.

When we rounded the house I saw, at the back, three terraces leading from the house to more grounds and a swimming pool. People sat around in groups, their voices carrying across the warm air. Somewhere near me, hidden by a great urn, a woman exclaimed in a penetrating English voice, "Who in the world are these people?"

I turned as I passed by and saw her—piled dark hair, long red silk dress, prehensile fingers, lean and bejeweled. I felt that she belonged to the Beau Geste age and should have raised lorgnettes to quiz me.

A man under medium height, wearing a beige suit of some silky material and a dark-green cummerbund that had been so fashionable with the British sophisticates a few years before, came forward to greet us. He had the strong Greek nose and dark eyes, and his hair was black and curly and springy. I wondered vaguely what he must be thinking in that moment before we were introduced—a dumb child in a simple white dress and a young woman wearing not one piece of jewelry.

But his greeting was charming and—I was certain—sincere.

"Louis has talked to me about you." His English was nearly perfect, his manners quiet and not in the least ostentatious. "Please come and have some champagne. And I would like you to meet one or two of my guests. To be introduced to the lot would be too much!" He laughed. "And Elaine—" He took her limp hand between both of his and held it warmly. "You've grown since I last saw you. I'm so glad Matt let you come." He spoke to her as if she were normal and understood, and for that I liked him immediately.

We were introduced to four people: an

elderly woman with a French title, who was charming; two men who were polite and both of whom seemed to have Spanish titles; and an Englishwoman, also not young, who was still a great name in the world of the theater.

Everyone sat or stood around on the flowering terraces with tulip-shaped champagne glasses in their hands, talking, laughing. There were a lot of very young people there, dressed with that expensive, almost throwaway taste that had the hallmark of great French couturiers.

I accepted the champagne but refused anything for Elaine. Matt had asked Kate to tell me not to let her drink anything in case she dropped the glass or spilt something. She didn't seem to mind at all—her sweet, vacant eyes looked all ways, only vaguely interested, but perfectly happy—I liked to feel—because she was with me.

To be taken round the villa with Louis was like being a specially conducted guest round a British stately home. We entered a great hall with veined alabaster columns and a magnificent painted dome. The floor was marble and silk rugs were scattered over it.

"They're priceless." Louis said. "Kirman

and Shiraz. You're walking on a fortune, darling."

The room into which Louis led me were full of treasures—too full—but then I had heard that Costos Machelevos had some Oriental blood in him which probably stimulated his taste for surrounding himself with the richest and the rarest objects.

"And now," Louis said, pausing at double doors, "I'll show you the whole object of the exercise."

"What exercise?"

"Bringing you over."

He opened the doors.

"It's a cinema," I said, and added, "Sort of," as I looked around at the casually arranged chairs.

"It *is* a cinema. But the big screen has been rolled up and a small one put in its place." He turned and pointed behind him. "You see that's where my camera will be set up."

"To photograph what?"

He laughed and touched Elaine's cheek. "Hands making shadow pictures on that screen."

"But you can't!"

"Can't what?" He was walking up the great room with its walls of blue silk, towards the screen. "You see?" He pointed. "There's a gilt chair for her to sit on—I've placed it carefully so that when she makes her shadow pictures, her profile will be seen on the screen's edge—and it's quite a profile that child has! Then, you see, there's the spotlight that will illuminate the screen and the magnifier . . ."

"Louis, I won't let you do this."

He stopped, turned, took me by the shoulders and kissed me. "It's all in the name of success—darling. And stop looking so dramatic. I'm not going to hurt the child. I shall be at the back of the room and I shall take masses of pictures of the guests watching Elaine—only it'll be an intriguing sight of the famous—the back view of their heads and shoulders taken in semidarkness while they're watching the screen. Machelevos is intrigued with the idea of including one of the studies in his book, and I may use a couple of them, back home as blowups in the studio."

"Doesn't it occur to you that Elaine has never seen such a huge screen and that her hands will show up out of all proportion to their size? She won't recognize them."

"As she doesn't recognize anything, anyway, I can't see that it matters."

"She watches what she does and she's meticulous in getting everything right. But she's used to small images. Louis, you can't put her through this—and with all those strangers watching."

"Oh, can't I? You wait and see."

"Elaine"—I turned to her—"come with me." I took her onto the dais where the screen stood, sat her down and then called to Louis, "Turn on the light, will you?"

He did so and the screen came alive. There was a huge book of animal pictures on an inlaid table; I opened it, found an easy picture and said, "Darling, look, a tiger."

For a moment she didn't understand. The place was strange to her and what seemed to interest her more were the gilded heads of lions that were carved at the corner of each arm of the chair.

"Elaine, *look*." I pointed to the book.

She bent her head, frowned a little and then turned to the screen. Slowly she raised her hands, and her fingers began to flow. The thing that was thrust on the screen was most certainly a tiger, but it was huge and she dropped her hands quickly, staring at the empty space where the shadow had been and then at me.

"Go on, that's fine!" Louis cried.

She sat for a moment quite still, then she started up and ran to me and laid her head in that way I knew so well, forehead against my shoulder. It wasn't fear, but it was a gesture of protest just as she did the same small act whenever I left her, protesting at my going. I understood. This was not her world or her way.

"It's no use, Louis. She hates it."

"It's strange, that's all. Go on, Justine, make her try again. She'll do things for you."

"No. It bewilders her. She's gentle and it'll worry her even more to have all those strange faces staring at her."

"I got her over here for this and she's going to give a performance—"

"Oh, no, she's not. Elaine is no circus act. What she does in the privacy of her own home or at Argus has nothing in common with what you want her to do here in front of this sophisticated crowd. Louis, face facts! They're going to be bored, too. They're used to slick cabaret acts."

"I don't care if they yawn. I want those pictures. I want people to see those heads in shadow and know that they are mostly famous people; it'll be a fun game for every-

one who sees the book, trying to identify the
stars by the backs of their heads." He took
Elaine by the shoulders and sat her down
again in the carved chair. Then he pointed to
the book.

Once more she bent over it, frowned and
raised her hands. This time she did not even
complete the animal, but started up and ran
again to me.

I put my arms round her. "Now perhaps
you can see that I'm right. The screen, the
strange room, everything here bewilders her.
I'm going to see Mr. Machelevos and I'm
going to tell him—"

"Justine, don't do that! You'll make me
look an utter fool."

"We'll all look much more foolish if the
guests are collected in here to watch a shadow
show—and the star performer just won't give
it."

"Perhaps if you stayed with her and tried to
persuade her."

"No." I took her hand. "Come, darling,
let's get out into the sunlight."

I gave a swift thought to the fact that the
women of Chrysolaki should be here to see
us. There would be a warlock as well as a

witch for them, or—in their susperstitious opinion—were only women evil?

I hesitated at the door. "Are you coming, Louis?"

"No."

"Then . . . then I suppose we had better go back to Chrysolaki."

"I suppose so. She's a dead loss, that girl of Matt's."

"She's not Matt's 'girl.' And I don't see how you can call her a dead loss just because she won't do something that was never really expected of her."

"Have it your way." He was bending over his hand-or-stand camera. "Machelevos can put on a film for his guests tonight. It doesn't matter that much. The only important thing is that they're looking at the screen."

I said unhappily, "we've been an awful wash-out, haven't we?"

He didn't answer me and I led Elaine out of the room, through beautiful connecting rooms and into the hall.

I wondered if Matt would be angry if he knew the reason why Elaine had been brought to Palacanthus. Anyway, the plan had failed and it no longer mattered. I had expected Louis to lose his temper, to follow us and argue. But it could have been the awe-inspiring magnificence of the villa that checked him, or it could have been that he had decided his other idea was just as good. What interested him was not a child's shadow play but the artistry of his idea and the excitement of its conception.

The sightless eyes of the marble statues in their niches gazed out at us as we went through the great hall between the green-tinted columns and the chairs almost too ornate to sit upon.

In a way, I could sympathize with Louis, for I understood his limitation so far as other people were concerned. His sensitiveness was in his eye, not in his understanding.

We made our way through groups of people. Tanned and jeweled hands held glasses refilled with champagne, and voices had risen as if the sun and air and heady drink were a little too stimulating. A girl was whirling in a solo dance on the lower terrace, her dress of rainbow colors floating like tongues of fire around her. Someone applauded her; someone called her name, "Zenia . . . Zenia . . ."

Costos Machelevos was down by the swimming pool talking to three people. His back was to us, and keeping Elaine close to me, we walked down the steps of the last terrace.

A group of young people, probably not more than seventeen years old, were standing on the clipped lawn, their laughter too loud, their hands flicking at one another in a kind of light horseplay that any moment could change its mood and become angry.

As we approached, one of them, a young man with closely curled black hair, saw us. He stood swaying gently and looking at Elaine.

"Now, there's one I like," he said. "Nice and really young, not like you aging monsters. I wonder . . . I wonder if she has ever been kissed—"

"Julian, stop it!" a girl cried.

"Stop what?" He didn't take his eyes off Elaine. "I really wonder if she's ever been kissed the way I'm going to kiss her now." He made a grab at her.

Elaine drew away, but too slowly, and he had his arms tightly round her.

"Let go!" I thanked heaven he could understand English.

He looked round, laughing at me. "Are you

303

joking? I'm not letting go of anything as pretty as—"

I hit him. It wasn't a hard blow, but it was my fist delivered at his cheek and he was so shaky on his feet that he crumpled and fell back into the crimson cushions of a chaise longue behind him. The garden chair twisted and gave way, and he went sprawling on the lawn and sat, looking up at me, giggling, eyes not entirely focusing.

"And don't try that again."

The two girls gave little screams of laughter and looked at me as if expecting me to introduce myself. I didn't.

I took Elaine's hand and walked on. Costos Machelevos must have heard the commotion, for he looked round, and seeing only a young man sprawled on the grass, resumed his conversation with his guests.

Someone touched my shoulder and I turned to find the elderly Frenchwoman to whom I had been introduced when I first arrived.

"May I apologize for that?" she said. "He is my nephew and I'm afraid he's not old enough yet to carry his drink. I'm sorry."

I murmured that it was all right. "But Elaine has to be guarded. You see . . ."

"I know. Costos told me. Such a tragedy. But she looks happy enough, as if the foolish things some so-called sane people do don't really touch her."

"Thank you," I said, "for understanding."

"Are we going to see Elaine's shadow pictures?"

"I'm afraid not. I'm just on my way to explain to Mr. Machelevos. The big screen bewilders her; she can't understand it. I'm afraid it's letting everyone down, but to be quite honest, I don't consider she should have been asked in the first place. We didn't come over for that, you see. We were only told that we might like to meet Mr. Machelevos and wander round the grounds. I'd no idea it was a party."

"A party?" She laughed. "This is nothing. Brilliant men sometimes have strange whims. Costos's is to fill his island with people—I sometimes think he feels that there is safety in numbers." She laughed again. "But then, I've known him since he was a little boy. Here he comes."

He joined us, holding a Greek cigarette in a long holder. With quiet tact, the elegant elderly woman left us, and I said, "Please forgive me, Mr. Machelevos, but I want to take Elaine home. I've been in your theater and we've tried to rehearse Elaine, but she won't do it. The huge screen and the strange room puzzle her; she doesn't understand the big shadows—I think she doesn't believe that they're her hands at all that make them. We *have* tried and it's useless. I think it would be better to go quietly rather than collect your guests and then find that the whole thing is a failure."

He had a way of looking one straight in the eyes and smiling, and I couldn't tell whether it was a polite façade behind which he held anger or natural good manners. When he spoke, I knew that it was neither.

"I'm sorry, Miss Charles. I'm afraid I'm at fault. I had no right to suggest your bringing Elaine over for my guests' amusement."

He wasn't to know that I was aware that the whole thing had been Louis's idea; he was taking the blame, charmingly and gently.

"Please feel free to wander round the island."

"I think I'd better take Elaine back." It would save him the embarrassment of his guests seeing us remaining on the island and yet making no attempt to entertain them. Better to go. But there would have to be his explanation. "Your guests," I said, "they will have to be told."

He laughed. "My guests live their lives either entertaining or being entertained. I have a new movie I can put on for them if they wish it, and the young can dance. Think no more about it. But I'm sorry you are going, Miss Charles. I have enjoyed meeting you."

"And I have enjoyed meeting you. I really mean that. And if Elaine had been . . . had been . . . different perhaps it would have been fun for her, too."

"If she had been a little show-off," he said with amusement, "or even a child with a great gift and a mature ambition. As it is, she just has the great gift. Oh, I've seen her, at Matthew Braddon's."

Elaine sat down on the path and reached out her hand to a clump of tall Madonna lilies. I drew her quickly away, saying, "I think she's tired."

"Then I'll get the launch to take you both back. And Louis—"

"No, we'll go alone. He has an idea for taking studies of your guests watching the screen. Perhaps he could take them watching some movie. He says it would make an unusual picture, guessing the famous from the back of their heads."

Costos Machelevos laughed. "I hope we meet many times while you are on Chrysolaki. Come when you like."

"Thank you."

"And now, if you'll go down to the landing stage, you'll find the launch will be there."

I left him to his guests, and the laughter and the talking followed us down the scented path between the tall trees.

The one thing I wanted was to be away before Louis found me. I was surprised that he hadn't come after me, but I guessed that, engrossed in the photographic studies he was planning, he had chosen to leave any argument with me until later. He had seen for himself that Elaine could be neither organized nor persuaded, and for that he could not blame me.

The sun was setting as the launch cut through the stretch of sea between our islands, and the waves were quiet, as the wind had dropped. There was a purple-grape bloom on the water, and a smooth blaze of crimson was spread like a feathered coverlet over the northwestern sky.

It was all so beautiful, so achingly beautiful

that I felt I could stay on the white boat, sitting in the gilded light, forever.

To my surprise, Kate was waiting for us on the beach. When we had climbed onto the little jetty and I had thanked the boatman, she came towards us, saying, "I heard the launch. You've been very quick. I imagined you'd be wandering round that marvelous island for hours."

I told her, as we walked up to the house, why we had left so soon.

"But that was very naughty of Louis! He shouldn't have suggested making a kind of spectacle of Elaine! And, anyway, how on earth could he think that those hard-boiled people would be interested in a child's shadow play?"

"That didn't concern him. His idea was to take photographs in the semidark with that special ray gadget he has and then include one of the studies in the book he is doing."

"Well, dear, since Elaine herself wouldn't play, at least he can't blame you."

I told her, as we reached the terrace, about the tipsy young man who had tried to kiss Elaine.

She said sadly, "I'm afraid that's going to be a problem. She's growing so beautiful and because she is retarded, there will be men who will think her fair game."

"Kate, she'll have to have a constant companion as she gets older," I said in alarm. "Doesn't Matt realize that?"

"What Matt realizes, he keeps to himself. He probably has some sort of plan . . ." She changed the subject as if the thought of Elaine's possible danger was something that frightened her. "I've got the car out so I'll run her back. What a pity"—she gave me a long look, taking in my yellow dress, my slender strapped sandals—"you should have been staying over there enjoying yourself, dear, not coming back here so tamely. It's a shame!"

"Oh, I don't mind," I said. But I did. I looked at the gray, forbidding house, the hot colors of the garden and thought longingly of the lovely spaciousness of the Villa Palacanthus. But Argus could have been cool and welcoming, too. All it needed was white paint and flung-back shutters, a disciplined garden, and an overall lightness that could never be achieved while it housed heavy furniture, too dark, too large for its rooms; and the clocks, chattering and mumbling like a frantic vocal chain that linked the d'Arrancourt dynasty.

I had dreaded Louis's return, anticipating argument: I should have stayed and rehearsed Elaine until she knew what she had to do; I shouldn't have let him down like that; I had behaved outrageously . . .

It was surprising, therefore, to find him returning just after ten o'clock full of triumph.

"It didn't matter in the least about Elaine," he said, and flung himself into a chair on the terrace. "Machelevos put on a film and had his technician stop it at various stages and I photographed the guests watching it. I took about a dozen and I think they've come out well." He pulled me down onto the double seat and put his arm round me. "When I've developed them I'll try them out on you first. You can see how many famous people you can recognize by their hairdos and the shape of their heads."

I was so relieved that I fell in gleefully with his suggestion. "I'll play. And if I guess them all, I'll claim a reward."

There was peace between us and I had no intention of upsetting it by telling him what he obviously had not heard about: that I had hit one of Machelevos's guests, a giggling youth who could not take his drink, and had knocked him flat.

19

COSTOS MACHELEVOS must have been psychic, for when the launch came for Louis the following morning, a huge bouquet of crown imperials was delivered to me. They were my favorite flower.

Wrapped in cellaphane, as though they had come from an expensive florist's instead of from his own grounds, there was a note attached. The language was English, the writing difficult to read; but the content warmed my heart:

There are occasions when a man is host to some who are not necessarily his friends. I know that I would never have to apologize for these, but for the acquaintances who sometimes litter my island, this can be necessary.

The comtesse told me what happened last evening when a silly young drunk made what you British call "a set for" Elaine. For him, I have to apologize to you, since I cannot apologize to that lovely child.

Costos Machelevos

Kate said, "Of course, you must have those flowers in your own room. They're yours, dear. Go and ask Ruth for something to put them in."

Ruth found a bronze urn and the crown imperials made my room glorious.

That evening, on the terrace, Louis was saying. "It's going to be easy having you over on Palacanthus with me. Machelevos likes you."

Kate shot me a quick glance as if dreading my refusal. Changing the subject awkwardly, I said, "I still have some postcards I bought in Hydra to send home. I've been terribly lazy. I'll go and fetch them and write them now."

On my way across the terrace I passed Ruth.

"A note has just come for you," she said to Louis.

I heard him slitting the envelope as I went upstairs to my room. The cards were in a drawer and I got them out, and was looking for stamps when Louis stormed in.

"Next time"—I swung round on him—"will you please knock? It's Kate's house, but this is my room."

He slammed the door with his foot and

thrust a dirty piece of paper at me. "Read that."

In the moment that I hesitated, I thought his face had the fanatical fury like that of the women at the door of the hut at Marathon.

"Go on, read it."

"I can't. It's in Greek."

"Then I'll translate." He snatched it from me and read aloud:

"Instead of going to the island, you had better watch the girl and the writer man. She is a witch and she will destroy—"

He twisted the piece of paper in his fist and looked at me, waiting. In that silent moment I saw the other side of the coin of passion—hatred.

"Well, haven't you got anything to say?"

I swallowed twice. "You didn't—finish—the last sentence."

"There's no more. Isn't it enough? God in heaven, *isn't it enough?* Hasn't it occurred to me that the writer of this is giving me credit for enough intelligence to know the rest. 'She will destroy' . . . Me . . . Me . . . *Me!*"

While the words tore out of him, I began to feel a peculiar calm. It was as if I were watching a hallucination and knew it—knew that none of what was happening had any place in my actual life; it was on some other plane . . . But it wasn't, and self-persuasion that I was dreaming was in itself a delusion.

"Talk, Justine!"

"A note, dirty, and I'll make a guess it's anonymous . . ."

"A witch!" He cut through my anger. "That's what they call you, and Braddon so besotted that he isn't thinking sensibly at the moment or he'd know, with the whispers about him still going around, that he should keep quiet and behave himself. After that business with Helen—"

"There is nothing between Matt and me."

"—and that dumb kid as the stumbling block . . ."

"I said, there is nothing between Matt and me," I shouted at him.

But Louis was beyond listening. Wrapped up in his fanatical sense of betrayal, he came close to me, looking down, his eyes blazing. "You couldn't be saddled with Elaine Braddon for the rest of your life, could you? But you didn't reckon on the villagers being wise enough to see through you. Justine, darling . . . *which—of—you—tried—to—kill—*

*Elaine—on—*Persephone?" He asked his question with a ghastly gentleness.

I backed to the wall, my fingers clinging to it. Shock was gone and in its place I felt only a curious objective puzzlement that I could look at Louis and see the contorted face of a stranger. But this was what quarreling was all about—the sudden steel barrier that alienated reason.

"Was it Matt Braddon who put the wrong chart on the boat, knowing that you could swim and that Elaine might panic and drown? She's strong—she could fight you, not understanding—if you tried to save her."

I could have pleaded; I could have wept. I did neither. The outrageousness of it all shocked me and I blazed at him. "If you can believe that disgusting note, then there's nothing more either of us have to say. And now please get out of my room, and tomorrow *I* will get out of Kate's house. I've had enough! I won't be a martyr, nor will I plead. Even if I have to walk all the way to Hagharos, I'll leave here and you won't stop me now, will you, because no man could live with hatred in his heart and see that person every day."

I moved away from the wall. Louis sprang,

caught me and flung me on the bed.

"Go and find . . . who wrote that . . . vicious note . . ." I spoke between struggling against him.

But he was too strong for me and he lay over me, his body heavy on mine. "How far have you gone—or rather, how close did you get to Matt? Like this? Like this?"

I tore at his hands, loathing contact which, with a blaze in his eyes, only desired to hurt and ravish.

Someone was coming along the passage. Louis lifted his head, listening, and I seized his off-guard moment to drag myself free. I ran to the balcony and stood with my hands on the still-warm stone.

"It's over," I said. "We've failed. Face it, Louis, please. It will make everything so much easier."

"Come here." He was close behind me and he turned me round and tilted my chin. "Do you imagine that people in love never quarrel?"

"Of course they do. But not in the way we have. You believe an anonymous note that tells you I run to some other man behind your back."

Louis traced the line of my face and he

must have felt every muscle tense and resistant, but it didn't worry him. "Do you really think I trust you? Oh no, not until you're married to me and I have a claim on you. I know Braddon, and I know, too, that places in the sun have bewitching effects on women from the north. Get this, darling. You are my love and nobody is going to take you from me. You understand?"

I understood. Possession was his god, not love.

"I will never be on the edge of your life, Justine. Do you understand that, too?"

I understood that also. He had to have total attention.

"And you will never go to Marathon again."

"There is something *you* have to understand, Louis. No one is going to turn me into a piece of mindless property." I walked past him, and to my surprise, he let me go.

Kate was sitting on the terrace, and I realized that as my room was directly over it, she must have heard at least part of our bedroom scene. I didn't care. She had to know about it, anyway, and as soon as she turned her head, looking over the back of the chair at me, she made it easy.

"You must tell me, Justine, what this is all about. Sit down, sit down."

I sat quietly, not knowing how to tell her.

Fortunately she was too avid to discover the truth to wait for me to find words. "One of the village children brought a note for Louis. He read it and then stormed up to your room. I heard you both talking—I couldn't help it, your voices rose." She leaned forward and touched my hand. "You're shaking. Justine dear, what is it?"

"I'm angry. I'm so angry that I intend to leave tomorrow. If I could go tonight, I mean if—"

"Take a breath; quiet down. You're talking to me, the onlooker, and if I can help you, you know I will."

"That note sent to Louis accused me of having an affair with Matt."

She caught her breath sharply, got up and stood with her back to the garden, looking down at me. "But how could anyone suggest such a thing? Why, you don't even meet except when you take Elaine home."

"Kate, who is it on this island who hates me?"

"After what happened at the hut and now the fact that Louis has had this note, we'll have to find out. My dear, we *must* find out."

A door in the house opened and closed and I thought it was the darkroom. I leaned my head back and closed my eyes.

"You're tired. It's been too much for you, hasn't it? I understand. I'm so sorry about it all, but I can't believe that Louis really took that note seriously—whatever it said in accusation. He couldn't; he knows you too well."

"I don't think either of us knows the other; I doubt if we know ourselves. At least one thing is certain, we've found out that we could never be happy together—and we've found out in time."

"How *can* you say such a thing. Louis adores you."

Her flash of indignation left me cold. A car was coming up the drive; Kate heard it too and went to the end of the terrace.

Left alone, I sat with the memory of words read long ago, returning like sad ghosts that had materialized: "Infatuation is a temporary insanity that is for a time so vivid that, like a gruesome pantomime devil, it acquires the mask of love."

321

Kate was returning and Matt was with her. The light streaming from the house behind us shone onto her face, and I couldn't miss the faint alarm with which she shot a glance at us both, as if afraid to interpret something more than casualness in our greeting. As it happened, neither of us spoke.

"Sit down, Matt, and have some coffee," Kate said.

"Thank you, but I can't stop. I came to ask a favor. I have to go into Hydra tomorrow and I'll be away the night. Ludmilla, as you know, is a heavy sleeper, and Elaine is in one of her waking and wandering bouts—"

"And you'd like me to have her here."

"Would you?"

"Why, of course. You know that. I'd be delighted. She can have the usual little room at the end of the passage next to Ruth."

"What would I do without you, Kate?"

She laughed. "Neighbors!" she said.

"I heard what happened this morning," Matt said. "At the hut. Ludmilla and Niko both told me—"

"Matt, it was an awful thing to have happened to Justine." She looked helplessly at me. "If I could only find out . . ."

"Don't worry. I'm on my way to do exactly

that at this minute. I shall go the rounds of the *tavernas*—"

"But it wasn't the men, it was the women," Kate protested. "And they won't be at the *tavernas*."

"It's their husbands I'm after. I'll leave them to put the fear of God into their wives."

"Oh, but please don't do anything that will antagonize them even more. Justine has had quite enough."

"I'd rather you did nothing about it." I heard my own voice, ice-cold, unemotional.

"There's a ringleader in the village—I suspect Ismene Stephanides—and I'm going to stop this at once. I'm sorry if you'd rather I didn't, Justine, but I know these people—"

"And *I* know what happened. I know they look on me as evil. What do you think is going to be the result of anything you may do? They'll say I've bewitched you, too. It's no use. Thank you, Matt, but on Chrysolaki it's obvious that I can't win."

"Justine dear, Matt is determined to protect you."

"As long as Elaine hasn't been upset by it, nothing matters."

"Nothing—matters?" Kate echoed.

"Because I'm leaving." The harshness of

my voice hid my pain—that was something no one must know about. "I'm going back to London and sanity."

Matt moved away from us. "It makes no difference. Even if you are among us only for another few hours, your safety is important. Goodbye, Kate, and thank you for offering to take Elaine tomorrow night. Goodnight, Justine, and whether you decide to leave here or not, the women sang their swansong this morning at the hut. They'll never harm you again."

But he knew nothing of the note, and I wondered what Louis had done with that grubby piece of paper. I prayed to all heaven that Matt would not hear about it—at least, not until I was gone from the island and his embarrassment would no longer be important to me.

20

LOUIS called my name softly, "Justine?"
I was undressed and ready for bed. I tied the sash of my robe and watched the door handle turn.

"Justine?"

"What do you want?"

As if that were an invitation, he entered, closed the door, and as I sat down in the low brocade chair, he flung himself in front of me.

"I'm sorry. Darling, I must have been out of my mind to have behaved as I did! Forgive me." He watched my face. "I've been in the darkroom making a bloody mess of every negative I've touched. My hands have been shaking and I wanted to smash the place up. I'm so jealous of you that it sends me nearly mad. I need you so much; I have no life away from you."

"Don't say that!"

"It's a madness and I know it. It tears and twists and groans in me, this need for you. I dare not lose you . . ."

The way he looked at me, his face humble and naked; the way his hands feverishly sought me, shaking like a penitent—oh, I couldn't bear that! Perhaps if I had loved him, I would have felt compassion for his self-abasement. I *did* feel compassion, but it was not for someone I loved: it was rather a deep pity that he was obsessed by his need to possess another human being.

"That note"—he seized my hands—"if you give me your word there was no truth in it, then I'll believe you."

"I've already told you."

"While I'm on Palacanthus I keep wondering what you are doing, imagining you with that stupid kid—"

"Don't call her that!"

"—and thinking, At least she's with her and not lying on the beach with some man." He dropped my hands. "You're tense and that means you haven't forgiven me. Justine, what do I have to do? Tell me . . . " He pulled aside the collar of my robe and pressed his mouth against my throat. "Sweet, we're together. Kate will be asleep. Let me stay—prove your forgiveness by letting me stay."

As if I had forgiven. Yet was I hard enough not to? But it was not a matter of forgiveness but of understanding, and I knew that there could be no miraculous reconciliation, no sleeping together. He was kneeling still and trying to draw me to him.

"Louis, please get up."

"You're hard!"

"No. Oh, no. Only tired and puzzled and wanting to be alone to sort things out."

"There's nothing to sort out." He pulled at my hands. "I'll make love to you so beautifully."

"Louis, I don't want to sleep with you. Now, will you please let me be?"

The lamplight was bright enough for me to see the sudden blaze in his eyes (How swift he was to anger! How superficial the persuasive tenderness!) "*You* don't want to make love! *You* want me to go! Well, my dear, there are two of us to be considered. And *I* want *you*."

"The dream is over . . ." I had no idea from what dredged-up regret the words came.

"Dream?"

"The one we both set out with when we came here. Perhaps it never existed except in our minds—or rather, in *my* mind. Perhaps I just translated what I felt into love, like finding the wrong word in a foreign language."

"Come and lie down with me and stop talking. You know what I shall call you?" He laughed softly. "I shall take the island's name for you—you shall be my tamed witch." He pulled me to my feet, but his hands—too urgent, too excited—were awkward and I stumbled. It gave me a moment's freedom from his grasp, and I flew to the door and dragged it open.

The light beneath Kate's door made a thin, sharp strip and I said loudly, "Goodnight, Louis."

He had seen her light also, and he swore quietly. "Kate has ears like radar beams! You did that on purpose. Goodnight, my darling, but just remember one thing. I'll make you pay for this." He kissed me just once, his teeth hurting me, biting into my lip, small and vicious.

The clocks in the next room hit the hour, trumpeting and grinding, backed by the soft titter from those gentler ones as if they were laughing at me behind their porcelain faces.

I listened and heard Louis's door close. Then I tore off my robe and dressed. I didn't bother to comb my hair, but wearing my softest sandals, I crept down the stairs and out of the house, leaving one of the terrace doors ajar.

Free of the oppression of Argus, I was able to breathe and to think, and slowly, with the painful sensation of learning something about myself, I knew that it had not been Louis's marvelous looks that had captured me, nor admiration for his fine gift as a photographer, nor even the gratification of his love for me.

Without realizing it, I had sensed in him an innate weakness that needed my strength, as my father had needed it. It was so strange. Louis had such power behind a camera—the eye, the heart, the integrity. But in himself he had an obsessive need to possess completely. He could not share. It was a weakness that was frightening and would have destroyed us.

I was walking along the track at the side of the olive grove, going slowly, kicking up stones as a child does, thinking. My mind was clearer than it had been for a long time.

A sound suddenly broke into my absorption. I stopped and listened. A car was coming towards me, approaching so swiftly that its headlights picked me out before I could dive under the shadow of the olives. The car's lights were pointing directly at me, dazzling my eyes. For a flash of a moment I was hypnotized by them, and then with a frantic effort I moved, plunging blindly into the doubtful security of the trees ahead. The car had stopped. I pushed myself into a thicket, arms stretched out to part the bushes, and with a cry which I tried to strangle so that whoever was driving the car would not be able to trace me by the sound, I hurtled down a bank and into a scented and half-silvered glade. I knew where I was.

I had entered the Paradise Garden not by the ancient steps but through the oleander and myrtle that enclosed it.

I managed to right myself at the foot of the bank just in front of a strip of fluted marble, luminous in the pale light of the sickle moon. I stood still, listening. There was no sound. Whoever drove the car might be looking for me in the other direction—or might not be looking for me at all. It could be a man and a girl utterly unconcerned about a frightened female running for cover.

I breathed more easily and crept along the side of the dell, keeping in the shadows. I knew that if I broke out of the Garden I would be a running target for anyone who wanted to—to what? Stone me? Attack me? For beyond the guardian bushes was a strip of open country and then the Dark Sister and the seashore. I sat down in the deep shadows and tried to get my breath back, waiting and listening.

The sliver of moonlight failed to touch the thick, dark ilex, but it turned the topmost leaves of the aspens to silver coins. A tiny piece of marble, like the molded curl from the head of a statue, lay at my feet. I picked it up and rubbed the slightly roughened surface with a finger, wondering who had dreamed the head and carved it perhaps two thousand years ago.

"Why are you afraid of me, Justine?"

If lightning had struck me I could not have reacted faster. I shot to my feet, twisted round and fell back against the trunk of a tree all in one movement.

Matt stood in front of me, his face in darkness.

"It was—your car, then?"

"Of course. I live just beyond that hedge. Remember?" There was a touch of laughter in his voice.

"But you followed me here."

"I did."

"Why?"

"An urge to know what made you, after

the shattering experience with the village women, go wandering out alone."

"Restlessness."

"I'm not surprised."

We were having a clipped, unsatisfactory conversation in a place that was too isolated for safety. Matt seemed completely at ease, standing facing me without attempting to calm the vague alarm he must have known I felt. I wished he would turn and face the moonlight so that I could see his face—even if only faintly—and then, perhaps, be reassured by someone too familiar to fear.

I felt forced to break the silence. "The Garden is so near you that you probably look on it as your property. Perhaps I'm trespassing. I'm sorry . . ."

"Do you have to be so confoundedly polite?"

"Not if you object."

"Then sit down. This bank is dry and soft."

I obeyed mindlessly but with all my muscles tensed to stop a ridiculous and inexplicable trembling. The moss was like a cushion and from behind me came the scent of honeysuckle and thyme. The Garden was hushed as if in an enchanted sleep.

But it was no dream, and our silence, on my part like that of a shy guest before an unnerving host, disquieted me so much that I said the first thing that came into my head.

"Why *do* you live here? I mean . . . the solitude . . ."

"That's it. I am, in a way, a sophisticate, and yet I like a certain isolation—which I suppose is a contradiction in terms. I couldn't write in London and so I chose Chrysolaki. But perhaps now that I'm well established and mature enough to say no to invitations which encroach upon my working life, I shall return to England one day. I don't know."

I laid my cheek upon my hunched-up knees and looked sideways into the shadows. "It's strange—"

"What is?"

"That this place is so deserted. I'd have thought that all the village lovers would have come here."

"The Garden is a long way from Kentulakis to come and kiss your girl."

"I'm glad. It seems that it is meant to be isolated. Even we are trespassers. Perhaps there are ghosts here of the old gods, although the gods don't die, do they? Only Pan—where did I hear that? That only the god Pan died? And this is just the kind of place he would haunt." I stopped, shy of my own fantasies, and leaned my head back, feeling the cool brush of petals. Behind me was a cluster of wild lilies.

"You are alone too much."

I turned to Matt in surprise. "Oh, I don't really mind. I have had Kate and Elaine."

"Ah, yes. Elaine." He was looking away, and his hands, clasped round his knees, were tense, the bones standing out whitely. "I think we will leave her out of this and talk about you."

"What—about—me?"

"Melodrama is easy to write about but difficult to speak of because, for all the horrible reality of it, people think of it as something applying to someone else."

"Matt, I don't understand."

I heard him draw a deep breath. "Very well, I'll say it in simple language. If you remain here, you're going to get hurt. Dear God!"—his voice exploded in the quiet—"and that's too gentle a way to put it. But it's a nightmare to know that you wouldn't be advised by me—or perhaps by anyone. You're willful, aren't you?" He turned his head to look at me, and for a flicker of a moment

334

there was rueful amusement in his voice.

"You said you would tell me in simple words."

"I did, didn't I? But I find I can't. If I could, then I'd be able to make you safe because I'd know how to combat the danger. And I can't. Damn it to hell, I can't!" The flash of humor was gone and a bitter violence broke out of him. "I'm in the dark, too," he said with a terrible sadness.

His own particular darkness—Helen's death?

"Melodrama!" he exploded. "I called it that, didn't I? And the whole bloody world here, underneath the sun and the moon, is melodramatic!"

I leaned back and the petals of a lily brushed against me. "You talk as if you hate the place, and yet you stay."

He remained silent.

"Why, Matt, *why?*" It was a desperate question, as if I suddenly had to know.

"Because I am part of it all. God help me! This is where life took a turn for the worse and nothing can ever be the same again."

"In other words, you are letting the past control you. I'm surprised. I'd have thought you, of all people, would know that the important thing is not what we can remember but what we make ourselves forget."

"Are you so strong that you can do that?"

Strong I? At the moment, hunched up on the bank with the lilies at my back, I felt like a curled-up embryo, small and feeble, making oh-so-clever remarks like some philosopher who had never experienced the grandiose things he preached.

I shuddered, pulling away from the cool touch of petals. "I feel my own smallness, Matt. The present seems suddenly such a tiny moment of time. The past, the Olympians and the Mysteries, control the Garden."

"While people believe in them, they never die. We create their immortality." His voice, which had held a dreamlike quality, changed, and he demanded with his earlier violence, "Who hid the chart of Chrysolaki's coastline? Who sent the women after you at Marathon?"

"If you had asked me why, I could have told you. They consider that I risked Elaine's life—and then the safety of their own children. I was the witch from the sea."

He reached forward and touched my cheek, and all the magic of the Garden was in his fingers. I laid my hand over his, the gesture as involuntary as my flight from the car's headlamps so short a time ago.

"Justine," he said, and took me and kissed me, not lightly, not even kindly.

Thoughts leapt into my mind and chased each other out like fighting armies. *Remember Helen* . . . Helen is nothing to me. *Remember Louis* . . . But that was over. Remember . . . Oh, God, please stop me . . .

Then I forgot everything but the fact that I was in Matt's arms and I knew the paradox of joy and fear as I cried over and over, with my mouth on his. "Matt . . . Matt . . ."

I wanted him wholly and completely. Every day for three weeks this was what had been growing. In the green shaded garden of Marathon the seeds had been sown for this night.

"Your face is full of light."

I knew it. I felt the narrow white blaze of the crescent moon and Matt's lips pressed against a pulse beating at my throat. We lay close on the bed of moss as on feathers. Time and memory were nonexistent, yet we were close only for minutes.

As if something had wrenched us apart, Matt broke away from me, got up and lit a cigarette. The unexpected exposure to the night air, warm though it was, was a shock after the fierce weight of his body, and the sudden emptiness with which I was surrounded was so intense that I shivered.

Matt's lighter glowed and snapped out; a dusting of smoke clouded the air between us and I thought with a vague irrelevance: I have never seen Matt smoke before. "Go back to England."

I sat up slowly, too dazed by the sharpness in his voice and the bitter change in the atmosphere between us to speak.

"Do you hear me, Justine?"

When I was shocked or hurt I had no words; only anger made me voluble. Matt was giving me an order, and when I still remained silent, he swung round on me. "Get away from this island—from all of us."

I pulled at a clump of grass because I needed action for my shaking hand. Matt leaned down and took me by the shoulders and lifted me to my feet. "Now, leave me here and go back to Argus and make your plans to go." But the way he held me denied the command in his voice.

I turned my face away, speechless, shaken by the too sharp transition from one mood to another.

"Your face is in shadow," he said gently, "and I'm glad. I don't want to have to see it, Justine; I don't want to know how I must be hurting you and knowing that I have to for your own sake. Listen . . . darling, listen. Get your mind free of the lot of us—" He drew my face to him so that it lay against his shoulder. "And don't say you understand, because you can't."

The awful thing was that I could. The muscles of my body, held against him, must have tightened and he felt my resistance, for he said, "I'm sorry. Damn it, there's no pleasure in remembering what has just happened—only regret and self-blame."

I leaned away from him, clinging to the tattered remnants of my pride. "You think I don't understand, but I do."

"And your tone proves that you don't. Justine, get one thing clear. My talk of regret isn't bittersweet; it's just bitter."

Because the Aegean magic could lay its finger on the most reserved of men and excite him to momentary madness . . .

"Blame the island." My voice was rough and too loud as I broke away from him. "Blame the night—the silly romantic ideas even the sanest people get. This place—this

Paradise Garden . . ." I felt sick at my own mockery. "Such a name! As if there was ever a paradise. It's all part of the myth, of . . ." My voice gave out. I swallowed, took a deep breath and said, "Goodbye, Matt." And knew that that was the end.

The patches of grass, the clusters of wild flowers, the hillocks of earth, all seemed to spring up like snares in my path, so that I stumbled and wove towards the steep bank. I didn't realize until I had left the Garden that I had been holding my breath, so that when I let it out it came with a choking that was punctuated with my own weeping.

Weeping for myself? I paused, resting my forehead against the red-gray bark of a pine tree, as if it had power to ease my pain.

It meant nothing to me that Matt had said, "Go back to England." I was going anyway. But I was not going so that his conscience would be made easier over an English girl sufficiently attractive to trouble him. I was going because Louis and I had fallen short of one another and because someone hated me enough to do me harm.

And Matt? "Put not your trust in princes . . ." How irrelevant were the thoughts of a disturbed mind! *Oh, darling, you are not a prince and I do not trust you. But heaven help me, I love you.*

I pushed myself away from the pine, and since I had come without my purse and had no handkerchief, rubbed my hand across my eyes as I used to do as a child. What was I crying for? What, in the name of reason? Yet, try as I might, reason had no place, only a tearing, emotional need for Matt.

The world under the trees through which I walked to the side gate of Argus matched my mood, covering me with pools of light and deep darkness.

I crept across the terrace, slipped through the French doors and closed them. There were no lights anywhere, and as I went up the stairs, slowly and carefully, with my hand on the banisters, only the clocks muttered and whispered as if they had been waiting for me and knew where I had been.

21

"THAT'S lovely, darling." Kate turned as I entered the room the following evening. "Look at this, Justine. All I did was to find a picture of an extinct dodo and Elaine has caught it so vividly that she might actually have seen one. It's remarkable, isn't it? Elaine, show Justine."

"She really does adore you," Kate said, "but then, you're so much closer to her age. I'm glad. Sit down, dear, and watch."

I chose a chair by one of the windows leading to the terrace. Kate had fetched Elaine from Marathon, and Matt had already left for whatever took him to Hydra. The previous night with him in the Paradise Garden had acquired a dream quality for me. I had nothing to prove that it had happened, that the moonlight had really covered us like a translucent cloak while we had lain, in love and enchanted. The time had been too brief and reality had mocked with its cold command: "Go back to England, Justine."

"It really is too bad that Louis had to stay late tonight." Kate sat close to Elaine, watching the flowing fingers.

Louis had telephoned that two stars of the film world were arriving at Palacanthus and there was to be a party at which he was required to take photographs. "And where is Justine?" he had demanded of Ruth, when she answered his call. She thought I had gone walking, but she didn't know for sure. Was she at Marathon? Ruth didn't know that, either. In her flat voice, Ruth said to me, "I have to give you a message. To tell you to remember what you and Mr. Louis talked about last night."

That I never go to Marathon again. I knew, and I hadn't been there. Not because I was obeying an order but because the very thought of the white house with the green shutters and the small prancing sea horses made me ache for Matt.

I had gone for a walk inland on my own, keeping well away from Kentulakis, taking the rough track that led to Aghios Christos, the Byzantine church with its reddish walls and great dome dominating the landscape. Rock roses grew out of its ancient stones and asphodel wove round it walls. That morning, for the first time, I had seen life there, as a little old bearded man came out and smiled at me.

"It's strange," Kate was saying. "This is all Elaine has, and yet she is so happy. It's merciful that she doesn't know what fear is."

"Oh, but she does!"

Kate blinked hard at me, her mouth opening to protest and then closing again.

"The other week," I said, "a little girl wearing a huge dark-blue cloak ran towards us and Elaine was frightened."

"Why should you think that had anything to do with memory? The child probably looked like some huge bird."

"Birds don't scare Elaine. Sometimes they fly out of bushes right across our faces and she just tries to catch them."

"But, Justine," Kate said patiently, "some of the islanders wear those cloaks in winter and Elaine must have seen them." She made a small gesture of dismissal. "You're letting your imagination run away with you. Elaine was probably just momentarily startled, that's all."

I gave in. "Perhaps you're right."

The shadows on the wall had vanished. Elaine had heard her name repeatedly mentioned and was looking at us, waiting for a summons, a gesture. But Kate just leaned forward and flicked a page of the book. "Here's one you haven't copied. Look, darling. It's a peacock. Isn't it beautiful?" Then, as the child bent over the book, Kate said, "Dear, don't try to believe in miracles. They're not going to happen in Elaine's case, and you must—you *must*—face that. There's nothing to hope for. What you thought might be memory is just an instinctive reaction. At least, that's what Matt says. And you can't argue with him—he's very, very clever . . ." She stifled a sigh. "I've tried to talk about Elaine to him, but when Matt says 'Enough,' then you stop."

Matt had said "Enough" to me the previous night in the Paradise Garden.

"Come." Kate had closed the book. "You've had enough for one evening. I'm going to help you to bed—you like sleeping here, don't you? It's fun, isn't it?"

Fun? I wondered what fun there was for that lovely child in being put to bed at Argus. Elaine watched the book being closed, then, as Kate turned to snuff out the candles, she lifted her hands and on the white wall came the familiar, unrecognizable shadow, the

345

bunched-up fist, the long witch's nose or serpent's tongue—who knew which, except Elaine? Again I knew that she was trying to make us understand something important to her, but it was in her own strange, private language and we could not interpret it.

Kate only smiled. "It's a funny little shadow, isn't it? I call it her signature tune because she's always making it. I wonder if it's a tortoise sticking its long neck out?"

But even as Kate spoke, Elaine's need to convey something to us had gone completely out of her mind and she was serene again.

Kate snuffed out the last guttering candle and Elaine waited to be taken to bed. As they went out of the room, I faced the fact that soon now, I would speak to Kate and feel the touch of Elaine's warm hand in mine for the last time. Somewhere along the line of our strange silent friendship, I had missed a vital clue that would have brought me complete communion with that lovely child. And when I was gone, she would return to her ivory tower.

I went into the kitchen and cleaned my shoes, which were gray with the dust of the island. Ruth was out. Although she had plenty of time during the day to take the long walks she so loved, and she chose the nights because she had never got used to the Aegean heat.

Back in my room, I put my shoes away, and as I closed the door of the old-fashioned wardrobe, something moved behind me. Nerves taut, I swung round. Elaine's cat stalked across the room. I laughed with relief and picked him up.

"So you came to find her?"

He gave a soft, protesting yowl and his paw shot out, claws extended, and tore at the skin on my hand. I dropped him and watched him streak out of the room. With a desolate flash of self-pity, I thought: *Even the cat hates me!*

I looked at my two empty suitcases. If I could only pack now, telephone to Hagharos for a mule cart to pick up my luggage, I could be away in an hour. If I could only escape, cowardlike, without more argument with Louis, without abortive attempts to explain, without placating Kate . . .

And then came the third wish. If only I could see Matt again . . . I plunged across the bed and hid my face in the smothering of the brocade coverlet. But nothing smothered my mind; it was so clear that for the first time I faced the lesson my stay on Chrysolaki had taught me.

The important thing between two people was not the quantity of quality of their faults, but whether they were faults the other could bear to live with. I could not have endured Louis's possessiveness and the lack of any independence I would have had with him. But I could accept and live with a man like Matt for all that—by some terrible accident—he had probably killed his sister. Something very powerful had been forged between us during our daily meetings at Marathon. Matt himself had recognized it—and denied it.

"Why—Justine!"

I rolled over and saw Kate in the open doorway.

"What is it, dear? You're unhappy."

I got off the bed and heard myself say, against all my decisions to withhold my news from her until I had told Louis, "I'm going away." It was so bald that it was almost cruel.

"But where?" She blinked rapidly. "You mean, you want to have a look at some of the other islands? Oh, but wait until Louis is free to take you. You'd enjoy it so much more."

"I mean back to England."

"But you can't!" She moved like somebody

suddenly springing to action, feet apart, body rigid. "Justine, you just can't do that. You've got another three weeks here."

"I haven't. I'm sorry, Kate. I broke the news to you so badly and baldly, didn't I? And you've been so kind. I could have loved my holiday here if I hadn't been so hopelessly involved."

"Hopelessly?" She picked up the word in a whisper. The fight went out of her and she sat down with a jerk in a low chair. "I don't understand. You and Louis—"

"We came out here to learn to know one another over . . . over and beyond just believing we were in love. And it hasn't worked."

"What else *could* you want to know?" Her wide, pained eyes watched me and I felt a dreadful guilt about hurting her. I wandered over to the mirror and spoke to her reflection. "It's no more Louis's fault than mine. We each want what the other can't give."

"You're so young; you have to learn to give and take."

"But there has to be a mutually agreed foundation. That sounds grand, though I don't mean it to impress you. It's true."

Kate put her hands to her face and I went

349

over and knelt in front of her. "Kate dear, please, don't be unhappy for us. Louis will find someone else. He'd never have been happy with me."

She dropped her hands and looked at me, anger flashing over her face. "How stupid you are! Louis loves you, and you just throw it all away with some grand talk about being temperamentally unsuited. He's my brother and I want for him what he wants for himself. He can't take defeat; it will break him."

"With countless other women wanting him? Oh, I know; I've seen them at the Yacht Club in England. Oh, really, Kate!"

"It's you he wants." She sat huddled in the chair, looking defenseless. I held out my hand, but she brushed it aside. "Do you know what he said to me? 'Without Justine, I won't live. I must have her.'"

I got up and went to the window, staring out into the darkness. The moon hadn't yet risen and the blackness was like a wall hemming me in. I knew that I had to be strong, to break out of the prison which the house and Kate's pleading for her brother was making for me. I knew that marrying Louis would be a fatal mistake for both of us, and I had to seal all the superficial channels down which compassion, doubt or persuasion could reach my brain and induce me to change my mind.

"This is only a mood, isn't it, Justine?" Kate's voice came from a long way off. I turned, but she was still sitting in the chair.

"It's no mood," I said. "And besides, how can I stay here when the people hate me?"

"Oh, Justine, they don't! What happened to you in the hut was just a dreadful misunderstanding. We'll sort it out, Louis and Matt and I, if only you'll be patient and not act on impulse."

It struck me for the first time that Matt had driven into Kentulakis for that very reason, to discover the ringleader of the attack. Yet when we had met in the Paradise Garden, the whole incident had been wiped completely from my mind. If he had discovered anything, I hadn't asked and he hadn't told me.

Kate had risen and put an arm round me. "I think we should forget this conversation and just go on as if it had never taken place. Be patient, dear, for another week or so and everything will be all right again. I'll explain to the villagers that you were only trying to amuse their children, that you come from a country where people don't see things as they do. Now, don't let's think of any of this again . . ." She kissed me on the cheek and then began smoothing the rumpled bedcover. "Have a little rest, then we'll go for a walk round the garden together."

Never any further than the garden for her at night, as if this were her entire world and if she stepped outside it she would go over the edge of beyond.

Left alone, I pushed the half-open shutters wide and stepped onto the balcony. Had I not been on an island, I would have got into a taxi and driven to the nearest airport. But to leave Chrysolaki was a major operation of time-tables and arrangements that, unless I carried all my luggage the ten kilometers to Hagharos, I was quite unable to cope with.

I shrank from asking Matt for help; I could not have sat by his side in the car while he drove me away from him.

I heard movement in the hall below. Footsteps sounded and then someone called up to me. "Justine . . ."

Kate was in the garden, a short, square little block of a woman dark against the night's faintly luminous darkness.

"Vasili Papadakis's wife is in a panic because she has cut herself and blood terrifies

352

her. I'm afraid I'll have to go to the village and see her. I won't be long. Her little boy, Angelos, has just come to fetch me. Will you be all right, dear, by yourself?"

"Yes. Yes."

"I doubt if it's anything serious. These people are so healthy that the least hint of sickness and they think they're dying. But Jock would be furious if he were called out unnecessarily, so I must go. And there's Elaine—"

"You don't have to worry. I'm here; I won't leave her."

"Thank you, dear. I'm so sorry—" Her voice receded as she disappeared round the house, and a minute or two later I heard her car speeding down the dark avenue.

I drifted round the house, listening for the launch that would bring Louis back, rehearsing what I would say to him. Ruth was still out, and only the chattering clocks broke the stillness.

Kate's taste in books was not mine, but I was bending down looking at the titles when the lights in the room went out. I spun round, heart thudding, dreading to see a shadow at my back. There was no one there, nor any light in the hall. I remembered that Kate, or

Louis, had told me that the primitive electric plant on the island could play strange tricks, and I felt my way towards the kitchen, allowing the door that divided it from the rest of the house to swing behind me. It could, of course, be a fuse, but when I found the light switch in the kitchen, that, too, had failed. The whole house was plunged in darkness. My first thought was of Elaine, but she would be asleep. Kate had once told me that although Elaine had times when she awoke in the night, she always went into a deep first sleep the moment her head touched a pillow.

The kitchen at Argus was huge, and I went cautiously from drawer to drawer, cupboard to cupboard, feeling for anything that would give me a light—matches, candles, a flashlight. I felt as awkward as someone newly blind, fumbling around on this dark, moonless night.

I found a flashlight at last and switched it on, going back to the living room, shining it around me. The relief the light brought me was short-lived. The walls of the house seemed, by the limited light, to close in, leaning towards me; and my imagination made living menaces of the shadows in the corners of the room.

I felt safer out of doors, standing on the terrace in the quiet. An outsize moth fluttered across the light, its transparent wings green-veined. I could hear a distant rustling—Niko's goat, probably, pulling at its stake.

I flashed the light in the distance for no other reason than a bored impulse to see how far its beams would carry. Something gleamed at the edge of the olive grove, and when I went to the far end of the terrace, I saw that it was the top of a car's hood which caught the rising moon's light at a place where the trees were thin.

Kate and Matt and Jock were the only owners of cars near Kentulakis, and the one I saw must belong to someone in Hagharos. But why should anyone drive out this far? There were no restaurants for good eating, no floodlit ruins, and as Matt had put it, "The Chrysolakians did not come ten kilometers to kiss their girls." The car was some way from Marathon and, anyway, Matt was in Hydra. Nor would anyone, coming to see Kate, park under the olive trees when Argus possessed a more convenient drive.

The place where the car stood was almost where I had seen one parked on the morning

Jock had come to Argus to fetch Kate's clock. But I couldn't imagine Jock taking silent walks through an olive grove when he could be swilling *ouzo* in a Kentulakis *taverna*.

The silence was unnerving. Was someone watching the house? Watching me? If I called, would I be answered by a voice I knew? I had never been overimaginative, but black fancies rose and chased each other across my mind. Standing on the terrace with the flashlight as the only light, I was too defenseless.

Devil-ridden, I ran back into the house, to four safe walls, and closed the terrace doors against my nameless fear.

Elaine would be asleep, but I needed to look on someone living and breathing—to see that sweet and silent child untroubled by blackout and shadows.

The door of the tiny room where she slept was open, yet I seemed to remember hearing Kate close it. Shading the flashlight with my hand, I crept to the bed.

It was empty.

I tore out of the room, searching the house, calling, crashing open one door after another, flashing my light in every corner.

"Elaine . . . Elaine . . ."

Stumbling and running, I combed the house, but it occurred to me that she could have wakened, sensed the unfamiliarity of the room and gone looking for her own. But she would never find her way back to Marathon. The sea lay on one side, and they said she had no fear . . .

"Elaine . . ."

I hoped wildly, against all hope, that I would find her standing in some corner in her pale nightdress. She was nowhere in the house, on the terrace, or in the garden.

There were too many ways to go. I ran up the drive and back again, cut across the dry, sparse lawn to the white side gate. It was open, and I went through, hesitating on the path that separated the house and the olive grove. I knew exactly where the car had been hidden, but when I reached the place, it was gone.

I swung my flashlight in great arcs but saw nothing except a pinpoint of light from the direction of Niko's cottage. Racing towards it, I traced him by the scent of the long, strawlike cigarettes he smoked. He was sitting on a low window sill softly singing to himself.

"Niko, have you seen Elaine?"

"No. No."

"You knew she was sleeping at Argus?"
He nodded.

"She has gone. And I don't know where she is. Please, Niko, please go down to the beach and see if you can find her. I'll search the woods. Is Ludmilla home yet?"

"I see her not long ago in the village. But do not be afraid, no one here will harm *Kyrie* Braddon's little lady."

"She can harm herself by not understanding. Will you search the beach?"

"I go. Of course, I go." He sped down the track, light and fleet of foot as a Greek athlete.

It was I who found her at the same merciful moment as I heard the familiar sound of the launch nearing our beach. The moon, fully risen now, picked her out. She was like a pool of light curled up under a tree, her cheek against the hard ground. I fell to my knees and touched her, saying as gently as I could, "Darling, wake up."

She didn't stir.

"Elaine!"

This wasn't normal sleep. I crouched, staring at the enchanting face blurred by the light, and then I started to my feet and shouted my lungs out, running towards the beach.

Louis was coming across the soft sand and I flashed my light at him. He stretched out his arms, laughing. "So you've missed me that much!"

"It's Elaine. Louis, I've found her in the olive grove and I can't wake her. I think she's hurt. Kate's gone to the village and there's no one to help get her back to Argus. Please . . ."

"Take a breath, darling, and kiss me first. Then we'll go and wake up the vagrant child. I'll bet she's putting on an act." His arms imprisoned me but I fought him.

"Louis, it's urgent." I turned and saw Niko further up the beach, near the Dark Sister. "It's all right," I called. "I've found her."

He lifted his hand in salute and lit another cigarette. I dragged at Louis's hand. "She may be unconscious, and I was in charge of her. I don't know what happened, she could have fallen."

"Wandering again," he said impatiently, "and not looking where she was going. That dratted child!"

I was running on ahead of him and he followed me with obvious reluctance. When we reached the place under the trees where she lay, he prodded her. "Come on, wake up. Don't play games."

"She isn't," I knelt by her side, trying again to shake her gently awake, but she didn't stir.

"I suppose this means I'll have to carry her back to the house. Damn the whole thing! This is Kate's business, not yours." He picked Elaine up and her head lolled back as if she were a pretty doll with a broken neck; one helpless hand hit against a tree as Louis heaved her more securely in his arms.

"Be careful!"

"She's not made of thistledown. In fact, I'm quite certain she's a lot heavier than you are."

We came out of the grove, and as we turned towards the gate that led to Argus I saw lights beaming from the living room.

"They went out!"

"What did?"

"The lights. I was in the house when it suddenly went dark. It took me ages to find a flashlight."

"It's that plant at Hagharos. It's hopelessly inefficient."

"But there's a light in Niko's cottage."

"Oh, he uses oil lamps."

"Elaine must have wakened before the lights failed," I said, walking along the path between the flower beds behind Louis and his burden. "If she had wandered down the stairs when it was dark, she would have slipped."

"God, this girl is heavy! Oh, look, there's Kate. Now we can dump Elaine and relax."

I ran on ahead and Kate watched me, stern-faced. "I looked everywhere for you, Justine. And Elaine—" She caught her breath sharply. "What have you done?"

"She must have wakened, realized that she was in a strange bed and gone to look for her own."

"Slipping past you?" Kate's voice was coldly incredulous. "When you were supposed to be looking after her?"

"The lights went out."

"They were on when I came home a few minutes ago." She turned to Louis. "Put her down on the settee. And be careful; don't swing her like that!"

"Swing her? In another moment I'd have dropped her. She's a dead weight."

Kate shuddered visibly, crossing the room and bending over Elaine.

"I suppose it must have happened when the lights went out," I said, "and I was in the

361

kitchen looking for candles or a flashlight. The baize door swung behind me, and so I wouldn't have seen or heard her come down the stairs."

"You mean you didn't prop the door open?" She turned a hard, censorious face to me over her shoulder.

"I was in darkness, Kate. And I didn't for a moment think that Elaine would wake."

Her fingers were on the child's pulse. "And you didn't see, either of you!" Her voice rose. "She's not sleeping. She's unconscious! Justine, get blankets. Louis, call Jock. Or, no, I'll do it. And then I must try somehow to contact Matt. Oh God . . . oh dear God, help me!"

"Calm down, Kate," Louis said impatiently from behind me. "From what I can see, she's breathing normally."

"Your experience is most certainly limited," Kate snapped at him and vanished.

362

22

I RAN to the large chest in the little store-room under the stairs and got out blankets and wrapped them round Elaine.

There were a few pieces of broken twig and dry leaves entangled in her hair, and I removed them, saying to Louis, "She hasn't got any cuts or swellings on her head, so I don't think she can be physically harmed."

"Being unconscious *is* being physically harmed," Kate said, coming into the room. "Jock isn't at home and I can't leave Elaine. Louis, go and call up the *tavernas* and get him."

"But if he's in Hagharos—"

"Then find him."

"The fuss you make! Elaine will wake in due course. What you call being unconscious looks to me just like a deep sleep. The trouble with you, Kate, is that you take on everyone's burdens and magnify them."

"*Go and get Jock.*"

Louis went.

Kate was rubbing Elaine's hands very

gently. "If only I knew what had happened, I might know the remedy," she wailed and turned on me. "You must have guessed that Elaine might be restless in a strange bed, why didn't you prop that door open while you searched for a light?"

"I didn't think—"

"No, you didn't think! But then"—her voice softened—"I can't blame you. The young are naturally irresponsible."

"That's not true, I—"

"This isn't the time for argument," she said quietly and turned back to the child.

I knew that nothing I could say would ease the situation. Kate had trusted me and something quite outside my control had conspired to put me in the wrong.

"As it happens, I needn't have gone into the village," she was saying, piling a soft pillow behind Elaine' head. "Papadakis's wife had only a superficial cut—I think she was more upset because she had slapped one of her children and sent him to bed crying. She wanted to talk to someone about that rather delinquent little boy. I needn't have gone—and this wouldn't have happened."

From the doorway Louis called, "Stephanides says that Jock hasn't been seen in

Kentulakis tonight. So he must have gone into Hagharos. It'll take ages to call up every *taverna* there, and he may not be in any of them."

"Then we must call the air ambulance people. I can't treat Elaine; I don't dare in case I do the wrong thing. *Louis, don't stand there. Do something.*"

"Is there room for just one more?" a voice asked from the terrace.

We swung round in unison.

"Jock!" Kate cried. "Oh, thank heaven! We've been trying to contact you. It's Elaine. Justine and Louis found her unconscious in the olive grove."

"I was afraid something like this might happen one day," Jock said. "I suppose she fell." He crossed the room to her side, bent over her and felt her pulse. Then he turned. "I can't do anything with a crowd around me. Please—" He swept his hand at us in a gesture of dismissal.

"Oh, Jock," Kate was crying. "How wonderful that you happened to look in when we needed you so badly!"

She might think it wonderful. I didn't. It was too coincidental, and as Louis and I went out to the terrace, I thought of the car I had seen parked under the olives.

"Let's hope *ouzo* doesn't cloud his examination," Louis said.

"Jock wasn't drunk."

"Darling, he can take more drink and stay seemingly sober than any man I know!"

I sat in one of the rattan chairs on the terrace and stared into the darkness. Everything was still.

"Come on, let's you and I go for a walk." Louis took my hand.

"No. I've got to stay. This concerns me."

"Don't be silly. It concerns Kate, and she knows it. She—" He broke off as Kate came out onto the terrace. She seemed to have gained inches in height and her voice came with difficulty, as if the muscles in her throat were too tight.

"What did you give her, Justine?"

"Give her? What do you mean? I gave her nothing."

"Elaine has been drugged, but you know that, don't you?"

"She couldn't be! *You* put her to bed; I only went up once—and that was when I found her gone."

Kate's face twisted with impatience. "Oh, come! You gave her something to keep her quiet, to stop her from doing exactly what she did do. You probably slipped a drug into some milk you gave her."

"I gave her no milk." Then, as Kate made a waving gesture of disbelief with her hands, I added angrily, "And I'm not in the habit of lying."

"I'm afraid it's all too obvious for protests, Justine. You knew that Louis would soon be back and you wanted nothing to interfere with your enjoyment. So you gave her a sedative—but you gave her too much!"

"She's all right? Kate, she's not going to die?" I was suddenly terrified.

"No, she'll be perfectly all right in the morning. You gave her a dose that would be merely normal for us, but to a child and one retarded, at that—"

"*I—gave—her—nothing!*"

"She must have wakened before the drug took effect and wandered into the olive grove," Kate went on, as if my voice had been a whisper she hadn't heard.

Jock called to Kate and she flew indoors.

"Oh, for God's sake, let's get out of here," Louis exploded. "And let Kate get on with her moan. She's really blaming herself. After all, she doesn't have to be nurse and lawyer and patcher-up of quarrels to these people.

Now, stop worrying. *I'm* your responsibility, not Elaine."

Kate was back on the terrace, darting like a jack-in-the-box through the door. "I've been upstairs to my room and . . . and we know now what Elaine took—or was given. My capsules, those prescribed for me by the doctor in Athens. I took one last night because I couldn't sleep and I found the bottle lying on my dressing table. *I* didn't put it there; I'm always so careful. But . . . but someone . . ." She choked. "Oh God, some-one—"

"Nonsense!" Louis cut her short. "Elaine probably woke, wandered into your room and began looking around, not really knowing what she was doing, and found the capsules. They're those orange things, aren't they? So, because they looked pretty, she ate some. She's not dying, is she?"

"Of course not! It's just a very deep sleep, and in the morning, Jock says, she'll be all right. Oh, how lucky he called. It's like a miracle."

"Yes, isn't it?" I said dryly.

Jock joined us, blue eyes bright. "She'll be fine tomorrow—I'm off."

"What do I do about telling Matt? Or, do

you think, as you think she won't have an harmful effects in the morning, we might say nothing about it?"

"With you ringing up all over Kentulakis to find me? The whole place must know."

"Oh, dear." Kate shot me a look. "And I did hope—"

Jock interrupted: "If you like, I'll tell Matt. I'll go along now."

"But he's not there, that's why I have Elaine for the night. He has gone into Hydra."

"Oh no, he hasn't. I saw his car only a short while ago passing your gates and he was driving towards Marathon."

"That's strange! I don't understand. Oh, well, perhaps the Hydra date was called off and he felt he would let Elaine remain at Argus. I don't blame him for wanting free evenings occasionally." Kate sighed. "It must be hard for a comparatively young man to have the responsibility of someone like Elaine."

"Yes, quite." Jock turned on his heel. "Don't worry. I'll see Matt, and as I've told you, the child will sleep soundly till morning."

Kate followed Jock off the terrace and

round to his car. By my side, Louis said thoughtfully, "So Matt never went to Hydra?"

"Or started out and changed his mind, or received a phone call that altered his plans."

"And got out his car and drove somewhere—and passed this house."

"Why not? Perhaps he went into Hagharos."

"Funny. Or perhaps, not funny at all!"

"Why make a mystery out of it?"

"Oh, it's no mystery, as I see it. Just a matter of a little subtlety and a lot of shrewd thinking."

"I don't think I want to talk about it."

"Darling, a few truths about Matthew Braddon will be good for you."

"No!"

"You don't need to be violent about it."

"I'm not, but I'm tired—"

"Then sit down, sweet, and listen."

"No. I said . . . No."

"All right, then, stand where you are. But you're going to listen." His grip on my wrist was firm. "Do you really think that a man can spend his whole life housing a subnormal child who isn't even his own? Oh, no, you're too perceptive to think that. There had to come a time when his odd impulse for sacrifice broke down. Elaine was becoming too great a burden."

"He loves her. He once said to me that *she* had taught him—"

"That no man's patience is inexhaustible. I'll bet she has!"

I twisted my wrist out of his grip and moved away, leaning on the terrace wall. Some petals from the white roses rising above the edge of the stone dropped silently at my feet as I brushed against them. I scooped them up. "They've got curled edges."

"We were talking of Matt, not rose petals. Why don't you want to discuss him?"

"Because you enjoy hating him."

"Oh, no, that's not true. But the facts are there. Elaine is a burden—"

"You're quite wrong about that."

He came behind me, seized my hair and pulled me back against him. "Why are you so sure he's not involved in what happened tonight?"

Louis was holding me lightly, but a new supineness, a strange, uncharacteristic weary indifference, made me stay where I was, physically close, but emotionally a millions miles away.

"You heard what Jock said, didn't you,

darling? Matt passed him along the road when he said he would be in Hydra. Suppose Matt knew that Kate had been called out—had, in fact, been waiting a long time for an opportunity such as tonight; suppose he parked his car somewhere where no one would see it, and knowing the house well, fixed the lights and then went to Elaine, dosed her and dumped her in the olive grove?"

It was outrageous and terrible.

"The lights—"

"Oh, he could refix the fuses while you were out looking for Elaine. And all this would be in order to lend point to his argument that she was beyond his control and in need of professional care."

"You can't believe what you're saying . . ."

"Don't forget that the villagers are quite certain that he was involved in Helen's death." Suddenly the persuasiveness went out of his voice; his mood changed, became impatient. "Oh, for heaven's sake, Justine, stop playing the three-wise-monkeys game! You don't see all, but you must see a little; you don't hear all because you don't speak Greek. But there's no need to behave as if there's nothing to say. Face facts. Matt is a writer, he can create situations on paper and, if he finds it expedient, in his life, too."

I walked into the house, my heels making too much noise on the hard, cold floor.

Kate was coming down the stairs, eyeing me half coldly, half pityingly. "I'm going to make some coffee. Both Ruth and I will need it through the night since we dare not take chances and are going to take turns watching over Elaine. Jock carried her to bed."

"Can I make coffee for you?"

"No, thank you."

"Kate, I'm sorry. I—"

"Don't, dear, please! I blame myself. I should have waited until Ruth returned from her walk before going into the village." She gave me a penetrating look. "Don't be too upset. You can't be expected to feel as we do."

"But I—"

She wouldn't let me speak. "It's such a pity that there is no way we can think of to tire Elaine out before going to bed. If we could, then she wouldn't need to be watched. But she doesn't understand how to be boisterous, and even trying to play ball with her is difficult because she just sits down and lets it bounce round her."

"Then give her something occupational where she can copy what adults round her are doing. Let her help Ludmilla in the kitchen, even if at first she does drop a few plates. Let her help make beds."

Kate's face had a frozen look and it was obvious that it cost her a great deal of self-control to speak patiently. "I think it has been proved that Matt knows best how to take care of Elaine, don't you?"

"No."

"I know you have strong feelings about things, but I think this is something that is no concern of yours—please don't think I'm being rude, dear. I'm just stating a fact." She touched my arm in proffered forgiveness and disappeared into the kitchen.

I called goodnight to Louis and turned towards the stairs. I wanted to see no one and to do no more talking. But Louis came striding out of the living room and caught me up on the stairs.

"We haven't fully discussed that note about you and Matt."

"There's nothing more to discuss—at least, with me. It's not true, but it seems I can't convince you and you won't even try to find the writer."

He said angrily, "You should realize that in this bloody close-knit community it would be impossible to find out who wrote that note—the writing is almost illegible and obviously disguised. No, that's not the way to shut up the gossips. But I know of one that's perfect. One that will mean you never go to Marathon again."

I pushed past him, and he leapt up the stairs ahead of me, blocking my way. "You're coming to Palacanthus every day with me. I wanted to ask Machelevos today about it, but he was caught up with this mob of guests. There won't be any trouble about it, though. He'll let you come. And then we will spend all our days together. You shall help me—I'll even teach you the rudiments of good photography. And in the evening, you can work with me in the darkroom."

"No, thank you."

He bent down and kissed me. "There's no argument. Now, let's call the night a day, shall we? From now on, we've got all the time in the world together, and you can go and lie in that big bed and imagine the marvels you'll see when I take you round the millionaire's island."

Frustrated and emotionally drained, I

375

found enough energy to hit the banisters with my fist. "Can't you face the truth? Just this once? It isn't any use . . . I've tried to explain—you can't force someone to love you, and I can't go on telling you that we would never be happy together."

"Then stop saying it." He was still laughing. "Oh, you little idiot, what do you want? Strings of love words—riches? You'll get them; Machelevos is delighted with what I'm doing. I'll have the world at my studio doors for this!"

"I want to do just what I am doing—go back to England." I glanced down into the hall. Kate had come out of the kitchen and was steadying the swing door, watching us. I appealed to her. "Please make Louis understand that I must leave here."

Louis said very quietly, "But you can't possibly get away."

"Of course I can."

"Not until I say so."

"It may be a long way to Hagharos, but if you won't help me get there, I'll find a way."

There was a long silence. I heard an owl hoot somewhere outside, and I put out my hand to push Louis aside.

"All right," he said. "So you get to Hagharos. Then what?"

"Athens and then London."

"Without your passport?"

"I haven't lost it."

"Then where is it?"

"In my suitcase where I put it on my first night here."

"You'd better go and make sure, darling." He was laughing.

A quiver of fear ran through me. "What do you mean?"

"Merely that your passport is no longer in your suitcase. I have it. I guessed, after that silly statement of yours that you would try to leave me, that you'd probably make a dash for it while I was at Palacanthus and Kate was working, so, this morning, while you were at breakfast, I kept the launch waiting and came back and searched your room. You're very trusting, aren't you, not locking up your personal papers?"

"In a private house?"

"So I found your passport and took it."

"Then you can give it back to me."

"Yes, when we eventually leave here together—at the very end of our seven-week holiday."

"Oh, Louis!" Kate moaned.

"It's all right, Justine is intelligent. She knows when she's beaten."

"But I'm not. You're going to give me back my passport tomorrow." I wasn't risking an invitation to his room that night.

He shook his head very slowly. "No."

"Then I'll go to the authorities and report it."

"Who, on this benighted island?"

"Jock."

"You think Jock Anderson would involve himself in someone else's quarrel."

"I hope so."

Kate was pacing the hall, walking curiously up and down on her toes. "What am I going to do? What am I going to do?"

"Just don't start wringing your hands like a Victorian tragic actress, that's all," he snapped at her. "This is our affair, Justine's and mine."

"But I'm involved, too. Justine—" She appealed to me. "You're being so impulsive, threatening to leave like this! You came out here to give Louis a fair trial and you aren't doing it."

"Three weeks and four days."

"And you promised seven weeks."

"We made a mistake; we were too hasty. Lots of people do the same thing and admit it and agree to part."

"You were in love," Kate wailed. "You still *are* in love. I won't believe—"

"What we had was a kind of fantasy thing and it burned beautifully for a few weeks. But it had no foundation in giving, only the excitement of taking. Nobody's to blame; it was part of . . . of our experience of living."

"How wise you make yourself sound."

"Oh, I'm not. I'm learning and the effort is painful. But, Kate, we never even got engaged. We said, 'Let's see how we feel about one another after more time.' We were honest."

"We said we were in love and that seals it as far as I'm concerned." Louis moved down a step so that he was on a level with me.

Kate murmured something, but what she said was inaudible against the sudden chiming of the clocks, hurling their interfusion of sounds at us like a Greek chorus.

When the noisiest had died away, I said, "Please, Louis, let me have my passport in the morning."

"No."

I found enough energy to lose my temper.

"I don't care whether you're holding the damned thing or not, I'm leaving tomorrow. What you've done, searching my room, is the final proof that I'd never have a moment's freedom with you. If you can do this now, when we aren't even engaged, what in the name of all that's crazy would you do if we were married? Your principles aren't mine, and that's important."

"Principles don't count in love or war. What is important is that you can't get away."

"Louis, please give Justine back her passport. It belongs to her. It—"

Louis turned his attention from me to Kate, and I seized the moment to race to my room. I shut the door, sat on my bed and tore furiously at the turned-down sheets.

I would give Louis just twenty-four hours to return my passport. Then, if it wasn't back in my possession by the following evening, I would leave Argus and take only my overnight bag. I would find my way to Jock's house somehow and ask him to drive me to Hagharos.

I tipped back, so that I lay across the bed staring at the ceiling. Louis, as someone I loved, was already a past experience. The thought of any individual attempting complete possession of someone else was insufferable. But the thought of the theft of my passport filled me with a fear of him. I dreaded what he might do if I stayed and, as much, I dreaded what he might do if he saw me trying to escape him. I had to leave while he was at Palacanthus. I wouldn't even wait for my passport. I would go to Jock.

Plans formed in my distraught mind and then changed and re-formed. I moved about the room, undressed, and then a wild idea crossed my mind that I might go and sleep somewhere away from Argus—on the beach, in the pine wood near the Green Sister, under the stars and away from the dark threat of the house. But in the end I climbed into bed, tucked the sheet over my head and tried to sleep. I kept waking and thinking, and then going to sleep again, but my thoughts ran like a continuous thread through the periods of wakefulness.

In a little while Louis would be for me just a vague regret buried in memory. Other people, far more important than he, would linger and haunt me for a long, long time.

Elaine, and what she had been to me, and what I had done to her. I had failed that charming child, but she would never know it because she had neither understood the adoration of the people of Chrysolaki nor the danger into which three times, all innocently, I had plunged her.

There would always be the animals: the one-horned goat and the donkey and Ariel, lying indolent in the sun at Marathon. There would always be someone to plait a little bracelet of grass for her. Elaine was safe—I had to believe that. Matt would never desert her and Louis's terrible hints were merely the dark twists of his own imagination.

I had had experience of Matt's seeming love and then rejection, but I would never believe that he would hurt a child. Not Matt.

The house was very still. I lay listening, wondering vaguely what it was I was missing. And then, suddenly, I knew.

Someone had stopped the clocks.

23

THE long black hours tortured me. I didn't believe in omens or portents; there would be no violent death at Argus because a whole collection of clocks had stopped at the same time. Nor could coincidence have played any part. The mechanisms must vary and so a human hand had deliberately silenced them.

I could not believe that in the whole of Chrysolaki, Kate had an enemy. But I had. And as the general idea seemed to be that I would eventually become a d'Arrancourt, I was as involved in the superstition of the clocks as Kate and Louis. *The clocks were stopped as a warning to me.*

In London I would have found such an idea incredulous. But I was on an island where the old gods impressed their will upon an isolated people. It was utterly beyond common sense, but I was afraid, and I lay until morning plunging into bouts of restless sleep, aware that the source of the hatred towards me had crawled nearer.

I woke at last to the relief of sunlight and sounds about the house. I stretched and tried to relax, hearing Louis below talking to Kate and her voice answering.

My watch usually kept perfect time and I had checked it the previous night before I went to bed. It was now five minutes to eight. The hand moved slowly. Four minutes . . . three minutes, and at last it was eight o'clock. If in the night I had had a foolish nightmare in which I had dreamed I was awake, then the clocks would begin to chime. None did.

There were footsteps in the passage outside my door and now I heard Kate talking to Elaine. The night had been so long that I had forgotten that she was still at Argus.

"You *are* a sleepy girl this morning," Kate was saying. "Never mind, you shall have coffee for breakfast just this once, darling, instead of orange juice. And lovely Mount Hymettus honey." Her voice, as always when she was speaking to Elaine, was too loud, as if the child were deaf.

Their footsteps died away and I realized that Kate would probably not even notice that the clocks were silenced.

I took a long time dressing that morning, wanting Louis to be out of the way before I went downstairs. Later, I would search his room for my passport, and if I didn't find it I would look in the darkroom. But I knew, even as I planned, that Louis would be prepared for such a possibility and that my passport had gone with him to Palacanthus. My only chance would be to get it when he returned.

I heard Louis call me twice from the garden and each time Kate hushed him. I moved very quietly about the room, hoping he would think me still asleep, although I knew perfectly well that he would not try to persuade me to go to Palacanthus that morning. He would have to ask Machelevos's permission first.

When I heard his footsteps crunch on the gravel leading to the beach, I ventured down-stairs. Breakfast was set for me on the terrace, and Elaine sat by herself in a chair at the very edge where the white roses leaned over and touched her bare arm. She was idly twisting and weaving, trying to make shadows on the stones, but the patterns were meaningless.

Kate came out, checking the contents of her purse. "Oh, Justine dear, there you are! I thought you'd like breakfast out of doors; we felt you were very tired last night, so we tried not to disturb you. You slept well?"

"Not very."

"Of course." She nodded. "I understand. Last night was distressing for us all. Louis looked awful when he left just now, as if he, too, hadn't slept much." She crossed to Elaine and laid her square hand over the child's restless ones, soothing her, but still talking to me. "Louis left rather early because he didn't want to keep the boat waiting as I'm afraid he often does. He said he wanted to catch Machelevos before he set out with some friends on a day trip on the yacht. He wants to ask if he can bring you over each day. The reason he'll give is that he needs someone to help him and he's sure there won't be any objection." She smiled at me.

"Kate, who stopped the clocks last night?"

"And Louis feels that if you are together all the time it will solve your problems . . . *What was that you said?*"

"Who stopped the clocks?"

"No one."

"Then you'd better go and listen for them."

She shook her head. "It always happens. After a time, people get used to any noise.

You just don't hear them any longer, that's all, dear."

"When I went to bed I heard them. I woke in the middle of the night and there was no sound."

I spoke the last words to an empty terrace. Kate had vanished, running through the house and up the stairs, her shoes with their thick heels clattering on stone.

There was a moment or two of silence, then a door slammed and she came running back.

"They—they couldn't *all* fail at the same time! I wound those that needed it only two days ago." She stopped and stared at me. "Justine, you didn't . . . you *wouldn't* have stopped them?" There was a flicker of hope on her face and I knew she longed for it to have been I who had silenced those ancient, relentless clocks. She longed for something positive to have happened to them, something human that would mock the superstition of the d'Arrancourts which was so dreadfully real to her.

I had been silent too long.

"*Did* you, Justine?"

"No. I would never dream of interfering with them and, anyway, I wouldn't know how to stop them. I'm not in the least mechanically minded. Perhaps Louis—"

"Never! If anything, he's more sensitive about them than I am because when he was little, my mother foolishly told him about the clocks, making it a kind of ghost story. You wouldn't believe it, but he used to be a very nervous little boy. The scared impression he had then has lasted. He wouldn't dare touch them. Justine, do you think perhaps . . . I mean, you could have been half asleep—"

"Kate, I've told you. I wouldn't even know how to stop them."

She turned swiftly and ran down the terrace steps and through the tamarisk hedge to the shore. She obviously hoped that the launch from Palacanthus hadn't arrived and that, incredible as it might seem, Louis himself had stopped the clocks.

I had no appetite for the croissants which Ruth made, the honey or the black cherry jam. I poured myself a cup of coffee and drank it, looking out on the blue, translucent light of morning. Tensions and fears were not confined to the dark; they were like an invisible enemy hovering over the bright garden. And beyond it, did someone watch me from the shelter of a tree or a vivid oleander bush?

Elaine had wandered towards the white gate. I kept a cautious eye on her and breathed more freely when she just sat down and seemed to be watching an insect's journey through the grass. She appeared no worse for the drug she had taken—or been given. Given? It was difficult to think that had happened. Yet someone had been near the house the previous night, someone whose car had skulked under the olives. Not Kate, nor Louis, nor Ruth . . .

"Louis was just getting into the launch. It was late this morning." Kate came breathlessly up the terrace steps. "He's as upset about the clocks as I am and he can't think of any reason why it was done, or who—" She broke off and said agitatedly, "I must go and start them again at once."

"The stopping of a few clocks isn't going to cause a tragedy, Kate."

"You don't understand. There are things . . ." She was away again, without finishing her sentence.

There are more things in heaven and earth, Horatio,

Than are dreamed of in your philosophy.

A hackneyed phrase packed with truth . . .

And the clocks? It was easy for an outsider to get into the house, for the doors were never locked. And someone, knowing the particular superstition of the d'Arrancourts, had crept to the room next to where I lay floundering in my nightmares, and stopped them.

I stood by the open front door and waved to Elaine as Kate drove off, and wondered if I would ever see Matt's enchanting niece again. That morning, while both Kate and Louis were away, I would have to make my plans to leave Chrysolaki.

I didn't go further than the beach, and sitting with my back against a rock, I wondered if Elaine was missing our usual morning companionship. Or was she as happy on her own as she would ever be with me?

The wind teased the waters beyond the shelter of the bay and I sat listening for the bell from Aghios Christos. It would toll for me as well as for the monks, for it was my chosen signal. When I heard it, I got up, shook the sand out of my sandals and went back to the house.

Ruth was in the kitchen slicing cucumbers. Her eyes flicked over my yellow swimsuit.

"I've got a melon here which I'm just going to put in the refrigerator. Would you like a slice?"

It was the first really friendly gesture she had made towards me and I accepted gratefully.

As I watched her gouge out the glistening black pips, she said, "Mr. Louis rang soon after you left this morning. I didn't know where you were and he was in a hurry, so he gave me a message for you. He has to go with Mr. Machelevos on his yacht to take photographs of some people. They'll be away the whole day and he may be home late."

It should have been welcome news, for it would have given me time to pack my overnight bag and find my way to Jock's house. But any journey would be useless without my passport, unless I went to the consul in Athens, explaining that I had lost mine. Then I would have to wait for a new one, dreading that Louis might come after me. If I could only have patience until Louis came home, I could perhaps persuade him to hand over my passport and avoid embarrassing explanations to strangers.

"Miss Kate is dreadfully upset about the clocks," Ruth said. "Ever since we came here, we have never found any need to bolt doors; we've always felt so safe. But now"—she chopped chives angrily—"now all that has changed."

She was right. Everything had changed at Argus because I was there and someone hated me.

I got off the table, threw the melon rind into the rubbish bin and rinsed my hands at the impeccable kitchen sink. Then I came back and asked Ruth if she would be kind and get me a Hagharos number on the telephone. I explained that I wanted to ask the operator to connect me with British European Airways in Athens. She seemed so unsurprised that I felt she must have returned home from her walk the previous evening and overheard some of our conversation on the stairs. I was also certain that she disliked the disruption of guests in the house and the fact that I was leaving might even have included the gift of watermelon.

She came with me to the telephone, and after minutes of what was, on my part, impatient waiting, got through to Hagharos. From there it took half an hour of my hanging on the line while she worked in the kitchen with the swing door propped open.

At my frantic call, "Ruth, I think Athens is on the line. Come and tell them what I want, please . . ." she came quietly, speaking in clipped, hesitant Greek and then nodding to me. "They are connecting you with the airline office and I've explained that you don't speak Greek."

The man at the other end told me that there wasn't a single seat on any flight out of Athens the following night or the next day. There might possibly be a cancellation but he doubted it. This was the holiday season, and I was, after all, a great distance away—on Chrysolaki—wasn't I? It would mean a night in Hydra, so I couldn't even hope to catch the plane from Athens for two days.

"Then please, please find me something in two days, if the plane only goes to Paris, or Brussels—I don't care."

He said in obvious surprise that he would do his best, took the Argus telephone number and hung up.

Kate and I had an unhappy lunch together, during which she told me that she had explained to Matt what had happened the previous night and had taken the blame on herself.

"You didn't need to do that. It would have been better if he had blamed me."

"What a strange thing to say!"

"He has already told me to go back to England."

"*Matt—told—you—that?*" She stared at me as if she had just heard that the earth was disintegrating. "But why? I mean—how did the subject arise?"

By a few mad moonlight moments in the Paradise Garden, Kate dear . . .

She repeated her question, still puzzled, still watching me.

I downed half a cup of scalding coffee. "He knew about the attack on me in the hut—after all, it was on his grounds that it happened. He thought it all horrible and . . . and I suppose he decided that I'd be happier away from it all."

It was feeble, but I hoped Kate wasn't observant enough to recognize evasiveness.

"Don't listen to him, Justine. Don't listen to anyone who tells you to go."

"We're going over old ground," I said, "and it's no use." I went on to tell her about my call to Athens.

"That was impulsive of you! And you won't get a plane, even if we'd let you go. Oh, dear, I don't mean we'd *imprison* you; I just mean that we want to keep you here, to give you time to adjust to Louis."

There was nothing to say except to ask her how much the call to Athens would cost. "I know," I said, "that it's expensive and—"

"You don't mean to insult me, Justine, but please—we are not paupers! Forget it."

Silenced and humiliated, I finished my meal without really tasting anything. Afterwards, Kate went to her room to rest, and I went into the olive orchard, lay on the stony ground, as if I wanted to punish myself, and tried to catch up on the night's broken sleep.

At teatime, Kate remained in her room and Ruth served me under the trees.

"Miss Kate is very tired; she works so hard at Marathon, and she is resting."

It was as good an excuse as any and might even be right, since I knew Matt was working to finish a book by a certain date and, to use Kate's own expression, was hurling written pages at her at such a rate "that I sometimes think I'm going to drown in them." At the same time, I had a feeling that she was avoiding me because a situation had arisen with which she could not cope.

After I had had tea, I went upstairs and opened the door of Louis's room. It was large and furnished, like mine, with fine old pieces; but it was also littered with shoes and shirts, old magazines and photographs.

I had heard Kate complain that he had objected to Ruth doing more than just making his bed and flicking an occasional duster, saying that his untidiness was his own affair and that when he had left for England, she could do what she liked in the way of tidying up.

It seemed useless to go in and search for my passport. I gave a last look round, closed the door on the chaos, and went back to my own room to pack my overnight case.

A bright idea occurred to me. I would try to persuade Niko to take me to Jock's house. None of the villagers would dare to bother me if he walked with me.

Dinner came and, as at lunch, Kate and I sat forcing ourselves to break the dismal silences with scraps of conversation that meant nothing. Kate kept saying, "I wonder what time Louis will be back? At least it won't be long now before the job is finished."

396

She smiled as she spoke, as if my plan to leave the island had been merely a passing mood. I didn't argue—it was useless, anyway—and when we took our coffee onto the terrace, I asked her if she had thought of any reason why or how the clocks had stopped.

"No, but I intend to find out. It was, of course, someone in the village, and the best time to find them all at home is in the evening. They know about my clocks and someone must have walked into this house while we were asleep and stopped them. It was a horrible thing to do."

"But, Kate, *why?*"

She sat in the shadow of the house, but I felt her head lift, her eyes watching me. "There's something strange going on, a kind of threat to our sense of security here. I can't think why, except—"

"That I'm here. And they hate me . . ."

"Oh, Justine, no!" She set down her cup, leaned forward and held out both hands to me in reassurance. But I felt that she was no more reassured than I.

For a few minutes she was fidgety, and then she said, "I think I'd better go into the village now. Are you sure you'll be all right while I'm away?"

"Of course."

"Louis should be back very soon."

I went to the front door and opened it for her, then stood waiting while she fetched her first-aid box, saying, "I'd better go and look in on the Papadakises, and see how Naida's arm is."

As she went past me and out of the door I said, "Goodbye, Kate."

She turned in surprise. "Goodbye. But don't sound so sad about it, dear. I won't be long."

I watched her climb into her car. Like the silent farewell I had given to Elaine, this too was final. I would never see Kate d'Arrancourt again.

There were so many things that would never be cleared up for me. Helen's death . . . And Matt . . . And Matt.

I walked as far as the Paradise Garden. The moon had barely risen, and as I reached the circle of trees that hid it, I hesitated at the broken marble steps that led down to the quiet, Arcadian dell. I realized that I had made a mistake in coming. There should be no nostaligc journeys before farewells; they only led to despair.

I stood at the end—feeling rather like a

398

child on the rim of a lost wonderland—and faced the fact that nobody could have taught me the lesson I had learned in the past few weeks. I had had to find out for myself how dangerous it was to act impulsively after a sudden shock. At such times reason is clouded. Mine was. I had been desperate to fill the emptiness left by my father's unexpected death. Nobody could have taught me, either, that a violent attraction is sometimes just a temporary infatuation and that, when the fire dies down, there is no phoenix to rise from its ashes.

So many mistakes made; so much still to learn. So much to forget.

I left the enchanted place that had nothing now to give me, and the scent of thyme and honeysuckle followed me a long way.

24

SOMEONE was coming round the side of the house, and we both stopped still at the same moment, two black shadows facing one another.

"Ah, Justine," Jock said. "I've just returned the clock, and as everyone seems to be out, I took it upstairs myself. I'm no artist, but I think I've done a reasonably good likeness of Kate and Louis."

"I'm sure Kate would want me to offer you a drink."

"No, thanks." I thought he sounded tense. "Go up and see what I've done. There's a third face on the panel, but I haven't filled in the detail yet. I think I'll have to wait."

My face?

"Go along," he urged, as if he were in a hurry. "Go up and look."

"I don't want to. It's quite idiotic, but I hate that room. I'm sure you've done a good job, Jock, and please don't think I wouldn't love to see the portraits, but—"

"I'm afraid you *must* go." His voice

became suddenly serious. "And when you've looked at what I've done, I want you to go straight to Matt."

He was drunk, of course . . . But he was too intent and too grave to be *ouzo*-sodden.

"I'm not going to Marathon. Why should I?"

"Good God, girl, I'm not playing games! Do what I tell you, go and see what I've painted on that damned clock." His pale-blue eyes willed me to obey; his manner was alien to his usual cheerful, haphazard personality.

"Jock, what are you trying to tell me?"

"What I've long suspected and what, between us, we have proved."

"We? Who is 'we'?"

"Don't waste time. Go and look and then make straight for Marathon. Go on . . . go on . . ."

"You're telling me to go to the one place I can't."

"Don't be so bloody silly!" Jock said, and walked away.

I called after him, "Why won't you come up with me and explain what I have to look for?"

"You'll see without me. And I've got something important to do. Now hurry—"

I disobeyed him. I went slowly, dragging each step, wondering where his car was, since it hadn't been in the drive; wondering if it had been Jock's car which I had seen twice in that remote corner of the olive grove.

The beating and the thrumming of the clocks thrust at me like a wave as I opened the door of the airless room. The alabaster clock, for which Kate had had a clumsy base made, stood in a niche near the door, and the strip lighting revealed a fairly good likeness of Kate and Louis.

There was a third portrait, so small as to be almost a miniature. It was merely sketched in, the face left blank. But the hair was drawn softly, fluffed out like feathers; the neckline of the dress was scalloped and there was a small star brooch at one side.

I stood shocked before it. If that tiny portrait were completed—and had Jock ever meant it to be?—it would not be I who looked out at that shuttered room, but Elaine Braddon, Matt's niece.

The truth was clawing at me through the clocks. So now I knew that Elaine was a d'Arrancourt. But whose child?

Some of the clocks growled in preparation for a strike, then one or two, a little faster than the rest, began to chime. The noise would have drowned any sound behind me, and I whipped round, nervous as a cat, aware that there was real danger now that I knew the truth. Whose child? Whose child? Had Helen been a blind behind which the real mother hid? Who was Elaine's father? And why had Jock done this, deliberately ripping open a secret by which heaven knew how many people would be hurt? Revenge? On whom?

"Go straight to Marathon," he had said. Into a trap, or to find out the truth? I had to trust Jock because there was no alternative in this place where, to run any other way, would be to run into possible enemies.

Hurry . . . Hurry . . . he had said, I ran out of the house and along the path, hesitating only when I came to the olive grove. Every tree seemed to hide a menace, every shadow to shift slightly. I changed my mind, swung left and made for the open country that ran along the base of the Green Sister. Because I could see all the way, I was less afraid. But I had forgotten that round a bend in the road there was a copse of aspens.

I stopped as I reached it, and listened. Everything was still, yet no sense of peace lay around me. I could not shake off the feeling that although this was not a way I often used, someone had anticipated my coming and lay in wait for me either in the tall grass or in the aspen copse. My flesh crawled at the thought that I had to pass the little wood, but hesitating, watching and listening, I saw and heard nothing and so shook myself out of my fears.

My footsteps were too loud on the stony path. The Green Sister towered above me, her tip of strange, primeval stones lit faintly by the thin curve of the moon. In the distance, pinpricking the night, were the lights of Marathon. Longing and dread tore at me. I fretted to be able to slip quietly away from the island; but a surge of excitement—half-scaring, half-wonderful—drove me on to obey Jock's instructions. *Go and see Matt . . .*

The scars of Chrysolaki would be with me for a long time, but eventually I would have to shake myself out of this sense of important loss, of some mistake of fate that had lost us to one another. I was young and healthy and I had a future. Nothing that ever happened to me would completely wipe out my love for Matt, yet it would be treachery to myself if I let him spoil my life. He had his place as part of a brief, wounding and marvelous interlude, and I was going to him now for one reason alone. I had to find out the connection between the Braddons and the d'Arrancourts; I had to know who Elaine really was.

Something moved ahead of me: a shadow among shadows. From a distance it could have been a lonely donkey or a goat which had broken free from its stake. It could have been, but as it drew nearer I saw that the shadow was a woman wearing a cloak.

Fear returned, no longer imaginary but real, for the woman was making straight for me in long, smooth strides. I knew by some instinct that it was no friendly passing of two people and I knew, too, that it would be hopeless to run.

Kate was coming towards me. I recognized her walk, the throw of her head. She was carrying the ebony stick with the serpent-headed handle which I had seen in the down-stairs cloakroom at Argus.

"You know, you really have behaved rashly, haven't you, Justine?"

She had waylaid me in order to argue about my leaving Chrysolaki. "I have to go, Kate. Please accept that."

"I'm not referring to your leaving the island. I mean—slipping off by a roundabout route to see Matt; hoping that since we were all out, no one would know."

"I have a good reason for going."

"I'm sure you have; but you won't get there. It's all over now—those lovely secret meetings with Matt on the beach, in the Paradise Garden." Emotion tore through her voice. "I saw you, so don't deny any of it. I watched you through binoculars from the roof at Argus. I must have missed so many of those meetings because I believed you when you said you were just going for a walk while Louis worked in the darkroom."

"You're so wrong!"

"And now, at last, you can stop lying." Her voice was utterly unlike her usual anxious, gentle tones, and she was obviously suffering from a deep emotional strain, for her breath came sharply between her words, punctuating them with a hiss.

"I saw Matt twice when I went for a walk and both times it was accidental."

"I told you to stop lying."

It was useless to keep denying something which she was obviously determined to believe. I stood my ground. "*Who is Elaine?*"

I thought I would shake her by my question. Instead she laughed, and the sound was so without humor or lightness that she might as well have wept. "You've looked into Louis's eyes enough times. Violet, aren't they—and very unusual. And his hair is dark gold—too beautiful for a man, but lovely on Elaine . . ."

"*Louis—and Helen!*"

"You understand, at last."

"Elaine is your niece, too."

"If I wanted to acknowledge her, but I don't. You can't realize how sick it made me to see you take her out, every morning, pretending to be so good to her, to care for her. And all the time, it was your ruse to get at Matt. Every morning, sitting in his garden—"

"*Elaine is Louis's child!*"

"Oh, do be quiet, you know it now. But did you think I wasn't perfectly wise to what you were doing? I've been doing the same thing for years—playing at loving that child because that was the only way I could get Matt. Yes. Matt and I. And now you know."

I leaned against a slender tree trunk, knowing that I no longer had any need to go to Marathon. I knew the truth.

"What are you turning over in your mind, Justine? Whatever it is, it won't do you any good. You won't see Matt tonight—or ever."

"You can't stop me."

The stick she carried moved, lifted a little from the ground, made a tiny circle as if in warning and then rested on the ground again. The stillness beat about me; I longed for someone to come—anyone, even the villagers.

As if I had spoken aloud, she said, "I have all the help I need in keeping you from Matt, my dear." She jerked her head sideways. "They're hiding in the wood and they're only waiting for my signal."

I took a few steps forward, trying to pass her. The stick shot out and I put up my hands to protect my face. "Don't be silly, dear," Kate said.

"This must be some crazy game! Kate, you can't be . . . be . . ."

"Be—vicious?"

Her laughter came again, cracking the stillness; the faint moonlight made a pale aura around her, so that she was like a great shadow in its midst—larger than life—larger than solidly built, not very tall Kate.

"You think I'm soft, don't you? Well, I'm not. Shall I tell you what happened to Helen?

Well, I shall whether you want me to or not. I killed her."

I had never understood before how people's legs could go weak with shock, but I had to cling to the nearest tree for support. I couldn't speak and Kate's eyes didn't leave my face—I could sense their stare although her back was to the moon and her face in the shadow.

"Helen came here to hand Elaine over to Louis. She had always intended to have her revenge on him for not accepting responsibility for the child. It was Helen's mother who prevented a court case over her—she adored Elaine. So Helen had to wait until her mother died for her great moment. She brought her child to Chrysolaki." Kate stopped suddenly, catching her breath in horror at her next thought. "As if we could have had a witless d'Arrancourt in the family!"

"Don't call Elaine that!"

She ignored me. "So"—her voice became smooth as if she spoke in a dream—"so I had to kill Helen before anyone knew the truth. She thought she was going to meet Louis that night on the Dark Sister and threaten him into taking responsibility for Elaine." Her voice took on a new vibrating note. "But when Helen slipped out of Matt's house, it was I who was waiting for her." I felt my blood freeze.

"It wasn't easy. Helen was strong. She grabbed me as she lost her balance and nearly dragged me with her. But I wore this cloak and I just slid out of it, so that, as she fell, she took it with her, flying down the cliff to the rocks below."

A cloak billowing like a huge bird with out-spread wings . . . That was what had frightened Elaine about the cloak worn by the little girl playing at being grown up. I understood at last. On that dreadful night when her mother had been killed, Elaine must have stood rooted to the place on the beach, terror robbing her of speech, the darkness screening the identity of the killer.

"My cloak was none of the worse for its baptism in sea water," Kate was saying. "Feel it, Justine. Feel how thick and yet how soft the wool is."

I backed away, silenced by horror at her obvious enjoyment of the scene. I could not see, but I felt her frenzied, trembling excitement at her own power. Somewhere among the scrub and thin cluster of trees were the villagers—her friends, my enemies—waiting her signal. Words read somewhere flashed through my mind: "Those who have killed once find it easy a second time."

I had to keep my head and fight rising panic. Talk to her; play for time—she seemed in no hurry, anyway, because she knew I could not escape. Yet time was my only hope.

The cloak took away all femininity; she was neither man nor woman. She was the symbol of hate and desire. But she was Kate . . . Kate who had chatted to me kindly on the terrace at Argus, who had tempted me at mealtimes to taste Chrysolakian delicacies, who asked with seeming genuine interest if I had enjoyed my morning, my afternoon. Smiling, always a little anxious to please, hurrying and fussing Kate d'Arrancourt . . .

"Dear God," I said. "What a consummate actress you are!"

The broken branch of a tree hung near me. I seized it and pulled. It snapped easily and with a swift movement I flung is sideways to catch Kate's attention so that I might have a chance to run. To run where? Marathon, along that track and half hidden by its trees, was suddenly a world away. Kate didn't even bother to turn her head; her blazing concentration was on me.

"The accident on the boat"—I whispered. "You—"

"I changed the chart while you were indulging Elaine and taking a long time to get her down to the beach because she was in one of her dawdling moods. I know them. The boat episode wasn't planned, though; it just happened that you wanted to go out in it and I seized the advantage. Clever of me, wasn't it?"

"You wanted us both to drown."

"Oh, no. All I wanted was for Matt to see how irresponsible you were. If he thought you'd endangered Elaine's life, it would be the end of your visits to Marathon—or so I thought." She swished the ground with her stick, making small, vicious movements, and I felt that she would have liked it to have been thrashing me. But before she attacked—and I was quite certain that she intended to—she had other things to say and every moment she delayed held an infinitesimal hope for me that something might divert her attention.

"I worked on the villager's superstition," she said, and slashed at a low cluster of scrub. "I told them that there would be nothing but

412

trouble while you were on the island, that you were evil. It wasn't hard to persuade them to believe me—you had already endangered the life of their saint-child."

"And you sent them to the hut."

"Warning them that their children were in danger."

I felt suddenly terribly tired. I knew it all; I wanted no more talk.

But Kate did.

"There must be a kind of streak in me somewhere—perhaps in different circumstances I might really have liked you. Because I decided to give you one last chance." She waited. Then, as I asked no question, she said, "The sleeping pills."

"You couldn't—you *couldn't* have wanted to kill Elaine!"

"Oh, no. I gave her just enough dope to make her sleep for a long, long time and frighten everyone—Matt most of all. If, after that, he had decided that you were dangerously irresponsible and lost interest in you, then you wouldn't be facing me now. But when I told him about it, he exonerated you. Do you know what he said to me? 'Whoever did this, I know it wasn't Justine.'"

I said, "There's one thing, Kate, that you

413

may not realize. Jock knows the truth about Elaine."

"That *ouzo*-drinking old man!"

"He has brought your clock back. There are two people painted on it—you and Louis. A third is sketched in—Elaine."

I heard the hiss of her breath between closed teeth. "That's a poor effort to make me leave you to see for myself so that you can run for help to Matt; the fish doesn't bite the bait, dear! Jock knows nothing. Nobody knows but Louis and I—and you, of course, but you'll never tell."

If she swung the stick at me, I would make a grab for it. I watched the circles it made as if restless to get on with its task of attack and yet holding back—she was still savoring her triumph. I wished I could see her expression and know whether she half believed my story that Jock knew the truth.

Desperately I pursued the point I had made. "The clock will tell the truth; everyone will know . . .."

Her laughter rang out, drowning my words. "A clock can be destroyed as easily as—" She lifted the stick, making a great arc, first back and then forwards with a vast swing, hurtling it towards me with such speed and ferocity that I flung myself sideways. The weapon didn't even touch me. Instead, it flew out of her hands; its weight, combined with the force she used, was too great for her to control. I saw it crash to the ground and there was a great echoing which could not have come from an ordinary stick falling to the ground. It was as if something had struck a hollow mountain, and the ringing continued long after the stick lay still, a booming sound like that of a great bell.

Kate hurled herself at me, tearing at me with her hands, trying to get her fingers at my throat. She was screaming obscenities in English and interspersing Greek words at the top of her voice as if summoning those who were waiting to help her destroy me. I heard her dress rip as I clutched at her; I knew the terrible need to use violence to stop violence. I was fighting for my life and I had to hurt her to make her let go. But she was impervious to pain.

"Kate . . . you're ill . . . Kate, for God's sake . . ."

Those who are mad are strong. Kate was strong. I felt my long hair being pulled round to make a noose for my neck; I heard hiccuping laughter. The blackness was not of

the night but of my own fading consciousness. I fell to my knees and there was a
rushing sound in my ears, I could not even
plead with her, for the noose of my own hair
was choking me.

My life, the great marvelous gift of life
which I had been given, was suddenly the
most important thing in the world. And it
was not going to be mine any longer to enjoy.

The two rock Sisters, the Dark and the
Green, were witnesses to death: Helen had
died by one; I was to die by the other.

I fell to the ground. Nobody knows what
the last thoughts are of those about to die;
nobody would ever know mine. They were
contained in three words—Matt's words that
I had read on a sunlit morning in Athens: *the
everlasting present*. The gift of life that should
be lived every moment to the full. Oh,
Matt . . .

I heard a shriek of laughter, and then Kate
began shouting sharp, staccato sentences in
Greek.

Her fingers gripped my shoulders, pressing
me down into the ground. "Do you know
what I was calling out, my dear, dear Justine?
I was saying to the women, 'Come out. I have
killed your enemy; I have made your children

safe. The daughter of Lucifer is dead. Come out and see . . .' " I opened my eyes and saw a melee of black figures, black skirts flying, voices shouting in a language that was alien to me. Kate had not been bluffing. The women of Chrysolaki had been there, awaiting her signal.

Hands tore at me; my clothes were ripped; the strand of hair round my throat loosened, and I choked, taking in great gasping breaths, then the grip tightened again. My fingers were weak with fighting, my wrists were scratched and I was sure that they bled. I saw a jumble of faces—hair flying, rough hands. Blackness came and went, and suddenly I had no idea what I was seeing. I was past knowing life from death.

A discovery flashed through me like a flaming dagger: The last of the senses to leave us is sound. For a moment I wavered, strangely beyond pain, in a kind of no man's land of semiconsciousness.

It was then that I heard another sound—high and piercing—in that strange momentary silence. It was like a cry coming from a throat that had hands too tightly round it or from someone who found sound hard to produce. It cut through that sudden stillness so startlingly that I tried to open my eyes. I could not, but my mind filled, as water fills a parched place, with a final, incredulous thought: *And Elaine screamed.*

After that, I gave a small, tired cry that never reached audibility.

25

I DIDN'T lose consciousness, after all. I was aware of being lifted up and of a sudden silence that was as terrible as the earlier screams had been. My eyes wouldn't open and my mind swung with a despairing thought: They're going to take me somewhere and . . . and what? Burn me as a witch? Fling me to the sea as an offering to something they revered and before which they crossed themselves in awe?

I heard a voice say my name—a man's voice—but I was too dazed to recognize it. I could be in Louis's arms, that golden man who had let Kate kill for him. I tried to move, to free myself, but there was no energy left. I was being laid on the back seat of a car; no one was speaking, but there were two people—two men. I lay, feeling a hand on my wrist, feeling another gently smoothing my hair. Gently? The pity of my enemies for what they were going to do to me?

I wasn't driven very far and I was carried into a house. Argus? I didn't know, and I was beyond caring. There were voices, stairs climbed, the softness of a bed.

"Justine, can you hear me?"

I didn't bother to answer.

"Open your eyes; do you hear, open them. You're safe and practically unhurt except for bruises and scratches. It's just shock. Are you bothering to listen? Well, you'd better. Open your eyes, girl!"

The voice was strong, and slightly threatening, as though I would be slapped awake if I didn't try on my own. I forced my leaden lids to lift, and it hurt to look at the single soft light in the room. At least I was alive; at least I could see. I tried to lift myself up and the weight of my hair seemed to drag my head down.

"I didn't tell you to sit up." It was Jock, who pressed me back onto the pillows. He was sitting on the edge of the bed in a green-and-white room. "You're at Marathon and everything is all right."

"What happened after—" Breathing had been fine until I tried to speak, and then each breath seemed to split into red-hot splinters. I put my hand to my throat. "The women . . . they . . . they came to attack me."

"We'll talk about it later."

"We'll talk about it now!" I forced myself to sit up. The fact that I was safe filled me with a false sense of well-being. I wanted to talk; I felt fine—as one feels fine in that moment of wild relief before reaction sets in.

"Why did you draw Elaine's outline on the clock?"

"For you to see and understand."

"It would have been easier to tell me."

"And not have been believed. You could have decided that I was a senile old fool jumping to wild conclusions. But you would have known that I would never have dared to draw Elaine on the face of that clock unless her relationship with the d'Arrancourts was a fact. You had to know the truth from someone, my dear. And while you were learning that, I was out looking for Kate. You thought she had gone into Kentulakis. But I was certain that she hadn't. Unfortunately I'm no sleuth and I never gave a thought to the possibility that you might not take the path through the olive orchard to Marathon. So, that's where I waited—dumb cluck that I was—certain that Kate would be watching and following, that because you were leaving as soon as you could get a seat on the plane for England, this would be the crisis night."

421

"You often watched this house, didn't you? It was your car I sometimes saw parked under the olives."

He patted my hand lying on the sheet. "You'd better rest now."

But as he rose to go I gripped his arm. "You've told me so much, you can tell me the rest. If you think I can lie down and go to sleep knowing only half—"

He grinned at me. "I may as well humor you."

"Why did you suspect Kate?"

"I'm a doctor, Justine, and I've learned to recognize psychopathic cases. Kate's condition was semidormant and it would be difficult to prove until a moment of great stress came to her. It came."

"She hated me for seeing so much of Matt."

"Of course. She was infiltrating his life so deeply that she believed that in the end he would marry her. But when she realized that it was over between you and Louis, she guessed what would happen."

"There was nothing—" I began. But there was. Kate could have followed me to the Paradise Garden. The irony of that was that she could have seen but not heard, not known that Matt had said, "Go back to England. Get away from this island, from all of us". . . Rejecting me. Kate would have loved me, perhaps, had she heard that.

"Someone was making trouble for you on Chrysolaki," Jock said. "But I knew the villagers wouldn't act on their own initiative; they'd never dare attack a foreign woman unless someone led them, and that someone had to be one they respected and admired. Kate, filling them with crazy ideas, stimulating their superstitions." He patted my hand. "You've kept me away from the *tavernas* in Kentulakis for some days, my girl, slinking here as I have, to watch and wait for the storm in Kate's brain to burst. And tonight it happened—only I was waiting in the wrong place."

"I was going to Marathon only because you told me to."

"I wanted to see you safe," he said.

"If only Kate had known! I was no threat to her. Matt wanted me to leave the island, too. And, as Kate loved him, that would mean—"

"*Love?* My dear girl, she didn't love him, she was just determined to marry him, which is a vastly different thing. Not that all her apparent devotion to Elaine and her conscientiousness towards her work at Marathon would have drawn Matt to her. He was grateful to her, but a young, virile man doesn't marry a woman out of gratitude. At least, not Matt."

"She killed Helen." I watched him, waiting for his shocked reaction.

He nodded. "She told us so tonight, screaming it aloud for all the island to hear. That's what happens when you go over the edge into madness—you become proud of your monstrous evils."

"Jock, where is she?"

"The Stephanides and some men are holding her until I can get back to the village. You came first. But I've telephoned for the air ambulance from Hydra."

Fear leapt back; I could imagine the women waiting outside Marathon for the moment when I would be alone.

"They'll let her go!" I cried. "Jock, you don't understand. They're on her side. They were even there, in the wood, waiting for her to give the signal to attack me."

"They weren't, you know!"

"But I saw them. They came at me—"

"They tore Kate's hands away and saved your life."

424

I leaned back on the pillows. Jock was wrong. I knew. "They hated me," I said.

"God knows, Kate worked on them to fear you, but last night *I* did the working. I got the men together and told them the truth; I warned them of a very real danger from a woman who was on the borderline between sanity and madness. They told their women—they're good, Justine, they would not harm except in terror to save themselves or their families."

"Then why were they there, waiting—"

"They weren't. When Kate dropped her stick, it hit a boulder that must have fallen from the top of the Green Sister heaven knows how long ago and not been noticed. The boom rang round the island. The women heard it and rushed out. Those with cottages near the Green Sister arrived to find Kate attacking you. You owe your life to them, my dear. Heaven help me, old fool that I am, I nearly lost it for you."

"Oh, Jock!" I put out my hand and he gripped it between his own rough brown ones. "Does Louis know?"

"Of course. He's with Kate now, and he'll have to take the responsibility for her. He's her only relative."

"He can't know—or can he?—that Kate killed Helen. He couldn't stay with her in that house knowing she had done that!"

"Oh yes, he could. He either guessed or knew—which it was will come out at the inquiry."

"He once said he'd kill me rather than let me go. I almost laughed at him, but he could have meant it. Jock, he could—if he were like Kate—"

"Oh, Louis wouldn't kill. He'll threaten and rage but he hasn't Kate's desperate, fanatical intent. He's obsessive where he wants something, but he's not mad."

"If he comes here for me—"

"He won't. He's got too much to do coping with Kate. One day he'll find someone else to fasten his possessiveness onto, and perhaps it will be some girl who doesn't mind being a doormat. The weak often dominate, you know, through sheer blackmail of the strong. And Louis is weak." He turned as footsteps sounded outside the door. "Here's Ludmilla with milk," he said. "It's wonderful for painful throats."

"Oh, my little lady!" She came and handed me the green mug and her peasant hands smoothed my hair back, my dark hair that

426

had nearly strangled me. "I tell *Kyrie* you better."

"Not now," Jock said. "Here, Justine, take this. Go on, swallow it, it's a fairly mild sedative."

"I don't want to go to sleep, if that's what this is intended to do." I looked with distaste at the little blue capsule he had put in my hand.

"Swallow," said Jock.

I swallowed, drank the milk and slept.

Matt was beside me when I woke. The shutters were open and the dawn had the color of a faded rose.

He said, "This is my first marvelous chance to kiss you awake," and leaned over and kissed me.

"Who brought me here?"

"I did. You're not very heavy, are you?"

"I was on my way to see you when it happened."

"I know."

"And tomorrow I was—I *am*—going to Athens to catch the first plane to London."

"Oh, but you can't."

"But it was you who told me to."

"God help me, I thought your going would be for your own safety. Instead I precipitated a horror which nearly cost you your life."

"I *was* going," I said, staring at the far wall, not daring to believe that his gentleness meant anything more than casual affection, pity, a reaction from his own alarm at what he had so nearly caused.

"Jock had already talked to me about his anxiety over your marriage to Louis; he knew that there was a psychopathic tendency in the d'Arrancourts. And only the night after he had spoken to me, something happened that threw a light on the whole question of Helen's death. Do you remember when we met at the folk-dancing in Hagharos, and Clytia and Louis were dancing? You opened your purse and dropped something?"

"My beautiful little ruby and turquoise pencil."

"It was then that I guessed who had killed Helen. You see, that pencil was given to my mother by her aunt—H.C.L.—her initials. As you know, it was made in the Kashmir in the eighteenth century. My mother gave it to Helen, but she had no feeling for old things and she probably tossed it across to Louis as I would toss a cheap pen onto a table. It was then that I thought I knew who had killed my sister."

"You thought—Louis—"

"Yes."

"But he didn't."

"I know that now."

I turned my head and looked at him. He reached out and twined his fingers lightly through my hair. "You didn't go to Hydra last night, after all?" I asked.

"I was to have met friends there who were passing through. The plane was late and they were going on to Istanbul without a stop in Greece." His fingers were cool against my cheek.

"If I hadn't dropped that pencil you might never have known the truth."

"I wonder? Things have a way of catching up on people. A lot that had been puzzling me fell into place that night while Clytia and Louis danced. There were no men on the island in whom Helen could possibly be interested. But twice Louis was over here at the same time and I realized that in between those times they could have met in London."

And become lovers . . .

"As soon as I found that it all made appalling sense, I decided that if you were not intending to marry Louis, you would be safer in England—I didn't dare risk loving you

429

here. I made a mistake in the killer, but at least I was aware of danger."

"I would have gone back to England and we would never have met again."

"Oh, but I would have followed you. Wherever you went, Justine, I would have found you."

It was strange, in such a moment when a singing joy ran through my blood, that I should lie so quietly, not even looking at Matt. But when he took my hand, I raised it and laid it against my cheek. We were surrounded by glorious quiet, and because of it, I remembered the clocks.

"Kate stopped them," I said. "I mean, the clocks."

"Did she?" He considered it. "Despite her superstitious fears? Well, it could have been just a small, sadistic act to unnerve you. Or it could have been her own symbolic way of telling herself that the crazy d'Arrancourt superstition was coming true. They were to stop when death was near. And, dear God, it nearly happened!" He turned my face round gently and I saw the lamplight reflected in his eyes like silver flames. "Oh, Justine, but you set a blaze beneath us all!"

"And went head first into traps laid for me

by Kate. But she was such an actress!"

"I think they call it psychopathic. But it's all over."

"There's one thing I don't believe has ever occurred to you. It's—it's my triumph, Matt, and you must let me have it. Elaine always knew how her mother had died. That's what her hands were trying to tell us when she made that odd shadow on the wall—a bunched fist and a finger thrust out suddenly. She had seen someone standing on the cliff—a kind of shapeless figure—and then a hand had shot out and pushed Helen over the edge of the Dark Sister. It was too dark for her to see who it was, but—" I broke off and turned to Matt and felt my whole face radiant with my discovery. "Don't you understand now? Elaine *has* got memory . . ."

Before he could answer me, the door opened. "I'm sorry," said Ludmilla, "but Elaine, she restless. She want to know—"

I sat up: my head reeled. The walls of the room danced. "*Elaine wants to know?*"

Ludmilla nodded as though she hadn't imparted news of a miracle. "Last night she wake, she hear all noise and she come out . . . follow *Kyrie* and see you."

"*And Elaine screamed.*"

"She shocked," said Ludmilla. "Shock make her not speak; shock make her well. It happen. It so."

"Oh, Matt, this is wonderful . . ."

He steadied my rising excitement. "She'll speak, but only ever a few words—simple, perhaps even unconnected. That is all, Justine. That is all."

"But it's a beginning."

"And it will stop there. Do you understand? She will be able to speak only as much as she knew before she was dumb. There can never be development. There are battles one wins, and battles one loses."

I didn't care. She would be able to make herself understood to me, at any rate, and to Matt. That first lovely impression of her the day we drove to Argus remained. She had neither prejudices nor frustrations; she had happiness and dignity.

I turned to Ludmilla. "I must see Elaine."

"Yes, she want you."

"So do I," said Matt.

THE END

ROMANCE TITLES
in the
Ulverscroft Large Print Series

THE SHADOWS
OF THE CROWN TITLES
in the
Ulverscroft Large Print Series